Praise for *Victoria Sees It*

"In *Victoria Sees It*, Carrie Jenkins pursues the idea of women's madness: its origins, its structures, and, most radically, its insights. When I began reading this beguiling story, I was put in mind of Charlotte Brontë, as the main character is a cross between the odd and serious Jane Eyre and the raving, attic-bound Mrs. Rochester. Jenkins's voice manages the rare feat of being remarkably intelligent and complex, while being fast paced and engaging. A brilliant thriller about the infinite corridors and wondrous nooks and crannies of women's minds."
—Heather O'Neill, author of *The Lonely Hearts Hotel* and *Lullabies for Little Criminals*

"Carrie Jenkins's novel is as intimate as it is intense. This rich thriller delves into the muck of academia—the sexism and classism and politicking that proliferates in the cracks of Cambridge and beyond. Her Victoria is a searcher, one with an astute awareness of behavioural quirks and an encyclopaedic knowledge of all things Sherlock Holmes and Hercule Poirot."
—Daniel Viola, Features Editor, *The Walrus*

"*Victoria Sees It* is delightful and disorienting, wretched and wry. Reading it is like rummaging through boxes in a crowded attic: you become subsumed, sifting through layers of memory while some barely-noticed haunted thing watches you from a dark corner."
—Ziya Jones, Senior Editor, *Xtra*

"For fans of Donna Tartt, this book—like most 'hysterical' women—is too smart to be dismissed."
—Sruti Islam, creator of the Weird Era newsletter and bookseller at Librairie St-Henri

Victoria Sees It

Victoria Sees It

Carrie Jenkins

STRANGE LIGHT

Library and Archives Canada Cataloguing in Publication data
is available upon request.
ISBN: 978-0-7710-4927-9
ebook ISBN: 978-0-7710-4928-6

Book design by Andrew Roberts
Cover art: RF Pictures / Getty Images
Printed and bound in Canada

Published by Strange Light,
an imprint of Penguin Random House Canada Limited,
a Penguin Random House Company
www.penguinrandomhouse.ca

10 9 8 7 6 5 4 3 2 1

Penguin
Random House
Canada

I had never seen with my eyes ever in my life before anything so unnatural and appalling and my gaze faltered about the thing uncomprehendingly as if at least one of the customary dimensions was missing, leaving no meaning in the remainder.

— Flann O'Brien, *The Third Policeman*

———

Having been is also a kind of being, and perhaps the surest kind.

—Victor Frankl, *Man's Search for Meaning*

Contents

Victoria Sees It

Prologue

I can never go back to Cambridge.

I don't mean like how Mrs. de Winter can never go back to Manderley. Cambridge has not literally burned to the ground. Not all of it anyway. It's still there. Still calling. What makes the place so magnetic? The magic of history? That's nothing magical, just a kind of mass hysteria. A *folie à plusieurs*.

But I suppose such things are necessary. Seeing the world as it really is makes you crazy. Accuracy is comorbid with depression, you know—major accuracy with major depression. We stay alive by means of the precise deployment of attention. Look at these seamless green banks, these ancient stone bridges arcing like half-moons, reflected to full circles in the flat jade water. These cloistered courtyards and these postcard-perfect weeping willows. Ophelia-esque, reaching down to greet the gorgeous swirling limbs of their watery counterparts. Punt on by.

Yet we must stick our poles into the mud at the bottom of it all. *The present builds inexorably over the empty fields of the past.* That's Dorothy L. Sayers. I suppose the way that I can never go back to Cambridge is the same way that her Harriet Vane

1

could never go back to Oxford, until she could, and did, and look what happened to *her*. Women must be put in their place, and their place is not a university. Sayers gets that. So she sends poor Harriet—who, let's be honest, is herself in a wig and dark glasses—into a thinly fictionalized 1935 Oxford that cannot deal.

Ah, but 1935 was such a long time ago! Water under the bridge, right? The problem is, it turns out you *can* step twice in the same Isis, the same Cam. Honestly, you can throw yourself in a thousand times over and nobody is going to stop you. Stagnant. Sayers writes us a river full of garbage and the bodies of suicidal girls and all we want to do is go there for a holiday. *That's* the magic.

As for me, however far away I get I can't seem to stop sticking my pole into the mud. The other week I agreed to a public online "chat" about my work. It was against my better judgment, but I am constantly being told we need role models for women in academia. It makes me feel guilty. Of course, as soon as the admins took a few minutes' unannounced break, the trolls swarmed. First the surface scum, the clinging weeds. I should make them a sandwich, I should be gang-raped, if a tree falls in a forest can they see a picture of my tits, why don't I kill myself. Then the deep undertow, the ones who might be typing from down the hallway and use good grammar. Women get all the breaks in academia, work like mine proves we are naturally inferior thinkers, positive discrimination is the only reason I got this job which I cannot do and don't deserve, why don't I give up.

Well, why don't I? I want out, but inertia is a killer. At least I got out of Cambridge. I don't quite know why I had to get so *far*. I suppose I thought it would help, to put some ground between us, and then I upgraded from ground to an ocean. Right now, I'm lying flat out on a hotel bed in Toronto. Did you know that acid indigestion can feel exactly like a heart attack? People die because they blame their starchy dinners. And yes, one way of looking at that is to say how awful it is that those people die. But the real, grinding tragedy here is that all the rest of us are in that much pain every day and nobody gives a toss because we *aren't* dying.

This would be a shitty insipid hotel room, beige and pointless, but for its one concession to non-generic decor, a drawing of a strange kind of dragon. Or it could be a snake. It stares right out at me, snout almost projecting from its two-dimensional plane, right over the sink where you'd expect a mirror to be. I don't miss having a mirror, the glass over the picture is good enough. When I wash my face, I can see my own two eyes reflected side by side in that snakey mug.

But this is all distraction, isn't it? I must, for once, stop distracting myself. I *must* focus. I am tired. To be fair, it's been twenty years of constant effort, pulling away in any direction, and that is exhausting. But when I let my mind snap back on its own elastic, it only ever returns me to Cambridge. Those months at the end of my first Easter term are *real*—they are as real now as they were then. As for everything in between then and now, that gets hazy. Hey, let me tell you a story with a weak female lead. It doesn't have a narrative arc so much as a trough, or maybe a cliff would be more accurate.

Perhaps that's an uninviting invitation. What do you want me to do about it? *What we can't say we can't say, and we can't whistle it either*. That's Frank Ramsey. Telling Wittgenstein off.

So take it or leave it. The one thing I'm sure about is that first year in Cambridge. That really happened. I can't get away from that, however far I run.

Twenty years and an ocean? It's nowhere near enough. I can never go back to Cambridge because I can never leave.

Part One
Corridors

When that I was and a little tiny boy

Chapter One

My mother stopped talking when I was born. They said it was "catatonia," which to me sounded like a country. So I thought she caught a disease when she was travelling there, and now her tongue was infected. Or had to be amputated. Perhaps they had to cut out my mother's tongue because there was something wrong with it.

I was born on her birthday. Just coincidence, there was never any connection between us. But even though she wouldn't talk, I saw her all the time. My aunt and uncle said I had to go. I remember once asking why bother when she didn't care, and everyone was very angry and I didn't understand. By the time I could have asked more questions I suppose I had got used to it. I didn't hate it, it was just a thing that happened, like breakfast or brushing your teeth. For most of the time I can remember, my mother lived in a tiny room in the corner of a red-brick building we called "the home." But for the first six years of my life she was in hospital.

I grew up there, grew into the hospital. As soon as I could walk, I was left to wander alone out of her room and off down the endless white-blue corridors. This was better than keeping me in with her, because I was so bored and curious about all the machines in there that I'd start pressing buttons just to see what they'd do. Once I pulled a red cable out of something—perhaps it was my mother's body—and set off an alarm, and a nurse came running tap tap tap down the corridor. My uncle had freckles and hairy arms, and when he was angry the hairs on his arms stood up in between the freckles and I would count them so I didn't have to look at his face.

In those windowless tunnels, nobody who knew who I was cared where I was, and nobody who knew where I was cared who I was. That's what being free means—we've forgotten this now. I hummed myself along, making up my own little tunes in time to my echoing steps. I'd turn corners and run into people, like kind nurses, or sad women, or serious adults in a big hurry. Quickly or slowly, they all passed me by because I wasn't their problem. I knew better than to make myself their problem. I kept my eyes straight ahead and looked as grown-up as I could. I remember the moment when I realized it was a grown-up thing to do to smile back when someone smiled at me, and I stored that away as something I could use in future: a quick signal that I really was old enough to be there on my own. Just enough to stop the foreheads of the kind nurses from scrunching up, and their heads swinging back around in concern as we went our opposite ways.

Of the others roaming the corridors, the sad women were the most interesting. I'd pause my own adventures sometimes to watch them pace up and down. I'd follow them into the ladies' toilets to see if they really needed to go or just wanted somewhere to walk to. They were with me but not with me, which was perfect. If they smiled at me, I smiled back. Sadly.

One time, a sad pink woman swung out into a corridor through a heavy white door, heading for one of the sitting areas. These were really just two faded brown armchairs and a table with an ashtray, next to a big machine that if you put in 10p would violently spit a plastic cup into a recessed tray. Often the cup then fell over, and the machine would dispense hot coffee directly into the tray. I got 10p once from my aunt so I could try it. I made sure to hold the cup in place even though it burned my fingers a bit. The coffee was the same colour as the armchairs, and tasted like the cup. The sad women came to these chairs to smoke, which smelled good with the coffee.

I had only just started following this pink lady when she broke the rules. She spoke to me. Her voice was clear and startling in the white space, like the sheer pink of her soft cardigan. Everything about her was sad and she smelled expensive. She wanted to know why I was there, and my name and how old I was. She pulled out a cigarette and lit it between bright pink lips, waiting for answers.

I told her I was seven and a half (I was probably five). I said my mother was upstairs, and I was just waiting for her. She nodded, calmly accepting these statements.

"I'm waiting for someone, too," she said. "I don't think she's ready to see me yet. What's your name?"

She'd noticed the evasion. I don't like telling people my name. It takes too long to say "Victoria" and it gets awkward in my mouth. I have to *perform* the whole thing. It might as well be an entire Shakespeare play. I could use shorter versions of the name, I know, but they wouldn't be me. I like my name, I just don't like saying it to other people.

"Someone," I said. The pink lady and I stared at each other for a second, then we both laughed at once.

Sometimes the sad women were going into the toilets to redo their mascara. This was a mesmerizing procedure. My aunt, too, always wore mascara. One of my earliest memories is sitting on the loo in our cramped bathroom, watching her flick at her lashes with the little black wand. Up up up. Only up, never down. The tip of her thin nose almost touching the mirror. She was very short-sighted, but had to do her eye makeup without the aid of her glasses. I asked her why she was doing it, and she told me not to worry about it because I was young and beautiful.

"Only old hags like me need to wear makeup," she giggled. She must have been about forty.

I'm thirty-nine now, and I wear a lot of makeup. I still couldn't tell you exactly what the point of it is, but I put all this stuff on my face in the morning, before I ride the bus to campus. It takes me about an hour to get it all on there. Why do I give up this extra hour of sleep? Couldn't I lecture a hundred undergraduates with a bare face? Couldn't I go to a meeting at the Dean's Office and have everyone look at my bare eyelashes? My eyelashes aren't so bad. My face is prone to cystic acne—I have big red bubbles on both sides of my chin, but I don't hate them. These jewelled cherries can be beautiful when I look at them the right way. I paint over them for the people who cannot. Private and secret are different things, I suppose, and my real face is private. I learned as a child to wear my hair pinned down across my forehead. Other kids teased me for being a "slaphead," and my aunt once told me nobody thought girls were pretty if they had big heads.

I was always afraid of loud sounds, and of angry people. And of the night. This is all quite normal. You know who else was afraid of the night? Zeus, that's who. It says so in the *Iliad*. Mrs. Schmidt, my classics mistress, would later teach me all about this.

"And Zeus," she would add with a wink at any available opportunity, "was a *very* naughty boy." Indeed he was. The original and biggest Big Man.

There was something else I was afraid of, though. Something I couldn't put a name to so easily. Something around my aunt and uncle's house. I knew it as a moving shadow, permanently in the corner of my mind. Something that would chase me, send me running desperately into the bathroom, into the bright light, to lock the door and read a book until it had gone away. Sometimes it waited, biding its time inside cupboards or under beds. But usually it was right behind me, just over my shoulder. If it came too close I could feel it, flakes of ice on my skin. It was always with me on the staircase.

The staircase was the main point of the house, the heart of its Victorian ambitions, for all its dark-carved banisters were dusty now, battered with the laying on of too many hands, and appearing to have at one time endured the attentions of a toothy puppy. I was never allowed a pet, and my aunt would point to the banisters as proof that animals ruin your house. She didn't say it, but I figured out that she had never intended to have any children in her house either. She taught me tidy habits and good housekeeping. In the evenings, she would shuffle me cheerily along the worn runner carpet "up the wooden hill to Bedfordshire," as if it were some trivial thing, but its height was unfathomably immense to my fledgling senses, amplified by a skylight of telescopic proportions. Swirls of old floral wallpaper trailed and tangled down the walls, green beanstalks fading into pale blue, each peeling join a frayed vertical plumb line from one plane to the next. I imagined the pattern must repeat to infinity, lift off into a skylit heaven, blues and greens rarefying to white light.

I lost a helium balloon in that stairwell. Once its string slipped the grip of my sticky fingers, even my uncle couldn't stop it. So up it went, and up it stayed, clinging to the invisible limit of the skywindow until it fell, deflated, weeks later, all dreams of escape spent into the sublunary air of my aunt and uncle's house. It dissipated down towards me as I waited below, daring myself to stand there long enough to catch the dead husk of my prize.

That shadow of the house couldn't follow me in hospital, though. Perhaps the disinfectant smell kept it away.

As I wandered the corridors humming my made-up tunes to myself, they began to take more specific forms. Tunes for walking straight along, tunes for turning a corner, tunes for climbing stairs. Tunes for doorways. Some of the doors that flanked the hospital corridors were closed, and although they had little windows at adult eye level, my own eyes were nowhere near. These doors were so much wall—I would never have opened one. But when they were already open, I'd stand and stare through, often into strange spaces. Entire rooms full of old beds and strappy equipment that looked like it might be for holding a person down. A ping-pong table with no bats or balls. A shelf of faded romance novels. I found small discarded treasures on floors, too. Even money sometimes. And once—one wonderful time—a little blue plastic Care Bear with a cloud on his tummy. I wasn't allowed branded toys—they were "tacky" and "commercial" and cost money we didn't have. I took him home, bathed him assiduously, and carried him in my pocket for years.

If I found myself in the hospital canteen and had 30p to spare, I would buy the delicious roast potatoes. I ate these so fast my chest felt like it was going to burst for a few beats, until a good swallow moved the starchy mass along and freed me up to cram in another forkful. Sometimes the hospital corridors smelled of those canteen potatoes. Sometimes other scents hung around: the perfumes of the sad women, coffee out of the machines, cigarette smoke. But underneath the changing surface notes was that clear, constant disinfected smell, the scent of the blue floors that sparkled like a hall of fame. I found these plastic pathways magical, with their little flicks of glitter under the brilliant lights. These corridors were the endless passages from the fantasy game I was occasionally allowed to play on my uncle's computer. Bright, clean, simple magic that can take you anywhere.

Somewhere on another level, all the things that mattered to my family were going on. Hospital space was infinite. It had room for them so I didn't have to.

———

Anyway the little shit talks all the time. Talks at me, talks about me, talks for me. Wears me. Like the whole nine months she was growing in my body, eating it away and it's the same now. Whenever she starts talking. I instinctively flinch, like someone's going to hit me in the face, only inside. I'd never let her see it. I'd never let her see anything.

Now she has my life just like she had my body. Hollow shells. All my stories—she's never even heard them and somehow they're hers to tell.

No, it's fine. It's not like I'm using them.

Chapter Two

And then it was gone. The home didn't have those infinite corridors, it was just a pathetic brick square. You could only walk around and around inside it, and all the nurses immediately knew who I was. I walked round the whole square the first time we went there, and burst into tears when I came back to where I'd started in less than two minutes.

Contained inside the brick square was a garden that felt like a fake smile. It had a couple of brown plastic benches planted in the centre, facing each other. My mother would smoke on one of these benches for hours every day, until her left hand grew a gross yellow bump on the back of its middle finger and her blonde hair went grey. Around the time the bump appeared, people started describing her as "stable." She was always thin, but she got thinner. I suppose objectively she smelled disgusting, although I quite liked the way she smelled. Whatever the weather, she'd be there in the middle of her small square world, silent, letting nothing out. I'm not even sure she exhaled the smoke.

I sat beside her on the plastic bench and talked. I wasn't really talking *to* her, to be honest, I just sat there and said things. But it was easier than talking when my uncle was around.

When my uncle got angry he called me a "stupid little girl." Every word of it stung in a different way, because he meant each one as an insult. But he was just wrong about "stupid," and it showed that he didn't know anything about me. I was clever. I was especially good at English and maths. So although we didn't have any money, when I was eleven my aunt encouraged me to sit the entrance examination for an all-girls boarding school.

On the morning of the exam we got up at 4 a.m. to drive the seventy miles to the school. My aunt helped me get ready in a new linen dress from the Red Cross shop, and she piloted me in her decrepit blue Beetle through the school's wrought-iron gates, up a long winding driveway, into a discreet car park tucked behind the main school building. Then we followed arrowed signposts, with a string of nervous girls and parents crocodiling into a huge gymnasium. Here there were highly polished, spotless wooden planks underfoot, and floor-to-ceiling windows on all sides. One side gave out onto the Victorian red-brick buildings of the school, and the other onto a manicured, greener-than-green terrace of playing fields that dropped away to the rolling hills and winding river beyond. We were in an Enid Blyton novel.

My aunt left me there and I spent an hour filling in the exam papers. They were easy. The only other task was a short admissions interview with the headmistress, a tiny elderly woman with pale skin and black-brown hair in a severely triple-wound bun. I admired its staying power. She asked me about Shakespeare and about current events and

I made a joke about *Alice's Adventures in Wonderland*. She looked at me in an unfamiliar way. It was part smile, and part surprise.

A week later, the headmistress phoned my aunt and told her I had the highest mathematics scores the school had ever seen. They wanted to offer me two of their best-paying scholarships, to run simultaneously, reducing their fees to a quarter of the usual rate. Even so, it was more than we could afford.

My aunt and uncle would send me to bed at around ten, but I never wanted to sleep. They made me turn out the light, so I would read clandestinely under the eiderdown, diving into this secret study space with a tiny torch, originally from a key ring, that was dim enough not to shine through the covers and give me away. The practice gave me headaches and might have been what ruined my eyesight, but it kept my mind alive.

The night of the headmistress's phone call I was put to bed on schedule, and had just pulled out my flashlight to continue *The Mysterious Affair at Styles* when I heard my uncle's raised voice. My aunt and uncle argued often, the sparks of sound seeping through the house's wobbly door-frames and porous floorboards, eventually settling into its nooks and crannies like ash. Usually I didn't listen because it didn't help anybody.

This time was different. I realized right away that I needed to hear the whole conversation, not just the loud side. I quietly snuck out onto the dark square landing at the top of the stairwell, from which, laying myself out flat on my stomach,

I could dangle my head through the space between the top two banisters. This afforded me a line of sight as well as good audibility, while I remained minimally visible.

My uncle was pacing. My aunt was opening a bottle of wine.

"And the government assistance will help," she was saying.

My uncle snorted. "Don't see why they get to tax my salary, just to pay for kids like her to go to some stuck-up private school. Nothing wrong with the comp. *Nothing*. Did me okay, didn't it?" He paused ominously. "Or are you saying not?"

"Of course, no, I just meant . . . she's gifted. She deserves a chance."

"A chance?" He was snarling now. "Of a better life. That's it, isn't it? She's better. Better than me. Better than this shit." He swung his arm around, knocked a china dog from the mantelpiece, and swore.

My aunt scurried around him and picked the dog up off the carpet.

"Fucking gifted. She's a little freak is what she is."

"For god's sake, be quiet!" my aunt hissed.

My uncle lowered his voice a little and growled, "Well, you know it. Look at her."

"You won't need to worry about it at all. Look, I did some sums, and when you bear in mind she'll be on full board at school, with all the money that'll save us here at home . . ." She held out a piece of paper torn from the notebook by the phone.

My uncle ripped it in half and dropped it on the floor. "I don't need to see more of your plans for how to spend my money."

"I'll see to her packing. I'll take care of everything." I saw my aunt's posture shift a little. "And she'd be out of the way."

This got no response except a hiss. "Little freak. Just like her mother."

"Please, James! You can't blame Victoria. She's a *child*."

"You don't fucking tell me what I can't do!"

My uncle snatched the open wine bottle from my aunt's hand and stormed out of the house, slamming the back door.

In the morning I woke up before everyone else, and went out to what we called the "back garden"—a sunless paved area between our house and the alley full of rubbish bins, where my aunt tended a row of potted plants with perennial optimism. There were several small pieces of green glass scattered around the fence. Aimlessly, I began to pick them up, and when I had them all I tried to put them in the flat-lidded dustbin. But with my hands full of the glass fragments I couldn't lift the lid properly, and I ended up dropping most of the glass and cutting my fingers.

I came back into the kitchen to wash them. My aunt was up now, listening to one of her favourite mixtapes while she did last night's washing-up. I stuck my hands in the sink and she asked what was wrong. I told her I had been tidying some glass in the back garden, and she flushed.

"Oh no! That's my fault, I dropped a bottle outside last night when I was taking the rubbish out. I thought I'd cleared it all up."

She hurried out to finish the job, as Tammy Wynette sang to me that *after all, he's just a man.*

Later that day, she told me she was coming to sleep in my room for a little while, because her snoring was keeping my uncle awake at night.

"And he needs to sleep very well, you see, so he is fresh for work in the morning. It'll be fun. I can bring up the camp bed!"

The camp bed was ex-army supply, a piece of khaki canvas slung across a folding frame. It was not comfortable. When we had to put up a guest overnight my aunt would set it out in the front room, covering it with blankets and donating her own pillow. It took up all the remaining floor space in my tiny bedroom. I never heard her snore, but we didn't have to share for very long. I started at the boarding school that September.

The school was huge. Better still, it was full of corridors and tunnels and passageways. There was even a footbridge over a busy road which connected the main building to another, newer block with multiple levels. This meant you could wander all over the entire complex for as long as you needed to, all the while appearing to be going somewhere. It was wonderful. During break times and lunch hours, I'd walk around humming to myself, imagining I was really an old woman who'd been given this one chance to go back in time and see what her secondary school used to look like. Sometimes I narrated it to myself. *Ah yes, this is where the home economics teacher tried to show us how to use a sewing machine, and Stephanie sewed a needle right through her finger. Poor Stephanie!*

In the evenings, the other girls made friends. They watched *Grease* on repeat in the TV room, pored over teen magazines, did each other's hair, and secretly passed round romance novels with all the sex scenes dog-eared. I read a huge brown hardback volume called *The Complete Sherlock Holmes*, with original illustrations from *The Strand*. It took me a very long time. When I had finished, I started it again.

Everyone shifted their conversations to whispers when I came close, and there were a few girls who walked into me on purpose. I vaguely registered this as strange, but I didn't quite get the message until one November morning in the first term. I'd spent the twenty-minute morning break walking around in the cavernous underground locker rooms, eating a bag of crisps and thinking about the haunting catechism from "The Adventure of the Musgrave Ritual":

Whose was it? His who is gone.
Who shall have it? He who will come.
(What was the month? The sixth from the first.)
Where was the sun? Over the oak.
Where was the shadow? Under the elm.
How was it stepped? North by ten and by ten,
*   east by five and by five, south by two and by*
*   two, west by one and by one, and so under.*
What shall we give for it? All that is ours.
Why should we give it? For the sake of the trust.

As the bell rang for the end of break and I came in to French, I saw that someone had written in large white letters on the chalkboard:

Victoria is a major wazzock.

Every social body has a kind of immune system, for killing off unwanted entities. I had to learn to evade it, and so far I hadn't learned anything.

I got careful after that. I worked out who were the right people to agree with, to look and act like. This system worked just the same as the other rules, really. The ones that the teachers made up. Except there wasn't a list of them written down in a booklet and handed out on the first day, so it just took me a bit longer to get square on the details. The most important thing was just to shut up or disappear when I couldn't get it right.

On exeat weekends, my aunt took me to visit my mother in the home. On the plastic bench, surrounded by her cigarette smoke, I started talking to her about boarding school. My teachers, classes, homework, exams. I was started early on French, in the upper third, and I remembered being told that my mother used to speak French a long time ago. So I practised on her. *Je m'appelle Rien. Ma tante n'est pas ma tante.*

I started talking to her about boys eventually, but only because I was supposed to. All the other girls were talking about boys by then and if you didn't they called you a "lezzie." This was one of many available forms of social death, like being square and not knowing the right songs. The seas of lava beneath a few floating stones. I saw a lot of girls fall in, and while some of them seemed to get another life, others just went away and I never saw them again. Once I had a handle on the rules, I found I could hop from stone to stone without really going anywhere, but without falling off either.

When I told my mother about school I sometimes told the truth, sometimes made things up. Generally my babble was a mix of both. It didn't matter, after all. I didn't look at her face much, because there was no point. There was nothing to learn there.

There was only one time I thought I saw her face move at all, and I'm not even sure if I imagined it. It was for a fraction of a second, what these days they call a "micro-expression." And it wasn't her mouth that moved, only something in her eyes. It was after A levels, when I told her I had met the conditions of my offer and would be going up to Cambridge that Michaelmas term to read philosophy.

I wondered if maybe, just for a moment, she felt proud of me.

———

Don't call it "home" for fuck's sake, I'm not a child.
This is the *home. The definite article. You need*
to understand the significance of that. How can
I explain? To Sherlock Holmes you know she is
always the *woman. Like there is only one. Only*
one moment. The moment when I nearly told her.
About me. I mean, about her. About us.

   Of course I could have told her at any time.
I could tell her anything. But what purpose
could it possibly serve?

Chapter Three

Being poor wasn't really an issue until Cambridge. Looking back, the girls' school must have worked hard to level certain differences. If you needed something for your classes—cupcake trays for a cookery lesson, a tennis racket, blue science overalls—there was one provided if you couldn't bring it from home. It's not exactly that I couldn't tell the difference between me and the other girls, but it was all below the surface, and usually it didn't matter.

Sometimes we'd be taken to historic stately homes on school trips, and the other girls oohed and aahed at the grand dining rooms and ballrooms, while I felt at home in the servants' quarters. In cool underground pantries, with huge sinks for washing clothes or dead animals for table. Kitchens with great blackened fireplaces and roasting spits, shelves and shelves of bright orange copperware, long, thick wooden tables bearing the marks from years of chopping. Low-ceilinged servants' halls, where I'd picture a footman belting out waltzes on an out-of-tune upright piano, the maids dancing after the evening meal was cleared away. Attic bedrooms, tucked out of sight on back stairs, where two tiny beds took up the entire floor, and I'd imagine shoving my own little suitcase under one of the beds and wondering who my cellmate might be. These were the spaces that felt right to me. But I didn't mention things like this to anyone.

There was one time I made the mistake of telling a girl my best dress had only cost ten pounds, and she yelled the fact out loud to everyone in the room. She didn't mean anything by it. She didn't know. Another time I showed a different girl my prized necklace of clear plastic crystals, a treasure from childhood. When I put my eyes up close, I could see the light refracted into little rainbows by each gem. She said it looked like it came out of a Christmas cracker. She was right. I could never bear to look at it again, all its magic evaporated—without that, it *was* worthless. People have this tendency to ruin things.

Still, at school it wasn't necessarily money but *cool* that made things magical, made people special. I didn't care about being cool, beyond the basics of avoiding extermination, so it didn't matter what I had or didn't have. There were all kinds of expensive extra-curriculars going on but I didn't really miss them because I was happy enough by myself. When I finished reading *The Complete Sherlock Holmes* for the fourth time, I discovered the piano rooms. These were tiny closed spaces arranged in sequence on both sides of a long corridor. This corridor wasn't exactly infinite like in the hospital, but it led to an underground tunnel in one direction and a broad hallway in the other, so it felt all right. The piano rooms were safe houses, where I could wait as long as I needed. We couldn't afford lessons but I sat improvising for hours, music that was good enough to pass the time without really going anywhere. I learned to pick out the tunes that I hummed to myself for walking, for going up stairs, for turning corners. At first the tunes were simply themselves, then over time I made them more and more complex, layered with harmonies, subject to variations of mood, tempo, and key. I figured out how to play the songs the other girls liked, too, and then they'd ask me to play for them while they sang. This was as close as I got to popular. If I say "I didn't have friends," that comes out sounding wrong: it's not like there was something I wanted that I lacked.

Don't misunderstand me here, I'm not a misanthrope. Humans amaze me collectively. This usually happens in big cities, from the balconies of high-rise apartments. What people are capable of, from that height and distance, has a wonder to it. I feel it at dusk when the gold light catches a hundred windows at once, and the tiny cars on city streets flash and dart like fish in a tide pool. But it must be said I do not care for humans close-up. What comes at me from them is always confusing, and most of it is scary. Their thoughts and speech always seem to be transmitting on the wrong frequency. Does that make sense? I try to pace myself to match other people's rhythms but I am always interrupting them, cutting into what they say. Or they're doing the same to me. So then we stop and try again, but we both start talking at the same time. Like when two people meet in a corridor and do the side-stepping dance for a bit too long, until it's not funny anymore and there's just this kind of desperation to escape each other. There is a constant low-level pain in social life, like indigestion or a headache.

I prefer dogs. And cats. They make sense. I cannot abide the idiocy that says you must be either a cat person or a dog person but not both.

—

In Cambridge the ground shifted. You don't ignore wealth there. I was hanging out with millionaires and I couldn't afford new shoes. The zeitgeist came to my rescue to some extent, as the after-effects of the recession meant I could get away with grunge as a look. Worn-out floppy black sweaters and scuffed black jeans, all day every day. Throw that on over a cheap black tank top, add a metric ton of black kohl pencil along your lower lash line, and you were doing something in the vicinity of that singer from Garbage who everyone thought was cool.

The College housed all of its students, so on the one hand I didn't have to worry about finding accommodation, but on the other I was stuck in close quarters with the millionaires and they were stuck with me. Minor royals from countries I'd only vaguely heard of, and the children of famous people. They tended to be loudest. I had ticked "low cost" on a form asking what kind of accommodation I would prefer, and been allocated a tiny bedsit in a complex called Hermes Court. This "court" was a strangely shaped red-brick array, evidently added in the 1950s to fit into a negative space defined by the surrounding seventeenth-century buildings. It now housed about a third of us freshers, tucking us away behind Great Court, and bulged out into the area above the Trinity Street shops. The smallest and darkest rooms were for the "low cost" freshers.

My room was on the second floor, and very plainly appointed. It was just big enough for a single bed, a small armchair, a wooden desk, and a three-shelf bookcase. The armchair was red, but there was no other colour. The entrance was from a long corridor of similarly plain-looking doors, though behind most of them, I eventually discovered, were rooms much larger than mine with nice views over the street. My window looked straight into a wall but I didn't care. I loved that room. It was *mine*, at least for the academic year.

A few feet away was a shared bathroom with three cramped shower cubicles and a well-worn plastic tub. Each of these ablution stations offered only a clammy, clinging white curtain for privacy, and because the entire room was lit by a single fluorescent light, pulling one's curtain across meant shutting out most of the light. Besides this, the corridor offered two tiny toilets at each end, and one "gyp room," a basic mini-kitchen of the kind suitable for people who either can't be bothered to cook or shouldn't be allowed to. I tried to stay out of all these common areas as much as possible.

The piano rooms were a short walk away, near the chapel. They were in a bright open space which felt all wrong, so I never used them. Instead, when the weather was good, I took my tiny harp and busked opposite the Great Gate. I had always wanted a beautiful concert harp, but they cost thousands of pounds. For my eighteenth birthday, my aunt had saved up a couple of hundred to buy me a tiny clarsach that sat on my knees. I fell in love with it even before it became a way to feed myself. When a day of busking went very well, I could even afford a bottle of cheap wine from the Sidney Street Sainsbury's. And it went well pretty often. Tourists come to Cambridge looking for magic, so they loved me and my pretty instrument nestled into the cobblestones, filling the little streets with plaintive folk songs and slow slip jigs. Wistful ghosts of a sonic past that might or might not have been real. It didn't matter, it was worth a couple of quid either way.

Occasionally, passing men stopped to sketch me as I played, leaving their sketches in my case in lieu of money. I mostly found this annoying. I did quite like one of the pictures, a soft and fuzzy pencil sketch with the stone wall of the College behind me. I kept it on the top shelf of my bookcase in Hermes Court. In another I was depicted naked, with bushy pubic hair and one misshapen breast almost as large as the harp on my lap. I threw that horrible picture away at once, and yet I can still see it to this day. I have no choice. One man's shitty image of me, grimly installed in my mind forever. Like it's his own personal gallery space.

Once, as I walked back to my room with my case full of coins, a rich kid stopped me. I recognized him as someone who lived on the corridor above mine in Hermes Court. But we'd never spoken.

"Hey! Why are you jangling?"

I showed him.

"Oh, *you* were the busker! Thought I could hear something. Very . . . pretty."

He meant the music. I think.

"Must have been a good day, for you to be jangling like that."

I said yes, it was, and we started walking together towards the door that led up to our rooms.

"So, after you collect it, do you donate all that money to charity?"

I didn't know what to say to that, so I just walked away from him. That was the end of our one brief attempt to get to know each other.

The rich kids didn't understand I wasn't from their world. Or perhaps they just didn't care. Cambridge had its own infinite spaces that contained such things for them. They call it "the bubble"—a pocket of airlessness, timelessness, unreality. Without oxygen, nobody can really breathe, but nothing can decay either. There's a lamppost halfway across Parker's Piece known as "Reality Checkpoint." The name is scratched into the iron—whitish-grey letters scored out through bottle green paint. If you walk by this in the mist, it can be unnerving. By legend, it's supposed to mean you are now leaving the Cambridge bubble—the "normal" world lies beyond. Town not gown.

The real joke is that nobody ever checked anything, there or anywhere else.

Deb was a rich kid. Not that we were kids anymore, I suppose. I met Deb in the second week of term, looking lost in the street behind the side entrance to the College, and I recognized her from our first lecture with Dr. Humberton. She'd annoyed me—and, I assume, everyone else—by asking questions that seemed to have nothing to do with the lecture. I'd hated her voice, and how slowly she talked, as if all the time belonged to her by default.

But for some reason I felt like I ought to help. This feeling was unfamiliar.

"Uhm, hi," I said, approaching awkwardly. "Heading to lecture?"

"Oh . . ." she said, looking around her. "Yeah . . . no. Sure." Ugh.

"Yeah you are or yeah you aren't?" I tried.

"Sure," she said, as if deciding only at this second effort, and even that was provisional.

So we went together, across the river that never seemed to move, towards the red-brick library—at this stage we were still too polite to talk about why it was shaped like a big red phallus—and round behind it to the raised building where most of our lectures took place.

Deb wore pink. Always. She liked to wear thin pink sweaters, and she was flat-chested enough to look good in them. Even her twinsets somehow never quite looked over the top. Her hair was all the My Little Ponies I never had: dead straight, pure blonde. It was so shiny she always seemed to be wearing a little crown of light. At the front, it flopped cutely over her eyes. She was everything I wasn't and she didn't have to try.

I didn't really like Deb, not at first. We just ended up doing everything together. Every Tuesday and Thursday morning I would find her—still unfeasibly disoriented—outside the back of the College, and we'd walk over to the raised building behind the brick library (which, by week three, we'd dubbed Big Willy) to our lectures. In the evenings we'd smoke and watch TV in the JCR. It smelled of spilled beer and stale cigarettes in there, which made it easier to talk. It bothered Deb that she was addicted to smoking and I wasn't: I could take it or leave it, but if there was money left at the end of the week, I'd take it. I liked how it made my lips feel, like they had a point. Deb used to say that if that's what it was about for me, then I was a non-smoker. I said fine, then I was a non-smoker who smoked. She said she liked her name shortened, so I started calling her Deborah-reborah. Then Deborah-reborah-reborah. Then Deborah-reborandeveramen.

She didn't have a middle name. Apparently, her mum had

hated her own middle name so much that in protest she'd given Deb no middle name at all. That made no sense to me. But Deb said it wasn't about making sense. It meant they were connected. I told her my mother and I had the same birthday but even so we weren't connected at all.

"You never talk about your mother," she said, and I agreed. It was several weeks into the term before we started to ask each other real questions.

"Why are you always sad?" she said once, out of the blue. I frowned. "I'm not."

"You are. You don't laugh at anything. I watched you the other day in the Humberton lecture and you never laughed once."

The frown furrowed itself in deeper. "It wasn't funny," I said. I'd honestly assumed the other students laughed out of awkwardness. Or perhaps in hopes of ingratiating themselves with him.

"He's pretty sharp," Deb said.

"Dr. Bumberton," I replied—and I unashamedly admit that we both found *this* hilarious—"is about as sharp as a six-minute runny poo."

We were still bent double with laughter when two guys burst in and changed the channel to watch the football.

When I went up to Cambridge, I stopped visiting my mother in the home. It was too far. I couldn't afford to take trains across the country all the time. So I stopped telling my half-bullshit stories to anyone. Almost my whole life I'd been spouting a running commentary into the dead air of the home, and now it went quiet. I would phone my aunt sometimes, but she only wanted to exchange platitudes and tell me how the weather was or what she and my uncle had eaten that week.

I wonder if my mother noticed the silence. I didn't, really. I had started talking to Deb. We liked to play with language, especially the Cambridge Latin. If you failed an exam, you were allowed to apply for an *aegrotat*, which meant you were ill on the day. We'd fantasize about getting an "I grossed that" by showing up for exams covered in putrid boils, or flesh-eating worms, so that the invigilator would have to send us away and all the other kids would vomit onto their scripts.

It took me a while to understand why Deb spoke slowly, but it was because her mind had gone on a three-mile hike between each word. I rush my speech because I want to get the talking over with, end the awkward social interaction. But Deb wasn't afraid of people. She was a still river with a killer undercurrent. I suppose people have a social speed setting, and connecting with them means you have to know the right setting. Deb's setting was slow but that didn't mean anything, except that's where her dial was set. When I meet people I do try to find their setting. It's better than giving up on a connection right away. It never seems to work though, not like it did with Deb.

One day I taught her a line from my old school chant: *Domino deo nostro serviemus*. She said it slowly back to herself: "*Dom-in-o de-o nos-tro* . . . serve me a moose?" and we crumpled into painful laughter that hardly paused long enough for us to eat or drink for the next forty-eight hours. Neither of us knew what sort of noise a moose made, so we experimented with a range of awful bellows and grunts. Nobody else found this funny, especially at night.

Sometimes when we talked until very late, Deb would curl up on the floor of my room. We didn't sleep much those nights, we just talked and laughed. Then, as the sky began to lighten, each of us would tell the other we were worried about her: she was not getting enough sleep. And we'd laugh at that until it was time to get up.

Breakfast would be a bleary meal of eggs and fried bread, watched over by a huge full-body painting of Henry VIII which dominated the Hall from the north end. Eating in Hall could be awkward, especially if you were wearing a skirt. The Hall seating, for members *in statu pupillari*, consisted of long wooden benches and long wooden tables, in straight parallel lines, perpendicular to the High Table. The benches made it incredibly hard to sit down in a skirt without showing the world your knickers. The College may have caved to the pressure to admit women students, but it drew the line at giving us opportunities to sit down with our dignity intact.

Fortunately Deb and I were not particularly concerned with dignity at breakfast.

"All you do is laugh at your own jokes," said a man sitting opposite us one morning. "It's the least funny thing in the world."

We both nearly peed ourselves at the realization that he was completely right.

There weren't many others in College I talked to. There was Pandemos, the College cat, a huge tabby with intermittently friendly tendencies. Students used to feed her scraps of cheese, and put out saucers of milk for her to drink. Pandemos was lactose intolerant. You could usually tell if the vomit in the stairways was hers or a student's by the quantity. Her presence was calming, though. I've heard it said that the reason cats smush their faces up against things is that they are "tagging" them as safe. I don't know if that's true but I liked letting Pandemos smush her face against me as she threaded round my ankles in the mailroom, or deigned to let me stroke her fur while she basked on warm stone windowsills in the sunshine. She seemed to care about very little except finding food and the occasional cuddle. She didn't even seem to mind that about half of what she ate came back out the wrong end of her. Because she was so round and large, it was often speculated that she might be pregnant, but I knew her for years and I never saw any kittens nor any change of shape. I could tell Pandemos anything. She couldn't have cared less about any of it.

Apart from Deb and Pandemos, I only talked to Gin, really. Or rather, she did most of the talking. Gin was a grad student, an American, working on her philosophy Ph.D., and she spent a lot of hours in the College library. Whenever I had an essay on the go, I did the same. Gin was what Americans call "put together," in a quiet way, with long light-brown hair and a soft smile. Her outfits and the leather satchel she took everywhere conveyed a scholarly look, in keeping with her bookish tendencies. We sat together round the pine tables in the College's working library, and we worked.

This library was an entirely different space from the College's show library, although the one sat right beside the other. The show library was designed by Christopher

Wren, and I loved it in a worshipful way. So quiet and cold, a little space out of the world. Its black and white diamond-tiled floor ticked and tocked under my heels, and the sound would bounce up around the book stacks, the shelves adorned with swirled wood carvings and packed with dark ancient spines. Sometimes when the sun was low, the light through the stained glass lit up the books in red and gold, like costume jewellery to the floor's harlequin outfit. Marble busts of dead white men guarded each aisle, but A. A. Milne's manuscript for *Winnie-the-Pooh* sat open in one of the glass cases, and somehow it made me feel a little safer to know that Pooh could make a home in here. Next to Isaac Newton's notebooks.

You couldn't talk in the Wren, though, that would have been all wrong. And there was nowhere to work unless you booked a space in advance. It was just a place you could be, like a temple, to stop time from coming at you for a moment. It was mainly used for ceremonies, but was also good for redirecting nosey tourists away from the student bedrooms.

In the working library, Gin and I could talk. When there was no one else around it felt fine to talk in there because we weren't disturbing anyone except the books, and these books were meant to be disturbed. They weren't like the beautiful manuscripts in the Wren: they were the working class of books. Cheap, scuffed, replaceable.

"Do you think that Mary who's lived in a black and white room all her life knows what it's like to see a red tomato?" She spoke softly and pronounced it *tuh-may-doe*. Gin liked to run thought experiments past me to see if they made sense, or check if I shared her intuitions about a hypothetical scenario, or ask how she might strengthen a premise in an argument.

"If it turned out that the stuff in our rivers and seas was not really H$_2$O but some other chemical substance, and had been all along, would that stuff still be water?" *Wah-durr*.

"Suppose one day you promise someone that you're going to kill your grandma. Is it now wrong for you to refrain from killing grandma, because you've promised, and breaking your promise would be wrong? Or is it still wrong to kill grandma because killing is wrong?"

All my grandparents were dead before I was born, but I didn't say that because Gin wouldn't have been interested. Gin never seemed to care about what was true, only what might be true, or what would follow from what, or what would happen under what circumstances. I didn't mind her casual intellectual company-keeping, but I never told her what I was thinking about, and to her credit she never asked.

Gin wasn't a friend, but she was the kind of person you can say is "a friend" if someone asks. Talking to her I'd sometimes feel that jolt of chemical release in my brain, the one that I think is meant to be a social reward, a signal that I have done something right (or at least well enough) so that my body wants me to remember and do it again. I don't think the mechanism works properly in me. I don't *like* the feeling very much. I can see how it's supposed to feel nice but it's also enervating, like a sudden intake of breath. It puts me on edge. I worry that I've set an expectation of social competence I cannot live up to.

Also, I don't think you're supposed to notice this sort of chemical event when it happens.

Chapter Four

That first Cambridge winter, there was a constant nip of wind chill. It was as if the city itself were animated by it: the whole place breathing cold air from the northeast, fresh and full of spirit. Deb and I would let ourselves be blown across the river to lectures like a couple of paper-chain dolls, conjoined at hands and feet, then afterwards we'd link our thick-coated arms to walk back to College at a forty-five-degree angle. Or we'd stand together, wiggling our bottoms in parallel, our mouths gaping in wide-open *O*s towards the wind, saying we were fish windsocks. I could really feel the rushing channel of cold air pass right through me, as we stood there performing this invaluable service for passers-by. We were vessels with a purpose. We meant something.

Other students hurried past. Most of them pointedly ignored us, but some looked at us like we were crazy. A few of the women snickered into gloved hands and whispered to each other, bending their heads close. It didn't matter that nobody else understood what we were doing. We made sense for each other, for ourselves, and that was enough. More than enough. It was joyous.

When we stepped out into the windy streets and cars beeped their aggressive horns at us for daring to be there, Deb would slowly give them the middle finger, sometimes using her other hand in a winding motion to "crank" up the bird. She could do it without even looking round—she kept right on walking. When men revved their engines at us for attention, she would hold her hands flat above her head and tap on it while blowing a huge raspberry, like the French knight on the battlements in *Monty Python and the Holy Grail*—you know, the guy who tells King Arthur they won't go questing for the grail because they've already got one. If the revving continued, she would start yelling "*Fetchez la vache!*"

I started to copy these performances of hers, and slowly we synchronized the routines until we could perform them with dance-like perfection. As if by mirroring each other we might deflect the rest of the world. Turn its evil gaze back on itself.

One night I dreamed that Deb and I really were wind-socks. We were floating far above ground in a cold, thick fog that swirled and eddied all around us. At first I was afraid because I couldn't see anything through the fog, but then it was okay because I could see Deb, and I could hear that she was laughing. Her body was a pink tube flapping in the wind, vibrant against the emptiness. I looked at my own body and it was flapping like hers, but mine was grey like the background. As I watched, it began to fade into the fog. Then the wind dropped, and everything slowed down. Eventually we were both silent and motionless. Deb remained as bright and complete as ever, just frozen. My own fish-sock body had all but disappeared, leaving a thin, grey, papery shell that would disperse in a fine ashy powder if anything ever touched it. But nothing did. Nothing moved, and I somehow knew that nothing would ever move again.

When I woke up she was right there, curled up on my floor in the fluffy pink blanket she'd taken to stashing under my bed for the purpose.

At Cambridge, time arrives in eight-week parcels named for the Christian calendar. The Michaelmas term, the Lent term, the Easter term. I never had much to do with the Christian religion; at school it was a kind of unexamined scenery. I didn't know what Michaelmas was. But I went home for Christmas. Or at least, I went to my aunt and uncle's house. There were piles of laundry in my room, and an exercise bike that looked like it had never been used. The seat still had the plastic cover on.

On Christmas Eve, my aunt drove me to the home, and left me in the cold in the middle of the brick square with my mother. My mother sat and smoked in silence, same as always, but I had fallen out of the babbling habit and now I didn't know what to say to her. I shivered and wished I'd brought a warmer coat. My mother was only wearing navy flip-flops and a dressing gown. They looked old. For all I knew they could have been the same things she had worn for the last thirteen years, since the day she came out of hospital.

I asked her if she felt cold. She didn't react, but it occurred to me that I had never asked her a question before. I tried some more. *Why do you smoke all the time? Are you hungry? Do you like Beethoven? Do you want me to go away?*

I looked down at my feet. My legs were crossed, and the top foot, the free foot, was moving around, wiggling, tracing some looping pattern of its own. It does that a lot when I'm not paying attention to keeping it still.

I sighed, and with the exhalation some stories came. I told her about my room in Hermes Court, about Humberton's lectures, about how I'd made a friend called Deb. I couldn't keep my face from breaking into a grin when I mentioned her.

Then something landed on my cheek. Maybe it was a snowflake. Or hot ash from my mother's cigarette. Do you know that it's impossible to tell sensations of hot and cold apart, when you can't see what's causing them? Put an ice cube on the back of somebody's neck and tell them it's a cigarette, and they will feel it burning.

Or don't, because that's a shitty thing to do. The point is, it's easy to present people with the exact opposite of what is real. Holmes understood this. *What you do in this world is a matter of no consequence*, he tells Watson. *The question is, what can you make people believe that you have done.* And then, *Never mind.*

On this occasion, though, I told my mother nothing but the truth.

While we were down from Cambridge that winter, Deb and I sent each other long letters with no words. Instead we would draw ridiculous cartoons of impossible animals, or philosophers we were studying, or people we knew from lectures, or each other. We'd stick small objects like toenails and dead flies to the pages with Sellotape, then seal up these missives in bulging envelopes and take them to the post office counter to be weighed in case they needed more than the standard first-class postage. We didn't need any help to decipher each other's signals. They were perfect.

Whenever I received one I would take it to my room and close the door, and laugh with such abandon that one day my aunt knocked gently and asked if I was okay, which made me laugh so hard that I couldn't answer her for a while, and she came in just to make sure.

She had such an anxious look on her face. It wasn't like her to be a worrier.

Back in Cambridge for the Lent term, College life started to fall into a routine. We studied Plato's *Meno*, a compulsory set text on whether virtue can be taught. There was also Hume and J. S. Mill. There was never a book by a woman. I had only one female lecturer, Professor Bell, a stern-looking woman in her fifties with short grey hair and a dry academic manner. She taught Descartes and Spinoza, and had such a posh accent that she said *fah* instead of "fire," and *ears* instead of "yes." Someone told me she was the daughter of a duke and could use a title if she wanted, but she preferred "Professor." I thought her lectures were okay but she always struck me as a bit cold in her manner.

As spring did its best to take the edge off the Cambridge wind chill, Deb and I discovered a shared secret love of McDonald's breakfasts. Their hash browns, surely the world's worst balance of fats and carbs to usable nutriments, became a weekly guilty pleasure. But these outings were as much about escaping Henry VIII's stale gaze and the institutional fried smell of Hall mornings as they were about anything. I'd heard that if you were locked in a McDonald's and it was all you had to eat and you had to stay alive, your best bet would be to eat all the packets of tomato ketchup because at least there are some vitamins in there. This was in the days before McDonald's tried to greenwash its menu with token salads. (They're only there so we all feel better about going into McDonald's. You know that, right? Nobody eats them.) The hash browns, glorious golden-brown grease patties, were followed in my own case by a day or two of gastric pain. *Truly, sir, and pleasure will be paid, one time or another.* I suppose I found the price reasonable. My gut was usually unsettled in any case. I blamed that on the cigarettes, the cheap wine, and my overall questionable diet.

Deb's birthday fell in March, and I decided to buy her a blue sweater. I had been saving for a month to get something good enough for her, and when I saw the right one in the window of Monsoon I instantly imagined Deb in it. How she would be beautiful in this colour; in something new. The price tag gave me cold feelings—I'd never spent so much money on clothes in my life. But sometimes you've got to take a risk. I bought some of the most expensive wrapping paper at Heffers, the prismatic kind that's hard to fold and doesn't stick to Sellotape very well. I hid the package nervously in my underwear drawer.

On the eve of Deb's birthday she slept on the floor of my room. She was unusually serious this time, and said her parents would be coming to take her out for lunch.

"I don't know how it's going to go," she half whispered, reaching out to hold my hand in the dark.

"I thought you liked your mum?" I whispered back.

"I love her. It's not that."

Deb sighed and slowed down even more than usual. "It's . . . there are things I'm supposed to do one day. Have to do. They'll want . . . to make sure I'm not attached . . ." "What?"

I could hear she was crying gently. "I can't. I'm not allowed to talk about this. Never. Not to *you*. Well, I mean, not to anyone. I'm not supposed to get close to . . . Oh god," she sniffed, "I can't. Please, forget it. Please. And promise me you'll never tell anyone. *Promise* me, like your life depends on it. Don't say anything to anybody. Not *anybody*, okay? Not even me. *Never* mention this again."

She was in deadly earnest now, and I was suddenly frightened.

"*Promise*, Victoria." Her voice wavered.

I had never heard Deb talk like this before. I squeezed her little hand tighter, and promised with my whole heart. Then I held on to her hand like it was a precious thing until gradually it relaxed its grip and she drifted off. I only half slept through the remainder of the night. The time was blank and dreamless.

When we woke up a few hours later, Deb went back to her room to get ready, then we went for a special McDonald's birthday breakfast on our way to lectures. I squished the holographic parcel, already bursting its inadequate Sellotape bonds, into my backpack with my files for the day.

As we walked to our seats with our plastic trays, I said, "Before our hands get all greasy, can I give you something?"

Deb pulled the package open with no difficulty, and shook out the blue sweater. She smiled, and said it was very pretty.

45

"Try it on!" I urged.

She pulled off the soft pink cashmere she had on and set it gently down on the back of the plastic chair, smoothing its folds before reaching her arms into the blue fuzz of my gift. It fit her beautifully; a little baggy, but in a classy way. She pulled her hair out through the crew neck, and it fell down her back like rays of golden sun in a perfect sky. She changed back into the pink one for lectures though.

I suppose the family lunch must have gone all right, because she didn't mention it again and things went back to just how they had been. Her clothing, too—I never saw her wear the blue sweater after that morning.

The week after her birthday, Deb came running to my room to tell me she'd won the annual College fiction prize for a short story she'd written. Of course she had. She was all dreams and wonder. I gave her a hug and we agreed to celebrate by going to Formal Hall in the evening.

Formal Hall cost about as much as I could usually afford to budget for three days' food, so I didn't do it very often. We had to wear our navy undergraduate gowns to attend, so whenever Deb and I were both going, we'd get ready early, pull our gowns up over our heads, and roam around the corridors of Hermes Court saying we were the ghosts of dead bats who'd just popped in to use the toilet and we were done now thank you very much only we couldn't find the exit. We'd pretend to try and follow the green "fire exit" arrows, which as it turned out led you in a circle around the entire second floor. We found this hilarious at the time, although now that I think about it, that could potentially have been a problem. We flapped up helplessly against the walls, and slammed into passers-by who were rarely as amused as we were. We were completely sober, this was just how we were with each other. Like nitrous oxide.

On the occasion of Deb's literary victory, our riotous laughter en route from Hermes Court to the Hall steps brought us briefly to the attention of Dr. Rumpole, a rather miserable-looking senior chemistry Fellow. He raised his eyes, as if to pray for defences against this invasion of his College.

"If you can neither understand nor respect the meaning of the undergraduate gown," he snipped, bony forefinger poking into my right shoulder, "you should not be permitted to wear it."

The rebuke punctured me all over, but as we walked away across the Great Court cobbles, more sombrely now, Deb whispered into my ear, "Rumpole Scumpole, stick it up your bumhole."

I took her arm and pressed it to my side, and we marched proudly in to her prize dinner.

The weeks ran round in their circuits and Deb and I trotted along to their rhythm, their structure as it pertained to us. Humberton's lectures on the problem of other minds marked the beginning of my week, although they were on Tuesdays. Other people's timekeeping conventions didn't matter.

Humberton was always immaculately dressed for lectures, but in a way that took you a while to notice. He usually wore a white shirt and juniper-green tweed jacket, with blue jeans that showed he wasn't trying too hard and brown leather shoes that were evidently expensive but not new. His jeans were often dusty where he'd rubbed his chalky palms. When it was warm in the room, or when he was getting excited about his subject, he'd take the jacket off and set it on the back of a chair, rolling his shirtsleeves up to the elbows to reveal tanned arms and a broad-faced gold watch. If we were sitting in the front row, I'd be able to smell his blend of fresh sweat and muted aftershave. It was a relaxing smell, damp and woody like soft rain in a forest.

In the lecture rooms, students perched at long wooden desks with long wooden benches attached. These arrays filled the room with parallel immovable rows. They were terribly uncomfortable places to sit for an hour. In most lectures I sat at the back, so nobody was looking at me and I could shuffle frequently to ease the abdominal pain that always came with sitting on such a hard surface. But for Humberton, Deb and I sat up front, and it was worth it.

He often got excited, and went off topic. One morning, he began explaining to us a conception of time as extending infinitely in one direction but not the other.

"So the question is: can you imagine time having a *beginning* but no end? Let's say time had to get started—we can say it started with the Big Bang. But now that it's going . . ."

The jacket came off.

". . . there's no stopping it. Time is never going to end. The future just goes on into infinity. Now, some people feel uncomfortable about this, but often that's just a general discomfort with infinity. They can't wrap their heads around the thought that something will never end. Not just that it's *possible* for it to go on forever—people are usually okay with that—but that it actually *does* go on forever. Well, if that troubles you, if you can't picture it, you could think of it this way. An infinite line looks like . . ."

He turned to the chalkboard with a smile, and drew a circle.

". . . this! It's just a circle with a bad memory."

The other students all laughed. I suppose they didn't think it mattered. They were wrong. It mattered. It gave me bad butterflies in my stomach and I had to step out of the lecture for a moment.

I stumbled on autopilot down to the women's toilets in the basement. I knew it would be cooler there. And it felt like the natural direction for me to head in. My digestion always having been somewhat ropey, I spend a lot of my life in toilets. Toilets are very important. Do not underestimate them. My trust in an institution can be measured quite accurately by whether I will sit down on the seat of its toilets. If I'm in my own home or in a hospital, I just sit right down. In those early days at the University, I would wipe the seats over with toilet paper, then sit down. In nice restaurants, I put a layer of paper down over the seat and then sit on top of the paper. In the public lavvies around Cambridge, I would not sit down under any circumstances. There I hovered, developing excellent thigh muscles in an unauthorized variant of chair pose. I judge toilets, too, when there is nowhere to put my bag (not on the floor or on the cistern—that's disgusting). If there is no such place, what I get from that is that you don't want women to be comfortable in your space. We have to carry all this extra baggage around, the least you could do is let us put it down for a second to crap in comfort.

In the building that housed the philosophy lectures, the gents was on the second floor, but the ladies was at the very bottom of the stairs, on a level below what you'd assume was the lowest one. This basement was a small, poorly lit space with yellow-grey tiled walls, and floors that were always a little damp. All that was down there was a cleaning cupboard and the ladies' toilets, and it was one of the places I felt safe in this building. Perhaps it was the smell of institutional disinfectant. And men had no reason to go down there, which meant that it was usually empty. The cleaners only came at night.

There was always a lot of graffiti in those subterranean toilet stalls. Layers of semiconscious scribble, accreting below the radar as the official conversations went on above ground. It generally comprised a range of uninspired variants on the same two thoughts: *X loves Y* and *Z is a slut*. Except that, on this particular day, I found someone had written:

> *You would think from all this wit*
> *Shakespeare himself came here to shit.*
> *And that, my friends, may well be true*
> *For Shakespeare had to do it, too.*

This is how genius works. It's an optical illusion generated by the way our brains process contrast. Light and dark. Blue and gold. Whatever: we will adjust to anything as a baseline. Little things look huge when there's fuck-all else going on.

I got myself back into Humberton's lecture as soon as I could. I hated to miss anything. I quickly tuned back in to his language, back in to the process of making detailed, tidy notes in my A4 pad, to be filed in my blue ring binder marked *Philosophy of Mind* once I got back to my room. Deb and I joked about Humberton but he wasn't a bad lecturer, really. He was interested in all kinds of things, so he went off on tangents that were interesting. He talked a lot about books. He said you can't read the same book twice because you're different. He said books are just mirrors. I think he meant they're good for seeing what's behind you. They say Machiavelli wrote a mirror for princes, and really that book is just a Rolodex of historical role models. So *Ruling Italy for Dummies* is all about the rear-view. A prince is meant to fig-ure out how to go on by looking backwards. And not just how to go on for himself, but for the whole damn country. How can that be a good idea? Unless you *want* everything going round in circles.

The only other lecturer I could stand was Professor Bell. We didn't really think about the same kinds of things at all, but because she was the only woman who taught me, she became a kind of role model, and a kind of mentor. You know the way women do when they're the only one. That's why I went to her for help.

This was well into the Lent term, during the whole situa-tion with Dave. Apart from Deb, I had never told anyone about Dave. I only told Deb once, and we didn't bring it up again because I didn't want to, but Deb had said maybe I should talk to Bell about it.

Do I have to explain Dave? Dave was a boy in my year. Or do I mean a man? I mean, he was eighteen or nineteen, like the rest of us. But no, Dave was a boy. I don't mean that as a pejorative—it's not a bad thing to be a boy. And *man* is hardly a term of approbation. Anyway, Dave had been taught to be whatever he was. His early education had evi-dently included lessons in persistence.

Dave was a minor irritation at first but he would not stop. It started with loud comments about my being "so fit," which he didn't mean. He wasn't even saying it to me, but for the benefit of whoever else was nearby. He'd pretend to swoon, or make humping gestures in my direction. Then he started throwing small objects at me in lectures. I ignored all that but I decided to talk to Bell when the holding started. Holding my arm while he talked and laughed, holding me in place when I wanted to leave. I don't want to talk about Dave. Dave is boring. He doesn't matter. What he was doing, it's so common. You can fill in any of a million Daves. Choose your own Dave. It's Bell who matters.

Bell agreed to meet with me one day after her lecture, and we found a spare room. A few printed handouts were still strewn about, remnants of the students' dash to the exit, this small careless mess only serving to emphasize the order of the room. The day's chalk dust was trying to settle, suspended for a moment in time by the treacly afternoon sun.

Somehow, in that room, all my words got suspended, too. The air became thick with them, like tiny physical particles. I couldn't make Bell understand what I was saying. Breathing was difficult, as if there wasn't quite enough oxygen to go around, and I was intensely aware of my own shifty feet. My poor cherry red Doc Martens, already tatty when I'd acquired them second-hand years before, looked so ungainly, cheap, ungraceful. Probably I was trampling semantics. But Bell was making vague sympathetic noises, so I persevered. I tried to avoid her eyes, but she would deliberately catch mine. Hers were round and grey, and there was something else about their effect that was striking. Some quality

I couldn't put my finger on—almost *behind* them, yet still visible from this side, if that makes any sense. I didn't understand it.

She was nodding gently, and saying, *"Ears, ears,"* which meant "Yes, yes."

Then it plopped out of her, like a heavy turd in a deep toilet bowl. "The thing is, Victoria, you know that if you complain about this it will go badly for everyone. For you too. It could even be bad for your career, if people were to think of you as a troublemaker. That sort of thing gets about, you know? You'd be taking such a big risk. And over . . . what? It's nothing *rarely*."

She meant "really."

Her voice was soft and sweet. Barely there, like finely milled icing sugar. My lips went cold and I stopped talking. I'd made a mistake. I had no mentors. A couple of weeks later, Bell gave a small talk in the department library about postgraduate study, at which she assured us all that there was no racism or sexism in the Academy anymore. It wasn't like when she was a young woman.

I met a few more Professor Bells later in my life. Perhaps it's my imagination, but I thought their eyes all had that same intangible, terrible quality.

———

For pity's sake I wish she'd shut up. What is
the fucking point of it, going on and on and on.
I don't believe half of it's even true. She contradicts
herself and goes in circles. Maybe I am the point.
Oh god, what if that's it, the meaning of my life,
to sit here and listen to the little shit talking
and talking and talking. If only she would just
disappear. Then maybe I could as well.

Part Two

Worms

But when I came to man's estate

Chapter Five

After the Bell incident, I suddenly felt that Cambridge was not a world where we could say what we meant. But I already knew it, really. Why else did we write in ciphers, speak in hypotheticals, scrawl drivel on toilet doors? Nonsense has always served this role in times of crisis. Weird echoes of the half-familiar that mean nothing—at least, nothing that could ever be pinned on anyone. The absurd is a cry of pain for when our symbols are overloaded, collapsing. The last thing left.

That's why the Nazis tried to ban it, you know. "Degenerate art." They exhibited it in "the insanity room" with a notice: *In the paintings and drawings of this chamber of horrors there is no telling what was in the sick brains of those who wielded the brush or the pencil.* History is a stuck record on this one: Jewish artists are crazy, queer people are crazy, women are crazy, ex-girlfriends are *super* crazy, our enemies are crazy, and crazy people are our enemies.

That was my conclusion, anyway, but I never spoke a word about it out loud. Except during Humberton's digressions, such extracurricular thinking was strongly discouraged. By the time we graduated, the *best* of us, the elite, the top of the class, would be writing very sane and sensible prose. We would forget how to read the nonsense codes, and that there was once a reason we needed them. We would call this training. Discipline.

If women are crazy it's because they contain multitudes, which is because they have to. And then they have to learn how to keep most of them tucked away most of the time. On the flip side, men aren't allowed to. Maybe that's why I'd never thought marrying a man would be a good idea. If I'd been allowed a few at a time, that might have worked. I don't know. With women, it's different. All their lives they're being flattened down in one dimension, so they get spread out in others. Kaleidoscopic. You know how if you unfold a cube, you get six squares? *One woman in her time plays many parts*, although in her case they do not appear in a specified order. They might be folded together, like a little chorus of supporting characters, all singing for their lives.

Or spread too thin, spun to rags and tatters. Go read a Plato dialogue, and then look at the fragments we have left of Sappho. One person's manuscripts so terribly important to preserve, the other's left to rot away. Full of holes, now. All that blank space on the page. What's left of Sappho is mostly nonsense. And yet what nonsense. Maybe I could have married Deb if I'd thought of it soon enough.

But by the time I'd figured out things like that, Deb was gone.

Deb went missing at the end of April. The Easter term had just begun: the exam term. The crunch.

The last time I saw Deb was at Humberton's lecture. We sat up at the front together as usual, scribbling commentary to each other in the margins of our lecture notes, and when it was over we walked out of the room, arm in arm, chatting and laughing.

"Bumberton's on good form today!" Deb said.

"You always think he's on good form," I told her. "You think he's the Platonic Form of good form. You *lurve* his good form."

She squished my arm and giggled. "I have to go to Big Bad Brain's lecture now."

Big Bad Brain was our nickname for Professor Bairn, whose parents had made the baffling decision to make their son a walking anagram by naming him Brian. As if they couldn't think of any other letters to use.

And that was it. Deb strolled away across the stairwell, I went back to the College library to work, and she was gone.

I knew something was wrong when Deb didn't come to Hall. Ordinary Hall was a cheaper, informal meal, earlier in the evening than Formal Hall, and required no special clothing. I sat there alone that night, with a small plate of lumpy mashed potato and floppy green beans, waiting. I could tell something was off. Even Henry VIII looked a little different, a little more ridiculous. A huge square with head and legs poking out. Had his eyebrows shifted from their usual position? I had to tell myself not to be such a weirdo. This painting had been in the College since 1567.

After dinner, Deb didn't come to the JCR to smoke either, and that was definitely not right. I waited for her for twenty minutes, then I went to her room and knocked on her door.

When that didn't work I went back to my own room. My head hurt terribly now, and my mind was noisy but useless. I lay like that all night, clothed and rigid on top of my bed, frozen in a panic response.

I called my aunt the next morning. I hadn't phoned her for weeks, but she hadn't seemed to notice. I plodded, slipper-footed, down the stairwell of Hermes Court to the payphone in the echoing lobby, and slid my card into the slot. I pressed the beeping metal buttons in their familiar order, but today it felt strange and wrong. I was all out of phase. When my aunt picked up, I must have sounded like an idiot.

"I had a friend . . . I need to talk to someone . . . she's gone missing."

"Hello sweetheart! Uh, what do you mean? Who's missing?"

"My friend Deb. She isn't here. She hasn't been here since yesterday."

My aunt laughed. "She probably went home."

"No, she wouldn't. I mean, she would tell me, she wouldn't just go away like that. She'd have told me when she was coming back. Or where she was going at least. Anyway you can't just leave during Full Term—you need an exeat, and you can only spend three nights out of town or you won't have kept term . . ."

She wasn't listening. She had never wanted to understand College life with its arcane terminology. Either that, or she hadn't wanted to try to understand it and fail.

"Maybe she met a boy!"

"What? No!" It was so obvious that Deb wouldn't have gone off with a boy that I hadn't considered it for a minute.

I didn't quite know how to explain why it was so obvious. All I found to say was, "She'd have told me."

"Why should she?"

"She's . . . my friend. We hang out together."

"Well, friends don't have to know where each other are the whole time, do they? Maybe she got sick of you breathing down her neck! Why don't you spend some time with your other friends?"

I didn't answer that.

"Your uncle sends his love."

I didn't answer that either. There was no way in hell my uncle had told her to send me his love, and we both knew it, and we both knew that we both knew.

The headset clicked that I was running out of credit, and I explained that I'd have to go soon as I didn't have another card. She didn't offer to call back.

"Okay, sweetie. Well, have a lovely week!" And in her sing-song voice, "Don't forget to study!"

God.

The next day I went to Professor Bell's lecture on my own. Deb was supposed to be there. I picked a spot on the horrible wooden benches that gave me a good view of the door, and I watched the door like an abandoned dog for the entire lecture. Deb didn't come. I don't know if Professor Bell noticed that I didn't look at her once that whole hour, but I didn't care, her lectures were always dead boring anyway. She drawled on about the *pay-Neil* gland (I knew from my own earlier reading that she meant "pineal") as my hope drained slowly out of the room, like the kind of dirty sink-water that leaves a rim of scum behind. I went back to my bedsit and went to bed and stayed there motionless for a few days. I'm not sure how many.

It should be long ago, but it feels so close I could touch it. The dire stillness of those first nights, when I lay awake in the dark and just *waited* for Deb. And then, when I got up again, the slow, dull dawning of the new situation.

What made it all the more chilling was how nobody else seemed even to realize that she was gone. Suddenly, it was as if Deb had never been there. That felt like an awfully cruel trick. Can you imagine waking up one morning and finding everything in your room has been shifted two inches to the left? You don't know what to do with that information. There's something hideous about it. Grotesque.

I supposed it made sense that the College would want something like this hushed up, and that the family would try to keep fuss to a minimum, so that the media would leave them in peace and so on. And I knew that Deb's people had money—the old kind, the kind that keeps itself quiet—so they would be able to arrange things. Cambridge is a weird place. The College is patrolled by these stolid men called porters who deliver the morning post but are effectively their own police force. Did you know that? It's a seriously weird place. Although none of them said as much, they all somehow managed to imply, in their attitude and expressions, even in their gait, that absolutely nothing out of the ordinary was going on. They *radiated* business-as-usual as they meandered under the Great Gate, touching their bowler hats whenever a student or Fellow of the College walked past. I guessed that either the College or Deb's family must have had the media in their pocket, too, because I never saw anything about Deb on the local news. I mean, there was no Twitter back then, and it's true you didn't hear about everything, but still, it didn't feel quite right to me.

I racked my memory constantly for what she had said, what *exactly*, that night when she had been afraid. When she'd mentioned some complication about her parents' visit. Something she had to do, or not do. She wasn't supposed to get attached. What had that meant? Why didn't I ask more, try to help? What kind of friend ignores it when someone reaches out to them like that? What the hell was wrong with me? Obviously it was something serious if she was under so much pressure to say nothing, even to me. But I had no experience of being a friend. So I had failed her.

Now I was useless. What could I possibly do? I had no idea what she had been talking about, and I had promised Deb—the last promise I ever gave her—that I would never, ever mention anything about that conversation to another soul. I didn't even know who Deb's family were. We didn't just Google stuff in those days. I had heard of some "internet search engines," but they had names like "Lycos" and "AskJeeves" and they were rubbish. It would never have occurred to me to use them to try and find out anything about Deb or her family. Right after she'd gone, I realized with a nasty start that I didn't even know if her surname was really Orton. That could just have been a pseudonym she used at the College for privacy. All we'd ever really talked about was the middle name she *didn't* have.

Anyway, her family would be the kind of people who evaded the public eye. Even if I'd had Google, it probably wouldn't have helped. It seems to confuse Americans these days, but there is this culture of old money. I met it in Cambridge, but I had already learned it from Conan Doyle and Christie. People who wore centuries-old heirloom jewellery that looked like nothing special, and carried incredibly battered leather bags. The only other people who could *see* these markers, these coded signals, were the others who belonged, who knew in an instant what they were looking at. People whose idea of researching their family history was pulling a dog-eared *Debrett's* off the shelf of some uncle's oak-panelled library, or wandering down a hallway of scruffily framed portraits that might include a Gainsborough or two but who's counting. People who (quite literally, I am convinced of this) would rather die than be photographed in a gilt palace with a stuffed child on a stuffed lion.

I tried so hard, so terribly hard, to remember if there had been anything else. Any other hint, any tiny sign of anything unusual. Anything else strange Deb had ever said, or anything she had done.

But there was nothing. Not then.

It was six weeks before the first clue arrived. There was still no sign of Deb, and my bitter, painful terror had strung itself out into a state of permanent jumpiness. I kept walking past her room, and I always knocked, but there was never any answer.

I was dawdling in the stone passage between the Hall and the College Buttery, sort of hanging out with the absence of Deb. It was still early summer, but the Easter term had come and gone. Exams were over and I knew that I hadn't performed as well as I should have. There was nothing you could do about that though, unless you'd actually failed something, and even then you could only apply for an *aegrotat* which, even if you got it, meant you'd be deemed to have received a bare pass. A bare pass was nothing I needed. I needed a First. If I didn't get a First, what would be the point?

It never occurred to me to ask what the point would be of getting one.

Since Deb had been gone I hadn't been eating properly. I glanced in through the open Hall doors at Henry, legs wide apart over the High Table, dangling himself at the diners below. *Semper eadem* over his head. *Nice thing for you to say, you giant wanker*, I thought. *You had something to prove about how replaceable women are.* Still, it made a good motto for canteen food. Right now, they were serving the usual varietals of solid English breakfast. I couldn't bring myself to go in.

It wasn't exactly cold anymore, but it was still Cambridge and a chilly breeze shoved its way along the passage each time the heavy oak doors opened to let a student in or out. For a second, I whimsically imagined the ghost of Deb slipping in behind someone. Deb in a pink sweater but transparent, the greying square stones of the wall still visible through her body. The ghost of Deb walked over to stand beside me, and turned towards the green felt noticeboards opposite the Hall doors. This was where little paper bulletins announced the winners of College prizes. Right then, I saw it. Something terrible, but at last, something real. Deb had won the fiction prize this year, and yet her name wasn't there on the board. There was the white rectangle, the typewritten print announcing *The Wharton Silversmith Prize in Prose Fiction*, but underneath, instead of *D. Orton*, it read *L. Smiley*. Who the fuck was L. Smiley? And then a painful spasm grabbed at the centre of my stomach. What if that was Deb's real name and I never knew it?

I turned on my heel and went up to my rooms to fetch a jacket, then headed out along the Backs. I needed to think. The idea that I might never have known Deb's real name was painful, but at least this was tangible. A starting point. A hypothesis. The scientific method demands that we begin with a hypothesis. How else are we to design our experiment?

The river was as immobile as ever, but now it made me angry. This was no time for sitting there, stagnating. Things couldn't simply *stay* like this, with Deb gone and no explanation. I usually think alone, but at that moment I needed someone. I needed to know it wasn't *just me*. But who? I couldn't trust Professor Bell. I didn't really know anyone else in College who had known Deb. The truth was, I didn't really know anyone else in College at all except Gin from the library, and Deb did not go to the library. Deb wrote all the time, but her writing flowed from her like waterfalls. She didn't pore over pine tables and sweat into pads of A4, like Gin and I had to.

I thought of Dr. Humberton. He would at least remember who Deb was: she'd been in his lectures. There were only thirty of us, and Deb asked a lot of questions. He *had* to remember her. And surely he'd have her real name on his records. I knew Humberton had an office in the raised faculty building. There was a decent chance he'd be in it, too—it was the middle of the morning, and a Thursday. I set myself in that direction. My chest was pounding.

———

*The little shit must be having a birthday today
too. Hasn't been here in a while thank Christ.
How old is she really? How would I know. I can't
understand time anymore. Maybe I never could.*

    *One birthday, Mr. Jones the geography master
makes her want to kill herself because he gets them
to colour in maps of Europe with colouring pencils
and then he critiques their pencil work. Their
colouring-in skills. As if that was the point of
anything. It's insulting because you know she's
not a child, she is thirteen years old. Or now
she is sixteen years old and she says she wants
a boyfriend and I can just tell she has no idea
what the point of him would be. Well the point
of anything, my dear little shit, is never what
you think it is.*

    *The first birthday was the last birthday. The
birthday. The night she showed up, I actually
thought she was a shit. It was dark. It felt awful,
but it always does, so I just went to the toilet. Then
I started bleeding so I went to the hospital. And
that was it. The hospital. The white light. The
yelling. The end of the line. The end of everything.*

    *And I was meant to love it, this birthday present.
Birthday past, birthday future. What a joke. They
gave up on that pretty fast though and took the little
shit away. Someone else will always do a better job*

loving things than I would. I have never been able to tune in, not that way. Maybe other people have a kind of sixth sense that I don't have. Or maybe I just don't want to. To be honest I can't tell anymore if it's on purpose. Does it matter if it's on purpose?

Chapter Six

"Think of us as beings in four dimensions," Humberton used to say. "We stretch out in time as well as space. Really, we're 4-D worms: little tubes tunnelling through time. Only we're not *going* anywhere in time. We're just pinned there. Like specimens in a box."

I ran across the bridge. I was moving as fast as my body would let me, but as I held the idea of Deb in me, in my memory, I felt her stillness. Like water that should be flowing. It was as if Deb didn't move anymore, didn't change. Even so, I told myself, she was suspended in the substance of reality. In the past, not just in my memory. Deb was gone, but she was still *real*. A bug in amber, not a dragon in a story. I pictured Deb trapped in brown resin, still as death, her pink sweater and blonde hair all turned the colour of Lyle's Golden Syrup. I shook my head, trying to dislodge the image.

Humberton's office was on the third floor, but before I could go up I had to go down to the basement toilets. I looked over the graffiti: the usual rubbish, and the rhyme about Shakespeare shitting here, but today I found, newly scrawled in another hand:

Even if that is true, would he honestly choose,
Over Stratford, the Sidgwick Site lecture room loos?
And it seems like a stretch, 'cause at least in my head,
For a guy who shits here, is he not kinda dead?

That's right, the newcomer had changed the metre from iambic to anapestic. And the original author wasn't even writing pentameters to start with.

Amateurs.

Business over, I ran all the way up the battered staircase, grey plastic worn bare at the centre where everybody treads, but still like new at both sides. Academic staircases are always battered in the middle. Too many of us going up and down all day. Of course you *could* walk at the edges, but it's awkward and people look at you funny. And what would you be trying to prove?

On the stratospheric heights of the third floor, the light was bluer and clearer. I slowed my thoughts and my body, in order to pass at a more respectful pace by the librarian's desk, through the little faculty library, and on into the open corridor with Humberton's office and those of a few other lecturers. I approached his door, painted a brilliant white like the surrounding walls, and stared at this blank slate for a moment.

I am sure Dr. Humberton didn't know then how important he could have been in this story. How important he should have been. I rarely spoke to him. He was the most popular lecturer in the whole philosophy faculty. A gaggle of students followed him everywhere, loudly attempting to converse in the same kind of language he used, with mixed results. Once

I had left Cambridge, I felt bad about how Deb and I had called him Dr. Bumberton behind his back. I did it in the same puerile spirit in which, in those early College days, I had pretended to hate any music that was popular. Now that I am a teacher myself, I try to remember: *Your quietest student does not love you least.*

His door was closed, but that didn't mean anything. All the doors on that corridor were always closed, because of the constant low mumbling and grumbling from the open-plan grad student workspace opposite. They were mostly grumbling about the fact that their workspace was open-plan.

I knocked, and waited.

I had a long wait ahead of me. Humberton, it turned out, had left town right after his last lecture and was on sabbatical for the next two years. I waited outside his door for fifteen minutes in hopes that he'd turn up, before I wandered over to the librarian on duty. I hate approaching people to ask for information, but sometimes it is necessary. She told me what some part of me already knew: there was no hope to be found there. Deflated and defeated, I went back to my rooms, fell onto the bed, and went straight to sleep as the College clock chimed for noon. At this time I had started to abuse sleep as others do drugs, bingeing for days then making ill-advised attempts to go cold turkey.

I woke briefly at 3 a.m. to the sound of a few late revellers, probably returning from a sweaty bop in the Dodson Party Room, vomiting happily in the hallway outside my door and bragging to each other about how direly they'd done in exams.

". . . the whole night before Histology with this absolute *scrubber* from Girton . . ."

I recognized the voice of Pierre from my matriculating class. Pierre was a medical student who had hit on me in freshers' week. I'd gone to the Freshers' Bop, because it was down on the freshers' week timetable as the activity for Friday evening. It was a mistake. The party room was a nasty underground square, like a concrete bunker, and it wasn't nearly big enough for the number of people trying to dance inside. The music was miserable and loud. Everyone was squashed together in near darkness with just a few flashing lights at one end of the room.

Not knowing what else to do with myself, I bought an orange juice for £1.50 from the "bar," which was really just a few second-years tucked in a corner with some cheap vodka, juice, and plastic cups. Then I decided to leave. As I was trying to get back to the exit, Pierre bumped into me. I think it was an accident the first time, but then he kept doing it and laughing.

"I'm trying to spill your drink," he yelled over the incessantly repetitive string sample of "Bitter Sweet Symphony" by The Verve. "Then I can buy you another one! I'm Pierre!"

"That's stupid," I yelled back as he shook my hand.

He laughed and shrugged, and I noticed that his hair all went straight upwards. I wondered if he spent time making it do that.

"I guess I'm stupid then!" he shouted directly into my ear. It hurt a bit. I couldn't tell if he had a slight French accent, or if I was just imagining it because of his name.

"I don't expect so, if you're here!" I tried to get closer to his ear so I wouldn't have to yell so loud. But just then the music shifted. Whoever was working the CD player had skipped ahead to "The Drugs Don't Work," and Pierre thought I was leaning into him to slow-dance. He enthusiastically put an arm around my hips and pressed them up against his own.

I squirmed away. "Ugh! Sorry, I mean, no," I mumbled, "I have to go."

He laughed again and said, "Want to come back to my room?"

"What? Oh! No, that's . . . that's fine," I said, and tried to back away towards the door. But there were so many people packed in on all sides that there was no space to back into.

I persisted in my efforts to leave, and Pierre kept dancing as if I were his partner. When I finally managed to pull away he started singing along with the track, miming heartbreak. Then two other men appeared, one of them whacked him on the back of the head and the other one handed him a plastic cup, and he went off with them into the crowd.

The next week, Pierre joined a drinking society and never spoke to me again. I remembered hearing he'd become a promising boatie, a possible future Blue. Now here he was, outside my door, swearing and belching. There were so many worlds overlaid in the corridors of Hermes Court. From most of them I only heard these strange echoes. I hadn't been wrong, there was just a slight French inflection in his voice.

Eventually, the future doctor drifted back out of earshot. There was always a legend floating around that one year a few of the med students had taken their corpse out for a night on the town. As I re-entered the half-sleeping state, my mind fed me a grim fantasy of Pierre and his laughing friends dressing up Deb's dead body, parading her around The Mitre

and The Baron of Beef. Pierre playing bar skittles at The
Maypole, like I'd seen him do in freshers' week, but with Deb
draped over his shoulder like a rag doll.

The next weekend was that of "Suicide Sunday"—after the
end of exams, before the appearance of the first results.
Undergraduates flung themselves into the Cam, ran topless
along King's Parade, sprayed champagne from bridges. Some
of the brave ones even stepped briefly onto the Great Court
grass until corrected by the hawk-eyed porters, guardians of
turf that wasn't theirs. But that was just the undergraduates
who wanted to be visible. I watched these scenes all weekend
from my windowsill, like a distracted cat. Unafraid, vigilant.

On the Saturday morning I woke up at 4 a.m., fully alert.
Not knowing what else to do, I walked mindlessly along
my corridor and up the stairs to Deb's room. I knocked on
her door. In the blanket silence that followed, I stared at her
name, tracing over each letter with my eyes. *D. Orton.* Here,
at least, that was still her name. Everyone living in College
has their name hand-painted onto a little black panel over
their door, even undergraduates. Surname and initial, in
perfectly uniform, subtly gothic white lettering. Thin hori-
zontal lines and a rather serious serif. The lettering would
appear and disappear as if by magic whenever students
changed rooms. You could sometimes see the calligrapher's
guide lines at the top and bottom where they hadn't been
fully erased. I stared at the letters, clung to their presence as
if they were still attached to Deb by some invisible thread.

I had slipped into being semi-nocturnal, preferring the
openness of nights when the streets weren't crammed with

tourists, and much less social interaction was expected of me just by virtue of having ventured outside of my room. The more drunk people were, the easier I found it to watch them without feeling obligated to engage in any way. Late at night, one could still find cheap food near the College at Gardies or the Trailer of Life, so despite a chronic lack of funds I started eating more (though not better), even putting on a little weight. Beyond the "Life Van," across the market square, was another institution known unaffectionately as the "Death Van," where a heap of empty fat and carbs was even cheaper and even more disgustingly indigestible. Life and death. Eat and shit. Since losing Deb, everything hurt so badly I didn't know how I could bear it. But somehow I had to keep it all moving.

On the Sunday, as I was heading back to my room very late with a half-eaten bag of chips in my left hand, my right hand reached out automatically to rap on Deb's door. Then the hand froze in place, knuckles just inches from contact with the wooden panel. A chill flowed slowly backwards from the knuckles, as if the blood inside the hand were being replaced with something else, something dense and thick, an icy slush.

Dr. Humberton's voice was replaying in my mind. Something from his lecture. From the day Deb went missing.

"Suppose when you die your body is cryogenically frozen . . ."

Here he had turned his back to us, rolling his crisp white shirt sleeves up to begin a drawing on the blackboard. A stick figure, lying flat inside a big rectangle labelled $-130°C$.

". . . and then three hundred years later this body is successfully resuscitated."

A second stick figure, this one standing. An arrow from the first figure to the second. Under the arrow, *300 years.*

"Now, in this thought experiment, humanity is capable of preserving a viable human *body* in a frozen state for much longer than the span of a normal human life. But here is your question: is the *person* preserved? That is another issue entirely. Who—or should I say *what*—is it that wakes up after the big defrost?"

In front of Deb's door, the slush that had been injected into my arm was still moving, forcing its way into the rest of my system. As it reached my brain and filled the space behind my eyes, I finally registered what I must have unconsciously seen. What had prevented me from knocking. I dropped my chips all over the floor and ran back to my room.

The thin, white gothic lettering over Deb's door said *F. Jameson.*

On the Monday, exam results began to appear. Class lists on thick cream A4 cardstock were pinned up naked inside a glass box outside the Senate House. Come and see: every student's shame or pride displayed to the world. As brutal as blood on white sheets. Undeniable.

I walked alone and blinking through the bright, cool afternoon to see them. My own exams, it turned out, had not gone as badly as I'd feared. Deb's name wasn't there, of course, as she hadn't taken the exams. But my name was among the Firsts. In fact, it was a high First, which meant I would be a Senior Scholar of the College next year. Of course I couldn't know, back then, what it really meant. That I had *momentum,* that inertia would be enough from now on. That I was set on my path, flung into orbit around this strange institution. My marriage bed was made that day and I had no idea.

I did not go back to my aunt and uncle's house for the summer vacation. It would have benefited no one. So I ended up sharing spaces around College with the few graduate students who also didn't leave for summers. Gin was there in the working library most days, and she would still turn to me from time to time with questions about an argument she was working on. But she never pried, never wanted to know what I was writing in the notebooks I drew out every day from my bag. I had asked her, just to make sure, whether she knew Deb. She didn't.

I was still making do with an old khaki backpack—you know, the kind from the Army and Navy Stores, made of canvas webbing—that I'd been given as a birthday gift years ago. It had seen me through most of secondary school, and it was a stalwart ally. Although it was frayed and dirty now, that was all part of the look. Still, it sat awkwardly sometimes next to Gin's beautifully aged soft leather satchel. You could buy a spiral-bound reporter's notebook for 10p from the post office next to Heffers, and my bag usually contained the two or three of these that I was currently working from.

In the notebooks, I was patiently recording everything— quite literally *everything*—I knew about Deb. All my memories, any clues I could glean as to what might have happened to her, every strange occurrence since her disappearance, every conversation I'd ever had that concerned her. All my observations and inferences. I was trying to get the sequence into order, from the moment we first met behind the College, down to the moment I was sure of having seen her last. We had parted to go our separate ways after Humberton's lecture, she to another lecture and I to the library. That morning had felt so entirely normal. I kept writing out the timeline. Whenever I realized I could include another detail or had put something in the wrong place, I started over on a fresh page.

I recorded how Deb's room had been empty for a while, until one day another student's name appeared above her door. How I'd looked for her in the matriculation photo for our year, before remembering that she hadn't been able to make it on the day of the photo because she'd had to go to the funeral of a cousin or something. How I'd plucked up the courage to approach a member of the Hall staff to ask about Deb, and how they had denied knowing her, although I was quite sure they'd handed her interchangeable pasta and rice dishes in the canteen on too many occasions to count. *Then again*, I wrote below this, *to the Hall staff we undergraduates must appear equally interchangeable.*

"This is going to sound crazy weird," said Gin one day, "but it's not weird I swear."

"What's not weird?"

"Would you want to be in a secret society?"

That made me look up. When I realized she wasn't asking another of her hypothetical questions, but extending a real invitation, my eyes opened wider and I pointed them straight at one corner of a particularly messy bookshelf behind Gin's hair. As if there might be something in that thick muddle of chemistry textbooks that would make sense of what she had just said.

Gin hurried on: "It's just a kind of debating society, like a book club, only we usually don't talk about specific books. It's really pretty normal. It's only a secret because it's, like, really old."

"How old?"

"Oh geez, I don't know, hundreds of years. It's called The Eleven. Wittgenstein was in it, and John Maynard Keynes. And Bertrand Russell. Oh, and like, the Bloomsbury Group, and one of the Cambridge Spies . . . uh, Anthony . . . Burgess or something? I asked the others about you last meeting and they voted you in."

"*What?*"

"Yeah, I know that sounds creepy. It's just . . . that's how it works. It's not weird, honest. But you have to agree that you won't tell anyone about it, before I tell you more. Is that okay? I mean, I think the main reason it's a secret is just that we don't want people asking if they can join, you know? We just invite the people we think are really interesting."

"You think I'm interesting?" It was a genuine enquiry.

"Yeah?" Gin said, as if my question was deeply weird.

This was making me nervous, and I felt awkward about the fact that I could not return Gin's compliment. So I selected another bookshelf to stare at.

"If you join you have to take a vow of secrecy. They call it a curse. It's kind of an 1800s version of some adolescent nonsense. But now that it's so old, it's funny. You're supposed to be cast into a pit of flame or something like that if you break the vow."

"Into a *what*?"

"I know, I know. I swear it's much less weird than that makes it sound. We just hang out and talk. Once a week. We present ideas to each other. In the old days there were always twelve members, so The Eleven was like a joke name, you see. It's officially called the Conversazione Society, you know, when we have to give College staff a reason we're booking out rooms or whatever. Nowadays there are usually about seven or eight of us."

I took a breath and swallowed hard. My stomach did not feel too good.

"When were the old days?"

"Well, in the 1800s. But I think its predecessor goes back to the 1600s. Probably something to do with Rosicrucians or Masons or whatever. I don't really know." She smiled. "I'm a philosopher, not a historian! I can lend you a book about the history if you want. It's probably quite interesting. If you care about the past."

"You don't care about the past?"

"Well, let me try this out on you . . . " and she ran McTaggart's argument for the unreality of time. I'd heard this before in one of Humberton's lectures. The gist of it is that if time is real, then every event has to be past, present, and future. But nothing can have all three of these properties: they are inconsistent. So time is an illusion. I told her my response, one of the standard moves. Nothing is supposed to have all those three properties *at the same time*, so there's no real contradiction there. An event can be future in the past, present in the present, and past in the future. No problem.

Gin nodded. "Yes. But doesn't the regress bother you?"

"You mean how now we just have nine inconsistent temporal properties, instead of the original three?"

"Yes."

"No."

She nodded, satisfied that the resolution was stable. "Not all regresses are vicious," she said.

———

*Call it vicious. Evil. Cruel. I see his face in here. I'm
not crazy, I mean I see him on the TV. Not TV. What
are you supposed to call it these days? I know the
things but not the words. That giant face. Always
eating, always talking, always consuming. Sucks
all the air out of a room, a black hole at the centre
of everything. A void. You'd have seen him, he's that
kind of famous. He explains mathematics, or
physics is it, or maybe it's philosophy. The shape
of reality. Explains stuff like that to the camera
but you won't see him. Unless you know what he
is. I mean unless you know that thing in him too.
And you'll have seen the one who makes his
excuses. There isn't a rapist bone in his body.
The woman with the big laugh. She knows. Rapists
aren't made of rapist bones, they're made of excuses
and all the air. If there's nothing left for me to
breathe, I can't talk. That's fucking physics.*

Chapter Seven

With Deb gone it always felt as though time wasn't passing in Cambridge, but of course it was. One minute I'd be walking down the cobbled lane beside the College, wearing my navy gown, and I'd hear the Great Court clock chime the quarters. I'd think *but this is exactly what it would be like if I had accidentally slipped into 1667.* Then someone's mobile would ring. That godforsaken Nokia drone, do you remember it? *Duddle-uh-duh, duddle-uh-duh, duddle-uh-duh duh. Duddle-uh-duh, duddle-uh-duh* . . . Christ. Human progress. Marked by such trails of audible trash.

Of course, if I'd strolled into 1667 it would be because I was already there, rounding that same bend, three hundred and thirty years before. Dr. Humberton had taught me about that, and how most of our beloved time-travel stories are inconsistent. You can't "change the past"—that's saying that something both did happen and did not happen, which is, to use the technical term, bollocks. Kind of ruins *Back to the Future.* But when you think about it, the whole idea of changing the past is selling hope to the hopeless, which is a cruel trick. A sick joke.

There was something so magnetic about the way Humberton said it. The way he used to ramble when he'd gone off-script. Like it wasn't about the words so much. Sometimes, I felt like what he was trying to do would hit me in the stomach. But that might just have been me. Or rather, my digestive situation. It was getting significantly worse by this time. Whatever I ate had to run the gauntlet of acid reflux, hiatus hernia, a selection of medically interesting food intolerances, minor blood sugar issues, and irritable bowel syndrome. It was a riot in there.

I kept trying to find out what could possibly have happened to Deb. I worked through every avenue I could think of, gradually filling up more and more of the 10-pence-a-pop reporter's notebooks from the post office. I stacked them in piles at the back of my desk, so they would always be handy to consult, and I kept one on me at all times. In these books I diligently listed all possible clues concerning Deb's whereabouts, recording everything as soon as it occurred to me. Memories that might or might not mean anything, weird explanations that came to me in the middle of the night but seemed ridiculous by morning. Records of interviews I was covertly conducting with unsuspecting College staff.

I even went to talk to the Bursar—a man who made me intensely anxious—because I knew that he must have records of her registration. The Bursar was sitting in his overly warm little office in one of the College's inner labyrinths, hunched over an enormous desk crammed with papers. Towards the edges of the desk, the papers had built up over the years into little walls that now defended him against student enquiries. Behind these fortifications stretched a flat morass of bills and letters. From time to time, he would rise to walk around the table and glide certain of the papers from place to place, like a minister pushing troops around a war-room map. The Bursar was a stolid man in his fifties, with white hair and blue eyes, who always wore the same grey suit. Students whispered that he was a Freemason. He was not an early adopter of email.

As on the few previous occasions when I'd had to see him to ask about rent or scholarships, most of his energy was devoted, not to the Battle of the Paperwork, but to an iced cream bun. This one had evidently come from a box at his elbow, which might originally have held a dozen. There were three left inside.

When a student enquiry came his way, the Bursar's goal, always, was to remove the distraction as swiftly as possible from his vicinity. I had scripted my question in advance so I could put it to him quickly and clearly.

"Good morning. Can you tell me anything about what has happened to Deborah Orton? She is a current first-year under-graduate who has gone missing."

The Bursar raised one bushy white eyebrow. He stared at the hand containing his half-eaten confection, and with prac-tised skill balanced a viscous squiggle of emerging cream per-fectly on top of the chewed side.

"Can't share any personal information about a student. Not without their written permission. Good morning."

He nodded at the door, and that was that.

Outside his staircase, my back to the ancient college wall, I wrote these words verbatim in my notebook. Just in case there might be something in them, something I had missed.

—

The morning after Gin told me about The Eleven, following several dull hours reading Rawls in the phallic library, I had to get something to eat. Outside the Sidgwick Site lecture rooms was a paved area that led to a little café called The Buttery. That was just a name, though. It was a café, not a real college buttery like the one next to Hall. When I had to go over there to get coffee between lectures, I always looked straight down at the paving stones, because this was one of those places that was high-risk for running into people in that awful grey zone: people I might be supposed to recognize. I'm bad with faces, but mortified when I fail to recognize someone I'm supposed to—or worst of all, call them by the wrong name. So I focused on the stones in order to have something to do. It was before we used phones for this purpose. There's something about keeping one's eye on the ground, too. You know it's at least not literally shifting.

I didn't like to step on more than one contiguous stone in any direction, which meant I often moved like the knight in chess. It probably looked a little weird if anyone was watching, but I don't think anyone was. I don't think people noticed me much. I had a kind of musical monologue that went with crossing these stones. It's similar to the one I use for going up stairs. They grew out of the little tunes I hummed as I walked around the corridors of the hospital or my old school. It's a means of focus; stops me taking in too much at once. I find it hard enough to get what I need from what I can take in. Overloading only makes it worse. I'm pretty sick of the tunes, to be honest— always the same few notes, day after day, year after year. But there you go. It's just repetitive, it's not the end of the world. *Worse things happen at sea*, as my aunt would always tell me.

My aunt was full of these aphorisms that seemed to make her happy. *The longest way round is the shortest way home. These things are sent to try us. If a job's worth doing it's worth doing well. A place for everything and everything in its place.* The same platitudes, over and over. Some of them flat out contradicted some of the others and she didn't seem to notice. *Comparisons are odious*, but then *Be a thoroughbred, not a pit pony.* Several had a ring of Ye Olde, which apparently lent them an air of gravitas in her opinion. *Don't spoil the ship for a ha'porth of tar. Ne'er cast a clout 'til May be out.*

My aunt's happiness was simple. At least it seemed to come simply to her, in situations I could never conceive of as being appropriate to such a feeling. Her sayings were family lore. Just not my family. I mean she wasn't really my aunt. She liked me to call her that, and I didn't care what I called her, so that was fine. She'd preface all her sayings with "As my grandmother used to say . . ." as if the lineage itself was the point. Perhaps it was. Perhaps her grandmother was happy like her.

My own maternal grandmother is a frozen woman on a mantelpiece who never smiles, who will never smile. I have inherited several of these mantelpiece women, frozen in their own little moments. Little clicks. Just like how your own present, your *now*, becomes frozen as soon as you think of it. Try it. Notice it existing. *Click.* I'm told my grandmother worked for the Secret Service during World War Two but was never allowed to say a word about what she actually did. Then after the war ended she was never a happy woman. She became obsessed with the cleanliness of her house. Beds had to be made every morning—and we're not talking duvets here but old-fashioned sheets and blankets, with hospital corners as a baseline standard—and she would inspect them. A single wrinkle meant failure. It got worse over time, until visitors were not permitted to stand too close to her windows in case they got steamed up. She would follow people around with a towel just in case.

I was almost all the way across the stones when Gin saw me and called my name. I was too close to pretend not to hear, so I looked up and she came over, smiling. I noticed and made myself smile back because that's what you're supposed to do.

"What's up?" she said.

I found this confusing; there was nothing wrong with me.

Fortunately she didn't wait for a reply but carried on, lowering her voice.

"Looks like we're meeting next week," she said, looking around with a furtive glance that struck me as only half play-acting. "You know—*conversazione*. Friday at eight. The Bainbridge Room in Queens'. You're coming, right?"

I asked at the Queens' Porters' Lodge for directions to the Bainbridge Room. It was tucked away behind the OCR, with a grand wooden door below an imposing stone arch. For a moment I was baffled that a student society would be able to book out a room with such a door for its meetings, but then I remembered Gin had told me it wasn't just students. Junior Research Fellows, and even a couple of more senior Fellows from Queens' and Caius, were members too. I'd forgotten to eat dinner first, and I knew there would be wine at the meeting, which would play havoc with my stomach for the entire night and probably trip a nasty headache. But that would just have to be. I debated for a minute whether to knock. Wouldn't that be too much like going in to a supervision? I decided on plausible deniability: a quick tap while depressing the heavy tab of the brass handle, then I swung the door open without waiting for a reply.

The walls of this room were gorgeously panelled in dark oak, the high plaster ceiling bordered by intricately moulded cornices. Gilt-framed portraits of old white men in black and scarlet academic regalia hung on each wall, and beneath the grandest of the frames an open fire burned in an enormous iron grate. The fire was surrounded by five armchairs, upholstered in maroon paisley. These formed part of a semicircle, with the ad hoc addition of three dining chairs, evidently taken from the grand table that occupied most of the room.

Years later, I would watch the Harry Potter films and laugh with something like relief at their depictions of an ancient magical school for witches and wizards, no more disorienting or unworldly than rooms like this were to my barely-adult self. All of the old Cambridge colleges were full of spaces like this, so that I was sometimes unsure whether I was seeing one I'd seen before or not. For all I knew, they might have been the same old white men on all the walls of all those rooms. The interior organization of the old colleges was labyrinthine too, as anything built and layered over centuries tends to be. It often seemed to me that the stone corridors and oak doors had rearranged themselves overnight, and everyone was treating that as normal.

As I entered, Gin introduced me to four people sitting around the fire, but I was preoccupied with the room and

I wasn't ready yet to focus on the people. I didn't catch what anyone was called, and spent the rest of the evening using every trick I knew to avoid referring to anyone other than Gin by name, but, perhaps kindly, nobody called me on it. They all seemed about Gin's age, and quite friendly.

"Get yourself a drink," said one of the men, gesturing towards the table. On the table there were several bottles of wine, a little stack of plastic cups, and an open bag of Jelly Babies. I added to this collection the moderately priced bottle on which I'd spent the last of my money for the week, and noticed that both a white wine and a red were already open. I poured a cup of the red (a mistake—reds are digestively trickier, but I wasn't thinking) and gratefully grabbed a handful of Jelly Babies, figuring that between them and the wine that would be about as many calories as a sandwich and I wasn't that hungry anyway.

The ritual of my initiation into The Eleven happened in that room, around that fire, with those five people. The man who'd invited me to get a drink read out the text that Gin had described, and I agreed with tipsy faux-solemnity to all of its terms and conditions. I recollect that there was, indeed, a mention of being cast into a pit of flame. It all sounded like nineteenth-century adolescent tomfoolery. Harmless.

By the end of that summer, it happened that I'd temporarily been appointed secretary to The Eleven. This was because several of the other members were away for the vacation, and nobody else was left who had rooms in College to store the Books. The Books were records of meetings dating back to the origins of the club, with a separate volume containing the signatures of all its members. I'd written my own name at the very end of the list during my initiation ceremony, and now I sat with this strange ledger in my room in Hermes Court, thumbing through its ancient pages. I found the signature of Bertrand Russell, and that of Wittgenstein, who had terrible handwriting which—to my mind—matched his awful messy thinking. I found Anthony Blunt and Guy Burgess, John Maynard Keynes, Lytton Strachey, E. M. Forster, Alfred Tennyson. And, to my surprise, Dr. Humberton.

"Oh, yes!" Gin had said, when I asked about him. "Ron is the *best* fun. He might come back for the Society annual dinner. You know, in December?"

It had taken me a full minute to figure out who Ron must be; I never dreamed of calling any of my lecturers by their first names. The fact that they had first names at all was entirely off my radar. Gin never called the other faculty by their first names either. Something felt strange about the way she did it with Humberton, but I didn't feel like I could ask more.

I very much wanted Humberton to come back for the dinner in December, but I somehow knew that he would not. I accepted this as inevitable. There's a kind of passivity that sets in when you're on a predetermined course: it doesn't matter what direction you're going, or why. Humans have this incredible capacity to fashion themselves a "normal" from whatever life hands them. And if it unravels they just start over, like there's a skein of wool they're constantly knitting and re-knitting into variations on the same garment, the same comfort blanket. *Normal.*

In this way, I became desensitized to holding the Books in my hands. These historical diamonds in rough handwriting, a treasure trove of poorly kept Cambridge secrets. I stashed them in the middle drawer of my room's little wooden desk, without so much as a locked box for protection.

My own notebooks about Deb's disappearance had grown into a disordered pile that now took up most of the desktop. This was starting to make things difficult. It was getting harder to keep track of my other work on top of the search for Deb, and sometimes I needed to write all through the night if I had an essay deadline. But the library closed at 1 a.m. So I ended up piling the books I needed for essays precariously on top of my notebooks, and then pushing piles to one side when it was time to write up my own six or seven pages of thoughts. We were permitted to submit typed-up work, but it wasn't particularly encouraged, and I rarely bothered. The computer room was in the opposite corner of Great Court, and often all the machines were in use. To clear myself a writing space I simply shoved, my forearm flat to the surface like a penny-pusher arcade machine, only in this case I hoped that nothing would fall off. Obeying the same gravity-defying physics that also governs those infuriating contraptions, stuff rarely did.

In fact there were surprisingly few catastrophes involving that desk, and only one worth mentioning. I was holding one of the oldest and most precious of the Books in my left hand when I suddenly realized the rollie I was lifting to my lips with my right had developed a great flying buttress of ash. This structure promptly disintegrated and buried itself deep into the Book's central fold, close to the ancient leather of its spine. Horrified, I set the cigarette down atop a turret of library books, its still-lit tip overhanging the edge, while I desperately squeezed the Book open and held it up to my face to blow the ash away. The spine creaked but did not break, and I managed to clear the ash in two puffs. But then, to my horror, I observed the thin line of spittle I had left in place of the previous airborne contaminant.

At that point it did finally occur to me to think: *The universe has made a mistake. I am not the kind of person who holds this kind of object.* Yet there it was, and here I was, and I'd proved my point by spitting on it, surely thereby failing whatever test the universe might have been administering to me. I laughed out loud, for a second, at the thought that I might apply for an *aegrotat* if I had failed the universe's test.

Hearing the laugh gave me a horrible shock, as if I were suddenly realizing I was not alone. The sound reminded me so palpably of Deb's laughter. Then I heard the sound break apart into broad sobs. There was no body in the room except my own. I was the one weeping. I set the Book down rapidly, not wanting to deface it still further with my tears.

On the open page, now slightly smeared with spit, I read the minutes of a meeting concerning Isaac Newton's alchemical work, in pursuit of the fifth element and the philosophers' stone. A substance to turn base materials into gold. I took a tiny reassurance from this, remembering how spectacularly wrong we can all be about so many things.

Beside me, the errant cigarette quietly burned itself out, its offence forgotten.

---

*The nurses watch me incessantly you know.
It's frightening how they watch me. Even when
I hide in my bed, under the sheets, they're still
listening in. What is the point of that? I have
no idea. It's none of my business why people
do things.*

Chapter Eight

There was nobody in The Eleven who became a friend. Then again, there was nobody I hated, and that was worth something. Our conversations in that wood-panelled room were probably not what you're imagining, if you're picturing Wittgenstein and Russell in a room with Keynes and the Cambridge Spies. Then again, history's not what it's cracked up to be. It's more Jelly Babies than genius. Only genius makes for a better story, so that's the one we tell.

There was nobody there I could have talked to about Deb, or about what was happening to me, but if there had been I would have freely admitted that by this point I was becoming worn. My mind was behaving like a kite on a windy day, shooting from one cloudy idea to the next, gently fraying at the edges, insufficiently bound to the earth. It often felt like I was watching my life from the outside. Or from another time. Looking in at something that didn't really belong to me.

Like my desk, the entire surface of my world had become overcrowded with Deb. It was as if, having been reduced to zero in all the customary dimensions, she was becoming infinite in another. Another plane, overlaid with my own, occupying all the space around me while I detected nothing. Except, perhaps, for a few leaks. Strange sounds or sights that didn't quite belong, but didn't quite not belong either. What if Deb was right in front of my face the whole time, invisible, begging me to see her again? It was a chilling thought, one I had to contend with often during that time.

There's a little passageway behind St. Catherine's College called Piss Alley. Probably it has a "real" name too, one that nobody uses. Piss Alley was rarely on my way to anywhere, but sometimes when I was upset and needed to walk without having anywhere to walk to, I'd find myself in places I had no reason to be. One day, about three in the afternoon, it had stopped raining long enough to convince me to go outside, and I was shuffling along Piss Alley when some graffiti caught my eye. It was out of the ordinary line of sight, on a door that looked like the back entrance to something. Possibly a college kitchen. There was a huge, dirty extractor fan at the top. From the greasy black grime around its frame, I reasoned that this door might not have been opened in a hundred years or more. It had once been painted dark green, but now more than half of it was spattered with dirt. Gigantic metal hinges secured it to the stone wall to the left. This graffiti was discreetly positioned on the right-hand side, about halfway up, almost hidden behind a heavy chain hanging on a concrete post for no discernable reason. Letters were in stark, new white paint: *What's missing from this picture*. No question mark.

No picture.

Perhaps the reason I noticed it was the perfectly formed

gothic script, which resembled the lettering above the doors in the College. The artist must have used a stencil to achieve that effect. It was a surprising thing to see in such a place. But it was much less weird, when I thought about it, than the self-rearranging ancient buildings, or the esoteric alchemical tracts secreted away in their libraries.

I looked at the words, head cocked like a puzzled dog, until the stink for which Piss Alley is named intruded unignorably on my awareness, then I held my breath until I emerged onto Trumpington Street.

I didn't think about the writing again for a while. The next day was the start of the Michaelmas term, and that was a distraction. I didn't stop thinking about Deb, but I had to get myself to lectures most mornings, and put enough hours into reading for my weekly essay to get by each supervision without feeling embarrassed by my poor performance, or—worse—being asked if there was "something wrong."

It wasn't until a week into term that I saw the white cursive script again, this time on a lamppost beside the Sidgwick Site, near to where I'd chained my bike. There it was, at handlebar height: *What's missing from this picture.* I'd bought my black and yellow bike in August for fifteen pounds from a graduating student—although it was not pretty, and cycling made my knuckles turn blue, it was a way to avoid running into people on the way to places and having to make conversation. And I could bring groceries home in its wooden basket. Anyhow, pretty bikes got stolen. You were better off with one that looked like a stupid wasp if you wanted it to be there when you got back.

I didn't know why a graffiti artist should want to write *What's missing from this picture* around the town in perfect lettering. But it was something to do, I supposed, and as such perhaps no better or worse than anything I was doing. When I got back to College and locked my bike to the racks at the front of the Great Gate, the words were there again. Only this time, they were right on the frame of somebody's bike: the next bike over, directly to the right of the spot I'd chosen for mine. And this didn't look like graffiti. It was more like a sticker or a transfer. It might have been part of the bike's original branding.

This time, I didn't like it.

I stood for a while beside the bike racks to catch my breath, staring up at the gate. The Great Gate is a battlement, a statement in its own right: Here I stand. The College. *The* College. I change for nobody, for nothing. Time is wasting its energy on me. The two brown-orange brickwork turrets are edged in zigzags of cream stone, with a crenellated parapet running between them as if we needed somewhere for Old Hamlet's ghost to parade up and down of a winter's night. Mullioned windows atop a huge, arched double doorway; and another, smaller door beside the Porters' Lodge for all-day, all-night use. A full coat of arms for Edward III, with small shields for each of his six sons. One of these small shields is a blank, because the poor kid died before he got his arms.

This whole situation is constantly watched over by another Henry VIII, but this one is uglier and more awkward than the posturing Hall Henry. This grey stone Henry holds a gilt orb in one hand and a wooden chair leg in the other. There are stories about what happened to his sword, so many stories that we don't have to worry about which one is the truth. His face is age-worn, eroded by centuries out in the Cambridge cold. Honestly, he doesn't look happy up there. Day after day, we all busy in and out under his stone robes, and nobody even bothers to look up and see what he's got going on underneath them. We don't care. The only creature I ever saw watching this watchman was Pandemos, the College cat.

My rooms were only a few steps away from him. Because I was a Senior Scholar in my second year, I had much better rooms now than the one in Hermes Court. I was allocated a set—a living room with a separate bedroom attached—on the attic level of Great Court, right beside the Great Gate. The proximity of the Porters' Lodge meant no loud staircase parties, and that meant slightly better sleep.

According to the porters, the rooms on the floor below me had once been Isaac Newton's laboratory. Certainly the decrepit gas hobs in the staircase kitchen, with their big brass taps built right into the wall, might have been Newton's own. And these were its only offering to the aspiring student chef. I lit them with matches, timorously at first, then eventually with blasé abandon. I boiled pasta in an old saucepan my aunt had given me as she packed me off to College, saving myself the extra quid or two it would have cost to be served the same thing or worse in Hall. In cold weather, the tiny kitchen steamed up quickly and I would throw its windows open to the icy air, looking down into Great Court. Watching people scamper back and forth like rats, along the broad, right-angled paths: beautifully cobbled, but paved in the middle for ease of walking. By evening the dawdlers had gone—at this time of day everyone was going somewhere, quick and purposeful, hurrying from lamp to lamp, staircase to staircase, before vanishing into one or another grand arched doorway.

My staircase also had a bathroom, up on my floor, above the kitchen. This was a bare room, just a tub and a sink, tucked in under the sloping eaves. But it meant this sixteenth-century building was still serving out its original purpose. Housing scholars of the College. Not taking a single day off in all those centuries. As if the very continuity of our world depended on it. Maybe it did. The College clock strikes the hour twice, you know. Perhaps it must: once to pass the time, once to let us know the time has passed. Metaphysics and epistemology. Very important not to let them shade into each other, to confuse what is real with what we know. A stopped clock, incidentally, is not "right" twice a day. It's never right and it's never wrong. It doesn't mean anything at all.

I don't care for baths. My body is unsettling at the best of times and I'd rather have less to do with it than a bath demands. When I was little, I used to inch myself slowly into the bathwater because it was always too hot. It had to start out hot, because as soon as it got cold that was it: there was nothing more in the tank. My aunt was scrupulously stingy with the immersion heater, which meant the hot water supply ran to a few inches at the bottom of the tub once a week.

"It's burning me," I'd whine, and my aunt would tell me about when she was a girl and had to bathe in cold water even when there were ice patterns on the windows.

"On the *inside!*" She'd pretend to shudder at the memory, then giggle. "As for you, the problem is you're not . . ." and she'd trail off, looking for the right word. "You're not *robust.*"

The night after that latest appearance of *What's missing from this picture*, I couldn't sleep. I found myself running a bath at about one o'clock in the morning. I looked like a little alien in the bathroom's flat square of mirror, my eyes far bigger than I remembered. I stared way back into the mirror, letting my gaze refocus as if I might somehow be standing behind myself. But all I could see over my shoulder were ghosts rising from the hot water.

The enamel was cold under my naked frame as I perched on the ledge. I clutched at the top of the tub with my right hand, nails scratching underneath the rim where it wasn't lined. *Why don't I just put some cold water in there?* I could not understand why I did the things I did. A whole foot went in, stinging badly where I'd made mistakes shaving around my ankles that morning. I had used a disposable razor that should probably have been disposed of a few weeks before. Now it sat beside me once more on the edge of the tub. *Why am I bothering to get in? Why did I bother to get undressed?* Both feet slid under the water. *Because a bath is good. A bath is a good way to look after yourself.* We didn't have the term *self-care* until later, when it became a promising commercial strategy and everybody picked up on it. The water burned more and more of my skin. Once I was properly in the tub, I reached across for the razor and sliced a red line into my thigh.

On the side of the tub, just above the waterline, one end of a curly black pubic hair clung for dear life to the enamel while the other end waved freely in the steam like an eel in a river current. I lowered myself down into the water until my head was at its level, and looked it in the face. Its ominous, eyeless mouth-end snaked around, weaving a charm for my strange eyes. Then it fell into the water, swam towards the red line in my thigh and attached itself there. Homesick for my body? If it was even one of mine to start with—I hadn't bothered to rinse the tub before I got in.

I watched the red line for a half-hour or so. It made the water pink at first, but apart from that it made no difference to anything. I might as well have been watching a video of myself. I closed my eyes. There was something I wasn't seeing—I kept being distracted by misleading signs, pointed down blind alleys by false clues. In the 1974 version of *Murder on the Orient Express*, Poirot is played by Albert Finney, with piggy little eyes and over-pomaded hair. He's just found the body of a man in a train carriage with twelve stab wounds. There are two different matches and a smoked cigar in the dead man's ashtray, together with a burned scrap of notepaper, and a stopped watch in his pyjama pocket. As Poirot's picking up a handkerchief with the initial *H* (or is it a Russian letter *N*?) he has this singsong line: *Has it occurred to you that there are too many clues in this room?* All that overload, all those attempts to distract him, send him spinning in the wrong direction, and he could see through it all.

Let us proceed by examining what I hope will prove to be the last of them, the burnt paper. By the final scene, he will have put everything in order. That was what I needed to do. Once things were in order, they would make sense. *Order and method.* I rinsed out the bath, went back to my bed, and lay down on my towel. My bedroom window gave on to Trinity Street, towards the post office and All Saints Passage. Across the road an old dog was sniffing, alone, round where the craft markets were held during the day.

—

It's inevitably halfway between states that things happen. On the knife edge between one resolution and another. When waking and sleeping become glazed and dulled, the liminal condition lives, breathes, haunts. Nyx is an ancient representation of the night, something more powerful than we can imagine. Hypnos and Thanatos are her twin sons: Hypnos is sleep and Thanatos is death. They are both very, very old, but Nyx is older.

I lay on my bed, looking out over the small square lawn in front of the College, beside the Great Gate. As it was told to tourists, the tree at the centre of that lawn was Newton's apple tree. People don't want history to be complicated. The simple legend sells. Maybe it was at least *an* apple tree. I couldn't have cared less what it was. But I was stuck there in a dreamlike semi-awareness of it, imagining all the ways Deb might have died in pain and fear. These were the worst moments, but I couldn't avoid them. When I closed my eyes, my thoughts all clumped together like clusters of cereal, and the dark air birthed these chimaeras. I lived through all of Deb's possible horrors, each time recombined in a new way. Half-asleep soundscapes would enfold me and I'd hear Deb's laughter, or the happy slow sound of her talking, then it would suddenly be silenced.

But this time I heard a different voice, breaking through the usual polyphony. It sounded like it came from the floor below. This was unusual. I rarely heard anything from the other rooms on that staircase. It was much nicer here than in Hermes Court.

The voice was quiet but clear and pure. It could almost have been a sound set ringing by the air itself, like a glass flute in the wind.

"What's . . . missing . . . from . . . this . . . picture."

The intonation was perfectly level. I could hear that there was no question mark.

Terrified, I tried to force my eyes open, but found myself fighting a heavy resistance that felt almost like paralysis. Still, I could have sworn that, for a split second, I saw the same gothic lettering on the sloping ceiling above my bed, but this time in a ghostly green, like glow-in-the-dark ink. *What's missing from this picture.*

Now I jump-started fully awake, prickling with cold heat. Pandemos, who had snuck in earlier and curled up on top of my duvet, hissed and spat, leaving a pattern of claw marks on my arm as she struggled to get away. I leapt to my feet and yelled out loud to the darkness: "I *know* what's missing! She's gone! She's *gone!*" I sobbed as I gasped for breath. "What am I supposed to do about it?"

The sound of my own voice was now the most terrifying thing, coming out of nowhere, out of no one, splitting the room down the middle. We say we are afraid of ghosts and crazy people, but really we are afraid of ourselves. Our real selves. Horror movie settings in ascending order of creepiness: a haunted house, a psych ward, a hall of mirrors.

I ran to flick on the main lights, so antiseptically bright that they killed all the night's illusions in an instant. The familiar walls returned. There was no voice downstairs. No writing on my ceiling. I looked down at my notebooks in despair, and as I settled into awakeness the rigid terror melted and morphed into white anger. The anger was suddenly overwhelming: a shapeshifter, a nightmare, an ever-expanding ogre that I would never escape.

"*Stupid . . . little . . . girl,*" I hissed at myself, grabbing armfuls of notebooks off the desk and shoving as many as would fit into the wastepaper bin. I slammed the bin down outside my door—leaving one's bin outside was an established signal meaning that the bedders should not come in to clean your room—throwing the rest of the notebooks in messy heaps on the floor all around it. Pandemos, who had recovered her calm much better than I, stalked out of the open door as if nothing had happened.

I dragged the door closed, cried myself back to sleep, and slept for three days. I even missed two lectures. I *never* missed classes. But this was the only response I could think of. To say: *fuck off*. To what? Myself? Cambridge? The universe?

What is this, a multiple-choice test? All of the above.

———

I can't starve it out of me, I tried. And I can't kill it. I could have killed myself, if they had let me. But it would come after me anyway. Death's nothing. Things keep going. People keep going.

Part Three

Doughnuts

But when I came, alas! to wive

Chapter Nine

Time scabbed over my sliced thigh, which healed up like Pandemos's claw marks. I got up again and went to lectures. What else was there to do?

The notebooks found their way back to me. My bedder had carefully gathered them from in and around my bin, the morning after I threw them out, and—assuming they were there by accident—kindly placed them in a tidy pile outside my door before taking away the rest of the rubbish. That's where I found them, when I resurrected myself on the fourth day. I sobbed with relief to have them again, although it was at the same time a heavy burden to accept. I knew that I would never be able to make another attempt to get rid of them.

I stashed as many as would fit in my desk drawers, and I made the overflow into three small stacks underneath the desk. At least that way they were off the surface and I could use it for work during the day.

And I did. *Nothing acts faster than Anadin.* My aunt loved saying that, and she would always add, with a giggle, *so why not take nothing?* But it turns out symbolic logic exercises are some of the best painkillers. Or all-nighter essays on immense metaphysical questions like why anything exists at all, why there shouldn't have been nothing. That kind of thinking utterly numbs you. Removes distractions. Feelings. Holmes understood: *All emotions, and that one particularly, were abhorrent to his cold, precise but admirably balanced mind.* But you have to replace them with something. I didn't believe in the possibility of nothing. Not as a genuine alternative. Not for me. It's an illusion that some people find comforting. I find it terrifying. *Nothing will come of nothing.* I'd hear that with my eyes closed, and an angry old white man would threaten me, shaking his impotent fist. (How long has he been there?)

Nothing does nothing to help Deb. That was the point. I needed to stay clear-headed, so I could find her. Of course, I didn't put any of this in my essays. I told nobody. In fact I barely spoke at all until the next meeting of The Eleven, when the polite young man who'd initiated me into the Society gave a careful but insipid presentation on the anthropology of ghost stories in Northern England, and the four of us who were present clapped kindly and asked him safe, encouraging questions. Then I went back to my silent life again.

I don't know how long I might have gone on like this, if it hadn't been for The Cop. Until I met her, I couldn't admit to myself how desperately I needed someone. Someone who could help me get back up. Correct my dreadful swerve. Set me on a path that actually went somewhere. A true ally, which meant a partner in the search for Deb.

"Hello down there!"

I think it was the first time a police officer had ever spoken to me. She was on duty, standing by the side of the road, keeping an eye on things. There was a half-hearted student protest going on.

I had joined this particular protest. Why? I couldn't tell you. I did things like that sometimes. I had no idea how to make the world better. I felt uneasy doing nothing at all, but I was also pretty sure that walking around chanting slogans for an hour or two on a Saturday afternoon made precisely fuck-all difference. The Cop who spoke to me was one of a few bored-looking officers stationed along the route to make sure nothing got out of hand, which it never did because student activism was well and truly moribund by the nineties. I've forgotten what the protest was even about. It could have been Huntingdon Life Sciences, or it could have been tuition fees. Such were the issues that got the kids out in those days. But if it had been tuition fees, the crowd would've been even smaller. So it was probably the animals. We were British when it came down to it.

The Cop was positioned on one side of St. Andrews Street, just past the Boots, where the protesters had decided—for reasons not discernible to me so far back in the flock—to sit down en masse in the middle of the road. I had sat there watching her feet at first, encased in very clean, very smart, shiny black leather. Then I'd followed the uniform, straight up through the black pressed trousers and reflective yellow jacket, to the bowler hat with its band of black and white dicing. It was a chilly day, late in the October of my second year. The Cop looked pleasantly warm. Her eyes, dead level under the hat, were soft like brown merino wool. I stared, and only when she stared back did I realize what I had done. I turned away. I would have moved, if I hadn't been sitting down.

But it was too late.

"So . . . what made you come out today?"

A question. Shit. Now she'd asked me a question. You can't ignore it when a police officer asks you a question. And what a question. She was asking, in effect, what the hell I was doing there. What was the point of it. *She* had every reason to be there, of course. I had nothing.

I probably mumbled something about dogs. Or cats. I remember that whatever I said was completely stupid, and I remember thinking that this was hardly important police business. But to be fair, we'd been there together for twenty minutes by that point and there was nothing else to do. So she made a conversation happen. And to my immense relief, this conversation was not a disaster. The Cop made sense.

Dr. Humberton had taught me the reason we prefer fiction to reality is that fictional characters make sense. They have focus, things they want, and they don't waste your time. The Cop was like that. She had something about her. A *manner*. I would almost say a swagger, except she had it even when she wasn't moving. I'd only seen this before in men. By this time, I felt deeply unsure about men. I liked how men dressed, and I had tried dressing that way myself, but I couldn't make it work because my body wouldn't fit in the straight clothes. Generally, I tried to avoid men. I knew that I certainly didn't want to have sex with them. Women had never occurred to me, not that way. But The Cop made everything really clear. It is such a relief when people do this. I don't know why we can't do it all the time. Within five minutes she had cut a straight path through my stupid responses to her small talk, told me I was pretty, and asked me on a date. By which I mean that she said the words "You are pretty" and "Would you like to go out on a date with me?"

She didn't speak loudly. She didn't need to. I can hear her voice even now, a crisp gold chime against the grey chatter all around. A signal, at last, through the static.

The Cop was very sensible-looking, always. She had brown, pencil-straight hair, and she wore it in a smart, short bob tucked behind her ears with bobby pins. Even when she wasn't in uniform it felt like she was. Her name was Julie, and she went by Jules, but honestly I only ever thought of her as The Cop.

Her body was straight like her hair. I wondered if men passing her on the street would look at her the way they looked at me, if they would talk to her breasts instead of her. In summer, when I wore a dress outside, men yelled things at me. I would stare dead ahead, like I was in a corridor with no exits, and as I walked away I'd imagine a giant hawk swooping down behind me and pecking their eyes out. That bird had my back, and it meant I could keep walking. But there was no joy in it, not like there had been with Deb. The Cop's body seemed to have its own armour, a kind of defensive magic that I envied. I only had my mind, and I wasn't too sure about that anymore.

I went on that date. And afterwards, I went to her flat. For the first time since Deb, I felt safe in another person's company.

In the morning she drove me back to Bridge Street in her Mini, and pulled up by the rising bollards that kept traffic away from the Great Gate during the daytime. Just as I was about to get out of the car she turned towards the passenger seat and said, "What about a quick brekkie at Fitzbillies?"

I knew Fitzbillies, a delicious and expensive bakery on Bridge Street. I knew, too, that I shouldn't be breakfasting on coffee and doughnuts—that's the kind of thing that could easily lead to a last-in-first-out crisis. But it was what The Cop liked. As the caffeine and sugar hit my system, my mind began to fill up like a hot bath. Just like always, it filled with Deb.

It seems ridiculous now, but only in the morning did I realize what an incredible opportunity I had here. This cop, *surely*, must know something. At least if Deb had been found dead, or whether there had been an investigation of any kind into her disappearance. All stirred up inside by worry and coffee and sugar, I suddenly blurted everything out. The Cop was still sort of a stranger, so it felt okay.

I told her everything I could think of. How Deb and I had become friends although I didn't really like her, how we'd walked to lectures, how eventually we'd spent every moment together, how she'd slept on my floor when we were up late. Her pink sweaters and pearls, our stupid games, our late-night laughter. How disorienting things were since her disappearance. I didn't get everything in exactly the right order but eventually I got around to all the important details, right up to Deb's name being replaced from the prize announcements on the noticeboard outside Hall.

I didn't say anything about The Eleven, or the graffiti, or the bath. All of that was irrelevant to the case. And I didn't talk about my notebooks, because that wasn't about the facts. That was just me trying to understand the facts.

I told The Cop everything that might matter. As I stuffed my poor body with a second jammy doughnut which it barely tasted, the words fell out of me in jumbles, and by the time I got to the end I was hyperventilating. Still, I gasped out the essential question: "What do you know about her? Orton. I mean, that's her surname. Deborah Orton. You must know something. I need to know. It's been—"

And then I ran out of breath. As my voice stopped, I noticed a rhythmic sound. My foot was wiggling underneath the table, tracing infinity signs.

The Cop brown-eyed me kindly but without recognition. "I don't know who that is," she said gently, "but if you want I'll ask the boys. See if anyone's heard anything. You want to get dinner? La Margherita?"

"Can't afford it," I murmured, looking away.

"You can if I pay." She winked.

That wasn't really true, though. Now I come to think of it, this must have been The Cop's first lie.

It was undeniable that I needed her. Needed her help: whatever had happened to Deb, it was clearly beyond my power to resolve it by myself. It wasn't just that, though. I slept badly in my attic rooms alone, but I could drift off peacefully when I was at The Cop's place. She was a calming person to be around. She told me she was from a military family. Her father and her brothers were all Forces. All keepers of the peace.

I would hang around the park at odd times of the day, watching Parkside Police Station for her to come out. My own personal thin blue line. When I felt like I couldn't put things in order anymore, it was restful to think that she was out there doing it for a living. Keeping chaos at bay for one more week, one more meal that I never paid for, one more night with her to divide the days I spent alone. To keep the weeks moving forwards.

Every time we saw each other I'd ask if she had any new leads about Deb. Often she'd ask me for more details—what colour Deb's eyes were, whether she had any distinguishing marks or scars, what kind of jewellery she could have been wearing the day she disappeared, that sort of thing. Every so often there would be something—a missing person she'd heard of in passing, or a case a colleague of hers was working—and I'd make her promise to follow up. I could never find the words to tell her how painfully grateful I was. Sometimes I would sit and stare at her without speaking. But I recorded everything we were discovering together in a new batch of notebooks.

Over that first dinner at La Margherita, The Cop told me about a blonde woman around the right age, who'd been found wandering through town in the middle of the night with memory loss. I leaned across our pizza excitedly, mashing red sauce into my T-shirt: memory loss would be a viable explanation, at least, for why I'd heard nothing from Deb herself. I asked The Cop what else she knew, and she said the woman had been taken to Addenbrooke's to be treated for dehydration, and was most likely in the psych ward by now. I asked if she would be able to find out what had happened to her after that, but she said that wasn't police work.

I nodded, and wondered out loud if I could go to Addenbrooke's myself. For a moment I saw myself adrift again in infinite white-blue corridors. Would this hospital have glitter floors, too? But The Cop said they wouldn't give out confidential patient information. Of course, she was right. The Cop was sensible. Level-headed. She didn't get stuck in stupid loops.

I saw on the local news next day that the woman with memory loss had been identified and returned to her family in Comberton, although she had not recovered her memory, and couldn't talk. I went to the JCR every day to watch the local news, but I didn't always get to see it all. If other students wanted to watch the football or something, they'd just change the channel without asking. When that happened, I'd make sure to pick up a copy of the *Cambridge Evening News* the next morning before lectures.

I tried to keep my feet on the ground during this time, but some of the mundanities of College life began to feel less important. I missed a lot of Hall meals, and binged on multipacks of Sainsbury's Economy crisps. I thought a lot about my connection with The Cop. How to make the best of it, like Holmes did with Lestrade, or Poirot with Japp. Snippets from the old Poirot stories often played in my head, in David Suchet's voice. Those ITV adaptations were the only thing in the world for which my aunt and I shared a passionate love. We'd curl up together to watch them in the evenings by the electric fire. (One bar only, even in the middle of winter—"Those things eat money and you have a toasty warm blanket!") We mimicked Suchet's pitch-perfect faux-Belgian accent, grammatical missteps, fudged idioms.

And when she opened the cupboard, she tried to focus our attention on the wrong object. So she used the briefcase as a . . . What is it? A bloater? Kipper?

And beautiful, poker-faced Hugh Fraser as Captain Hastings: *Red herring*.

The second time I went for dinner with The Cop I wanted to talk about the woman from Comberton, even though I knew it wasn't Deb. She'd gone back to her family, to her life, but had her life come back to her? The Cop looked at me over the plastic McDonald's table and tilted her head to one side as I went on spewing questions. What would it be like to lose your past like that? Would you become a stranger to yourself? Or would that perhaps be the closest to actually *knowing* yourself that you could ever really get? At least, as an adult. It comes more naturally to children, I said, because they are not constantly suffocating themselves with memories. Memories, if you let them, become a crowd of ghosts following you around. Stuffing you further and further into your former life, until you can't breathe. Or did she keep diaries, perhaps? At least then she'd have some little splinters of her personal past, written by someone who'd for a time used her body, borrowed her voice. Would that past-woman feel like a twin sister? I never had a sibling. I'd often wished for a sister, but The Cop said I was lucky because siblings were awful and got in the way.

I took a breath when she spoke, realizing I'd been going for a while, and asked if she'd heard of anything else lately. Any other possible news of Deb. She smiled slightly and said I'd actually jogged her memory about something, with all the ghost stuff.

"By the way," she added through a mouthful of cheese-burger, "that was weird."

A woman had been buried alive in a disused well on the estate of Wimpole Hall. Once she'd slipped in, she must have dislodged the structure of the well, and the sides had caved in over her, stifling any sounds of crying for help.

"Not that she would have been able to do that for very long anyway—the soil would have filled in her mouth and lungs quite quickly. Her eyes were open, and her mouth was full of dirt. They found a worm in her ear."

She leaned over and wiggled her fingers at me, as if telling a scary story to a small child. "And her fingernails were very long—they keep growing after you die."

"Out into the soil," I said. "Like roots?"

"What?"

"From a plant that doesn't know it's dead?"

The Cop blinked. She was completely unperturbed by the facts, however grisly. She told them like they were the most ordinary thing on earth. It was my question that was wrong.

Anyhow, she explained, the local officers had ascertained that the woman had most likely fallen in by accident, and they weren't treating the death as suspicious. She'd been wearing a tracksuit, and The Cop asked if Deb could possibly have gone running out there, but I said I had never heard of Deb going running. Or wearing a tracksuit.

"What colour was it?" I asked.

"Kind of light grey, they think. It was really manky of course, when they dug out the body, but it looked like it would have been grey originally. Seem to think it could be a girl from one of the farms round the Wimpole estate. Probably went out there at night for some reason without a torch, couldn't see where she was going, fell straight in."

She indicated the action with her free hand, finger-legs walking to the edge of the invisible precipice, then flat-palming the table with a slap.

I had heard of Wimpole. It was one of those grand country houses owned by the National Trust—the kind we used to visit on school trips—just a few miles south of Cambridge. I asked The Cop if she wanted to go out there with me at the weekend.

"Why? Whoever it is, she's not still down there in the well. They'll have taken her away by now to be buried. I mean, buried again. I mean, buried properly. Somewhere else."

"I still think I'd like to go."

"What for?"

I paused and smiled at the floor. "You're a wise fish," I said.

"What?"

"No wise fish would go anywhere without a porpoise."

"Oh, I know this one! That's the Mock Turtle."

I nodded and smiled, and she looked pleased with herself.

"I bet the grounds of Wimpole are beautiful right now," I proffered, "with all the autumn colours."

She weighed this for a moment with a fake-serious frown, nodding and rubbing her chin.

"Yes," she said eventually, "that's a good porpoise. Okay, we'll go."

So she drove us down that Saturday. It was a soft day with thin sun, the kind that calls for wool scarves and thick socks. A short drive between flat, wide fields and big skies.

We plodded round the woods and the farmland, inhaling air thick with rich scents of leaf mulch and cow dung. "Good country air," my aunt would have called it. Damp oak leaves caught on our boots, and we pocketed the green-gold acorns and chocolatey conkers. I told The Cop I liked the trees with the blood red leaves, like steaks in a butcher's shop window. And the yellow five-fingered ones that waved at us. I said they were a chorus of jazz hands: this was the end of Act One, only we wouldn't have time to stay and see the rest of the show. The Cop tipped her head to one side, then gave me a playful box about the ears.

We swiped at the last of the year's bumblebees, still making drunken demands of the dying berries and brambles.

"Time, gentlemen bees!" I called, but then I felt a pang of remorse knowing most of them would have no homes to go to after mating season. I had to keep stumbling into a half-trot to keep up with The Cop, who was a good head and shoulders taller than me, with strong legs that she used to full effect. When we passed a tree stump covered in gorgeous bracket fungi, I jumped up onto it and swung my arms out wide.

"Season of wasps and rotted appleness!" I declaimed. "Gross bosom-friend of the revolting mould . . ."

The Cop looked bemused at this, and it occurred to me to wonder if she'd studied Keats. I didn't quite like to ask. As I jumped back down she glanced around to make sure no one was looking, then kissed me on the nose like a performing dog.

Neither of us said anything about the woman in the well. I didn't know where the well was, and The Cop, if she knew, didn't mention it. All I wanted to do was snoop around a bit, just in case there was anything that struck me as a reason why Deb might have come out here.

There is a folly in the grounds of Wimpole Hall, made up to look like the ruins of a medieval castle. A round stone tower with mullioned windows and narrow slit crosses, sitting askew on its foundations. Pretending to have been beaten into an odd angle by centuries of resistance, relentless effort to maintain its space against all comers, to deserve its moment in time. Crumbling portions of smaller buildings lie scattered about as if to suggest that they've fared less well in these imaginary struggles. Playing shattered visage to the tower's vast and trunkless. *Nothing beside remains*: that has two readings, you know. "Nothing else is left," or "These things are nothing but remains." Smaller again, but more resolutely real, pale grey field mushrooms ran fairy rings around my feet. These days, of course, the Wimpole estate Folly is genuinely old.

"Huh . . . *built in the late 1700s,*" The Cop read out loud from the visitor's guide. This is the thing about the past: even real history is full of fakes. Or even its fakes are real, if you prefer to look at it that way.

It's called a folly because it's supposedly a pointless building, though I could think of plenty of good reasons for making this. But my particular interest came from a memory of having seen, in the pages of the Books of The Eleven, a reference to its construction by Capability Brown at the order of Philip Yorke, the second Earl of Hardwicke, after the first earl commissioned a design from an architect called Sanderson Miller who was known for his follies. Miller lost interest though, and the architect who worked with Brown was one James Essex, who, it turned out, was also responsible for the

bridge at the back of the College. A triple-arched stone structure. Solid-looking. The water completes the arcs so that
when you punt up to it, it looks like you are facing three dark
circles. You must choose one, before your boat crashes into
the walls between.

Anyway, the debate recorded in the Books had concerned
the "ethicks or morality" of the first Earl's decision to commis-
sion such an extravagant and pointless piece of gothic frip-
pery. One member had pointed out that building a folly was
a way to provide income for the local poor without "undue
charity which promotes idleness and intemperance," while
another argued that it must have been done at the urging of
his wife Margaret, presumably thus forestalling any question
of a rational basis for assessment. I believe this was recorded
on the same page as the minutes of the meeting to discuss
Newton's alchemy. Certainly it was close by. Perhaps the page
before, or the page after. And for some reason, although the
quest for Deb was always at the front of my mind, what I'd
read in those pages was never far from the back of it. I felt as
if something there were important, but I couldn't put my finger on exactly what.

Maybe it was Cambridge, something about the place itself,
that made the occult feel close. Feel almost normal, almost
expected. While I thought this all through, staring at the folly,
The Cop had gone on ahead. So I said to nothing in particular: *"And those that are fools, let them use their talents."*

As I passed by the foot of the tower, my eye was caught
by a glint in the mud, a small reflection of the autumn sun
almost buried at the base of a tree. This tree had five roots,
like a hand plunging into the earth. What was it grasping for

down there? I bent down to retrieve the source of the glint, which turned out to be a small silver-coloured skull. Probably dropped from a necklace, or a key ring. I pocketed my find without telling The Cop, who was still a few feet away, and briefly revelled in the idea of removing evidence from the scene of a crime without notifying the police. I didn't recognize it as Deb's, and it certainly wasn't her style, but I thought it was worth keeping just in case it turned out to be suggestive in some way later on.

On our way out through the gift shop, The Cop said she wanted to buy me something. I chose a room spray, the sort you can only get from the National Trust. *Recall the beauty of our historic gardens*, read the label, above a tasteful illustration of a bluebell. An unseasonal choice for autumn, but such trivialities as a few months seemed irrelevant to a scent with such self-conscious pretensions to a different era. An era that quite possibly only exists in the imagination of the kind of person who wants their home to smell like a National Trust gift shop. Who feels like these really are somehow "their" historic gardens.

Then The Cop and I drove back to The Unicorn in Trumpington, where she bought us pints of Strongbow and split open a bag of salt and vinegar crisps to share. We felt out of place in the bar with our muddy boots and jeans, so we sat in the beer garden, snuggled close together, and watched the sun give up on the day. Somewhere, a church bell chimed the hour. It was only five o'clock, although it felt like nine. This bell rang out its five tones just once; all it had to do was tell the time. Still, it preluded the announcement with those familiar decorative notes. The so-called Westminster Chimes. They are really the Cambridge Quarters, you know. Big Ben borrowed them from the Church of St. Mary the Great, whose role in the world is to be the University's anchor. Undergraduates must reside within three miles of Great St. Mary's to count as keeping term.

"Ding dong bell," I said, and shivered.

The Cop pulled me in closer, and affectionately rapped her knuckles on the top of my head.

"Who are you calling a ding-dong?" she said. *Actioni contrariam semper et aequalem esse reactionem.*

I clutched the silver skull in my pocket, and buried my face into the warmth of her donkey jacket.

———

I see it in his eyes because it's in mine. I don't look in mirrors.

And I don't look at the little shit when she visits because her eyes, when she came out of me, her eyes didn't have it for that one moment and I can't let her catch that from me. From my eyes.

I would do anything to stop the little shit ending up back in here. But what chance did she ever have. Did any of us have.

Chapter Ten

I was still attending the meetings of The Eleven during this time, but not finding them very interesting. I was more intrigued by the book Gin had lent me sketching the Society's history, and even more so by the Books themselves. By now, Michael—one of the Society's affable grad students—had been appointed as secretary, relieving me of their care. Still, I couldn't shake the memory of what I had read in them, nor my inexorable feeling that it *mattered* somehow.

On the inner cover of one of my notebooks, I had transcribed a particularly arresting passage from the records of that meeting at which Society members had discussed Newton's alchemical research. I didn't make a note of the exact date or who was present, but I remember that I had one of the oldest of the Books in my hands when I copied out these strange words:

The Philosophers stone therefore is one but it hath many names & before thou knowst it it will be very difficult: For it is watry, aery, fiery, earthy, flegmatick cholerick, & melancholy.

Quite the multitasker, it sounded like. All things to all men. Capable of spinning everything into nothing and vice versa. Tricksy. In a feminine way, as light can be so full of every colour that it is invisible, and the perfect woman adapts so precisely to the requirements of her situation that she and all her labours disappear. No wonder we evade scientific understanding.

I bought a cheap leather choker from the market so I could wear the silver skull I'd retrieved from the mud at Wimpole's Folly around my neck. I washed the skull carefully at the handbasin in my room, and threaded the leather through the little loop welded to the skull's crown. With my black tank top and old Docs, it could pass muster as a grungy icon. It showed I didn't care about death: I was okay with being made of dirt and bones, bits and pieces. With being weak and temporary. I would have liked to get a tattoo that told the same story, but I couldn't afford one so I drew on my skin with biros. Mostly abstract swirls, or combinations of words that I thought sounded cool. *Green and dying. Towards Zero. Plus c'est la même chose.*

During the day, lectures on second-order logic and set theory kept my mind quiet, kept me ticking over in a neutral gear. Although it all went nowhere, the battery didn't die. And then in the evenings and at weekends came the work that really mattered, the search for Deb. With The Cop to help me, I felt for the first time as if progress on that front was really possible. I was no longer being shut down and swatted away at every turn. The Cop and I made a powerful team. I had the drive and determination, she had the resources and reach. She could see when I was at risk of spinning out about it, too, and knew just what to say to bring me back down to earth.

On top of all that, I was really starting to like her.

Our next lead took us to the Jesus Green Lido.

Jesus College used to be a nunnery, but, as legend has it, not an entirely virtuous one. The college now bears a "real" name chosen in hopes of making this history smell a little sweeter: The College of the Blessed Virgin Mary, Saint John the Evangelist and the glorious Virgin Saint Radegund, near Cambridge. It doesn't seem to have occurred to them that an institution which needs to mention virginity twice *in its name* is protesting too much.

Anyhow, Jesus College is the name that stuck. I'm sure there's an explanation. And Jesus Green is named after the college. Following the Cam out east brings you to Jesus Green and then on to Midsummer Common. Both are huge lawned stretches of city park bordering the river, stuck in another possibly fictional era where such a use of prime real estate was viable. Maybe the 1930s: the Lido on Jesus Green is a long, cold, open-air pool in the style that was popular in that strange transitional decade. It is accompanied by a row of changing huts, and a grassy terrace where it might be nice to sunbathe during the two days a year when it's warm enough. Picture moustached men in long bathing suits describing the water as "bracing" and "character-building," and you have the idea.

Then again, the whole place might be more at home in the 1330s. Midsummer Common is to this day still a *common*, where local residents have the right to graze their animals.

There was a woman drowned in the Lido that November. Officially it was closed for the year, but it had been specially refilled for a private event hosted by someone with more money than sense. And one woman had died in the unheated water. I actually heard about this case even before The Cop told me, because it was on the local news one evening.

The next day, when The Cop and I met to get lunch at Gardies after her shift, I asked her if we could go over to the Lido. So we plodded there with hot white-paper parcels of chips in our navy-fingerless-gloved hands—I'd shamelessly bought a cheap pair from the market to copy hers—and as we walked she filled me in on the details of the case.

It looked as though a group of young people—"possibly intoxicated," The Cop said through a mouthful of grease and steam—had broken in to the Lido in the dead of the night, after the private party had ended. It wasn't hard to break in there if you could climb a fence. And it seemed likely that this poor woman had got into difficulties after her friends had left, since nobody had raised the alarm. An attendant, arriving to clean, had found her body in the morning.

As we approached, I could see there was police tape across the main entrance, but everything else looked intensely normal. Chillingly normal. The Cop's face didn't change as she told me the woman who'd drowned was probably killed by her own heavy clothing—an all-over-sequined ballgown which flared out from the waist. She was still wearing it when she was found.

"It would have been more or less impossible to swim in that garment, even sober."

"Doesn't that make you feel . . . I don't know, heavy?" I asked.

But she shook her head. "I don't get emotionally involved. It's my job. Training," she said.

I thought of Pierre, and of that rumour about the medical students taking their corpse out to party. To become a doctor you have to be able to desensitize yourself. Ignore certain things, pretend they aren't there, until you're not pretending anymore. It's sink or swim.

"What colour sequins?" I asked. I had spotted something twinkling in the grass a few feet away.

"Blue and green," said The Cop.

Suddenly I imagined a dead mermaid, her shimmering tail lying bloated and listless against the surface of the water. I shook my head vigorously. This image was horrible and I wanted it gone.

"Deb wore pink," I said.

"Oh yeah. I think you mentioned that before."

I had mentioned it several times, in fact. It was a sea blue sequin that had caught my eye, but I said nothing about it.

The Cop asked if I wanted to go inside the Lido itself. We could check the place out, she said, see if any officers were still around, if they had any updates. But I said I didn't need to. I knew this could not be Deb. So we kept on walking. When we finished our chips, she collected my paper and scrunched all the rubbish together into a tight ball. Then she threw the ball into a park bin from a good ten feet away, taking a casual aim then popping it straight in through the middle of the open lid.

"*Shot!*" I said. I was impressed and wanted to cuddle her, but there were lots of people around.

The Cop grinned at me. "Training."

Later that day, I went back on my own and found the sequin. I don't know why, but I wanted it. The little green-blue spangle. When I got it back to my room, I washed it in my basin, then threaded it onto my leather choker beside the silver skull. I had to make the hole in the middle of the sequin a little bigger, but it was easy enough to push a wool needle from my sewing kit through and wiggle it around until it fit.

I wondered if any of the other students knew I had a sewing kit. Once, a student from Professor Bell's ethics lecture tore his shirt sleeve while gesticulating excitedly outside the lecture hall, explaining the lecture to two nearby women (who had also been in the lecture). He took the shirt off, and threw it in the next rubbish bin they passed. It was a perfectly good shirt that would have taken thirty seconds to mend. I thought about going back later to take it out, but if anybody had ever noticed me wearing it, the humiliation would have been more than I could bear.

The next week, after a morning shift, The Cop told me about a hang-gliding accident. A woman had been tow-launched out of Sutton Meadows with a hang-gliding club. She had soared for hours. At some point during those hours—I guess we'll never know how long she'd been going—she lost control, and eventually landed near Steeple Bumpstead.

That's thirty-five miles away, and the most stupidly named place on Earth to crash down in. But The Cop relayed all the details straight-faced.

"It's not funny," she said, and I suddenly realized I was giggling.

"Oh god, of course it's not funny that she died!" My face flushed hot. "I'm sorry. I just meant . . . the name of the place."

"Gliding can be very dangerous," she said. "It's not for amateurs."

"I think the sky is dangerous for everyone," I said. She took my hand in hers and put both into her coat pocket. Then she told me about her big brother Elliot who was in the RAF, and how I shouldn't be scared, because people like him were up there keeping the sky safe for people like me.

I told her I had never even been in an aeroplane, and I was terrified of the idea. It baffled me that anyone could want to fly one for a living. I couldn't imagine having nothing to stand on, no support, nothing there to stop you going into free fall.

"Uh, that's what the plane is for," she said, knocking me on the forehead, as if to check whether anyone was home. "Flying isn't dangerous if you know what you're doing. Way safer than hang-gliding. And trust me, anyone who's flying a commercial plane with you in the back knows what they're doing. It's what's in here . . ." She knocked on my forehead again. "That's what's scaring you."

What *was* in there? A bunch of goop, I supposed. Finely tuned, carefully evolved goop. I'm not afraid of that weird material, just perplexed by it.

"I'm not scared of my own brain," I said. "I'm scared of plummeting to my death. It's totally different."

"Not your brain, you numpty. Your *mind*. Your fear is all in your mind."

"My mind . . ." I refocused. I wasn't sure I believed in minds, at least not if they were supposed to be different from brains. Certainly I had never seen a mind.

Then again, was it seeing that mattered? Galileo supposedly dropped a cannonball and a musket ball from the Leaning Tower of Pisa, so the people could see for themselves how the two objects would land at the same time. Now that's a good story. The visuals are spot on, tinged with military history, and it has a strong hero: the kind of genius we all want to know and love into existence. Sherlock Holmes is just like this. Do you know how many people play "the Game"? Its one rule is that the Sherlock Holmes stories are not fictional.

Anyway, that was Galileo's big gimmick, getting people to look and see for themselves. Look through his telescope and see the Galilean moons and know *the truth*. Game over, right? Well, it's a pretty good way to crash and burn your narrative arc, that's for sure. Someone's going to have to introduce a very different kind of drama if you insist on playing it that way. How else to keep the story moving along, create some tension? Holmes knew what he was doing, keeping all the important details to himself until the bitter end, the big reveal, when everything would come together. And Poirot, beloved Poirot, he understood that seeing for oneself wasn't all that. Poor old Japp says that Inspector Miller won't miss a single clue, *he's got eyes that see everything*, and Poirot absolutely zings him: *So, mon ami, has the London sparrow. But all the same, I should not ask the little brown bird to solve the problem of Mr. Davenheim . . . It is the brain, the little grey cells, on which one must rely.*

So was that what I was afraid of? Reliance? I can't rely on something as flimsy as an aeroplane to keep me in the air. I don't belong up there with Cosimo's stars. Then again, maybe they don't belong up there either. Or to Cosimo de' Medici. Or to Galileo. Is it even possible for a moon to belong? *One might be tempted to answer that, if your tube shows something which cannot be there, it cannot be an entirely reliable tube, wouldn't you say?*

There was nothing about the gliding accident on the news yet, so I asked if we could drive out to Steeple Bumpstead and see what was going on. It was only forty minutes and The Cop said she didn't mind because country driving cleared her head after work. Out past Addenbrooke's on the Babraham Road, the landscape flattens and makes the sky wide. I watched it expand around us until it engulfed The Cop's little car and we became comfortably tiny, peering out through the windscreen at the vast acres of crops. Our progress was slow. Negligible, when one could see it to scale. I watched the road signs passing, and imagined what they might look like to someone who did not know our conventions. Our symbols. How far could you get by looking at the shapes alone, probing them for some physical resemblance to a real situation that one might encounter on the roads? And then, what about the words? How do words look when you can't read them? What if you don't even know they're words? There's a Sherlock Holmes story about criminals using little stick figures as a code, because to outsiders they don't look like bearers of meaning at all. But anything *can* be a word, if we decide it is one. And what about the other direction—can we undo that decision, once it's made?

The crash site was in a huge flat brown field, a few huge flat brown fields over from the village of Steeple Bumpstead itself, to the north and east. A handful of people were milling around, every now and then looking up at the huge blue sky as if they half expected someone else to fall out of it. One of them was insisting to anybody who would listen that this very field was the "Bloody Pightle," a locally famous spot where some guy was supposed to have been burned in the sixteenth century for being a nonconformist. Going to the wrong kind of church in the wrong kind of way.

Crash or burn. What's worse? I turned to ask The Cop what she thought, but she wasn't paying attention. She was chatting quietly and discreetly to another officer on the other side of the police tape. They nodded briskly to each other when they were done, in mutual recognition of their shared professionalism.

"They are about ninety per cent sure she's called Alicia Botham. I'm sorry." Then she looked confused. "That came out wrong."

I nodded. I was confused, too—I couldn't locate the proper feeling. Was I disappointed? That a dead woman turned out not to be Deb? I desperately didn't want Deb to be dead. Still, there was another kind of desperation in not knowing.

As we drove back down the lane to the village of Steeple Bumpstead, The Cop turned on the car radio. We heard on the news how a team of cosmologists, measuring the redshift of supernovae, had figured out that the rest of the universe isn't just moving away from us, it's *speeding up*. How must it feel, I wondered, to discover such a desolate truth? I reflected on how much The Cop had come to matter: the world as I understood it was accelerating away from me. And except for The Cop, everything and everyone else were going along with it. She was the only person on my side in this tug-of-war with reality.

There wasn't any point hanging around Steeple Bumpstead. The Cop and I decided just to pop into the post office before we set off again, to buy some Polos and cans of Coke for the drive home. On the counter, they had for sale a stack of laminated printouts of a corny poem about the village's name. *Once Steeple Bumpstead had a Steeple / Beloved by all the village people* . . . There were several stanzas of this crap. But then there was this bit that I liked about how the weather-cock on top of the steeple had flown off, *And left the place no means of knowing / Whatever way the wind was blowing.*

Next to the confectionary and the wobbly poetry was a little stand with cheap cigarette lighters, decorative key rings, and assorted small useful items like paper tissues. One of the key rings was decorated with a tiny white plastic wing; perhaps it was meant to represent the wing of an angel. It caught my eye at first because of the poem, but when I picked it up it felt like it belonged in my hand. The Cop saw me holding it and smiled, then she put it on the counter with our Polos and Coke. She pulled her black leather wallet from her back pocket, handed a crisp fiver to the sweet old lady minding the shop, and secured us all we needed for the time being.

It wasn't up to me. None of it was. When they decided I had bled enough they started cutting. My body was split apart and she was taken out of the middle and then there was nothing left in there. Nothing alive, nothing dead, nothing nothing nothing nothing nothing. I am full of it.

Chapter Eleven

The little white wing found its way onto my choker with the skull and the sequin, as the cold of autumn turned the corner into winter. December set in, bringing bitter mornings and dim days. This cold was not like last year's living cold. This cold stopped the blood in my fingers, turning them funny shades of red and white.

Still, however bad it got, women would go out to Cindies wearing almost nothing. Cindies was a nightclub, the only one people seemed to talk about as if it were an actual club rather than a kind of glorified student society or college bop. At the same time, everyone laughed about what a shitty club it was. Mostly cheesy dance music, '80s nights, and foam parties. Hot, dense energy bouncing wall to wall in a closed environment. Compressed and wriggling bodies. To some, an image of hell. It wasn't even really called Cindies, it was called Fifth Avenue. "Cindies" was a remnant of a brief but luminous previous incarnation. In Cambridge, language doesn't change fast, and certainly not for such trivial reasons as accuracy, which buckles easily there under the weight of *tradition*.

I had never been inside Cindies, but often saw drunk students streaming back through the market square as I collected my late-night greasy snacks from the Life Van or the Death Van. Women in tiny black skirts and sparkly boob tubes laughed and yelled and puked and hugged each other, seemingly impenetrable to the sub-zero night air. Perhaps they didn't even notice it was cold. Like young children at the edge of the sea, oblivious to their blueing lips and chattering teeth because their sandcastles are all-important. Who am I to say they're wrong? I'm not building anything so spectacular myself.

One night, as I circled indecisively around the terrible food options, I saw a trickle of revellers dressed in Cindies clothes approaching me. Something was different, though. They were strangely subdued. As my eyes followed the trickle back towards its source, it became a stream, then a flood. The entire club had to be emptying all at once. But why so early? It was barely midnight. And why was their customary exuberance so eerily muted? This felt like a parade of shadows.

Eventually, a louder group came by, led by a man I recognized from my year. He was one of those whose flow of speech could not be brooked by any force in the world. Even when he wasn't actually speaking, you could see the floodwaters building behind an inadequate dam, and it was impossible to relax knowing it could burst at any second. When it did, he went off indiscriminately in all directions.

Now he was dishevelled, with what looked like grey dust in his hair and clothes. He was flanked by a gaggle of men who responded with expressive faces, yeahs, whoas, and other markers of an appreciative, non-obtrusive audience. Social ecosystems form and flourish like this in the strangest of circumstances.

"It's gotta have started in the bogs, right, think about it, where those guys were running out, you know, probably faggots, like what were they doing in there anyway, when 'Come On Eileen' starts up just as I'm about to duck in there myself for a quick waz, thought I might need to barf too but first I couldn't open the door, and like the handle was all hot, and then, fuck man, everything suddenly goes mental, the whole bar is on fire and it makes sense you know because, right, think about it, that's all pure alcohol, *pure alcohol* right, so it goes up like *fffffwoosh* . . ."

He made an explosive gesture with his hands.

". . . so then there was the alarms going off really fucking loud, but some of those dumb bints in there, they're so off their tits that they're like *wwwwwwooooooooowwwwwwooooo* and they start jumping up and down and they're all *come on, Eileen, ta-loo-rye-aye* . . ."

For added verisimilitude he was jumping and singing now, his grimy beige polo shirt drenched in sweat, yet he continued to narrate seamlessly and without ever apparently needing to breathe. I thought to myself that he could be really good at the didgeridoo, or musical theatre.

". . . then the bouncers and the guys behind the bar are all there on the dance floor and they're like *ladies this is an emergency* but they're like *wwwooooowoooooooo* and trying to dance with the bouncers but then the fucking bar explodes man, like we're in a fucking James Bond movie, and suddenly everyone can see the place is fucking on fire, right, and they're like shitting themselves, so then everyone's running out screaming . . ."

He jogged a few steps in a mincing, tottering impression of a woman running in heels.

". . . so there's the fire engines outside and there's the pigs there right, and they're like *nobody leaves until we've talked to you all* but Jiz Harvey, you know Jiz from Peterhouse, he's off like a fucking rocket because he's scored on the way out here and now he's paranoid as fuck, and this copper *slams* him down, but anyway the rest of us when we get outside and there's the fucking fuzz, you guys saw it, right, they must think it's arson, fuck man . . ."

I reflected that the audience of this monologue must have been present for the entire adventure, but that one might as well tell a firehose one is already wet. His voice trailed off, Doppler-like, as the group passed, and I walked quietly through the alley behind the Church of St. Andrew the Great, towards the scene of the disaster.

The actual fire must have been put out, and now the night air smelled of smoke and damp ash. I couldn't see The Cop, and I didn't dare approach anyone else. There was a smattering of journalists and photographers around but they seemed mostly to be leaving. I hovered near the dying babble of the aftermath to overhear someone—maybe a firefighter—say over a radio that six people had gone to Addenbrooke's. Three, it seemed, were dead on arrival. One killed by the explosion, two in the crush to get out.

I skirted round the building, down a short flight of steps into the narrow brick passageway that led to Christ's. This was the edge of Lion Yard, an awkwardly modern, ugly 1970s addition to the city centre. The floor of the passage was laid out in zigzag tiles, grouted in between and scattered with grey chewing-gum splotches and occasional cigarette butts. I noticed a pattern in the gum, approximating a smiley face with a lipstick-stained butt for a nose. We want patterns, especially faces. Crave them so much that our brains have evolved to see them everywhere.

There was something sparkly trodden into the dirty grouting, right where an earring would have graced the flat countenance. I dug it out with my fingernail: a little crystal attached to a metal link. Probably from a pendant necklace. Or, indeed, a real earring, erstwhile of a real ear. It reminded me of the plastic baubles on my once-beloved necklace, the one I hadn't worn since my classmate pointed out how cheap it was. This crystal looked the way they used to look, before she said that. I guessed that one of the Cinderellas fleeing this burning ball had dropped it in her hurry. I pocketed it for myself with no intention of seeking her out. No Prince Charming, me.

Under the street lamps, it looked as if there were a tiny rainbow fire burning inside the crystal. Best it stay trapped in there, I thought, where it can't do any damage. Back in my rooms, I scrubbed the dirt from under my fingernails, rinsed off the crystal in my basin, and threaded its metal link onto my choker.

I caught up with The Cop the next day, and I asked her about the people who'd died in the Cindies fire. I'd heard on the news that one of them was a young woman, but didn't learn her name. As we meandered from Parker's Piece towards the Grafton Centre, The Cop told me the woman who died was Madeleine somebody. She was local, not a student.

"A townie?" I asked.

The Cop stopped and looked round. "Uh . . . so you know, that's not always the best word to use when you're talking to one."

I suddenly felt my face burning. I had heard other people use the word, and I knew what it meant on the surface, whom it referred to. I had just never thought about the *weight* of its meaning. Its undertow. I had never had to think about that.

"I'm sorry, I didn't mean . . ." I said.

She smiled and said, "S'okay. Just don't do it again or you'll be cruising for a bruising!"

She air-boxed me several times, bobbing and swerving to avoid my non-existent counterattacks.

I wore my choker every day. The skull, the sequin, the wing, and the crystal bunched together and weighed it into a V-shape. This little collection seemed complete now, and I stopped adding to it. I wore it for myself, not for show, tucking it away into my thick Cambridge-winter sweater.

The last lead I got from The Cop was a suicide. This was well into the Lent term. Even now, it's the most difficult one to talk about. I should say her name, at least. I owe her that. Caitlyn.

If the woman from Comberton had lost her past, Caitlyn had lost her future. I don't mean the easy way, the same way as everyone who dies. Even after we realized she wasn't Deb, I kept asking questions. In the Botanic Garden on Trumpington Road, The Cop and I sat staring side by side at the lake. Cherry blossoms and crocuses lay scattered in the grass like discarded sweet wrappers. The Cop told me Caitlyn was a "brilliant student." I said they always are, and The Cop nodded softly.

"She was a mathematician in her final year, on course for a First, perhaps even a starred First," said The Cop. "Usually about fifty Cambridge students try to kill themselves in a given academic year."

We sat in silence for a minute, as the ducks chattered softly in the background. There had been murmurs since forever that someone needed to do something about the brutality of the place, or at least about all the "Suicide Sunday" jokes, but it was Cambridge and nothing was going to stand in the way of a tradition. What *could* be done, anyway? It's not like suicide rates were official policy.

"She left a note," The Cop added eventually. "Said she had lost her way."

"Yes." I thought about it, and nodded. "A map extends in four directions. It looks comprehensive. All the points in the two-dimensional plane. But we are supposed to *know*—to know without being told, I mean—that there's an up and a down as well. They're just not depicted. They can't be, given how this kind of representation works. But as long as we know about them, we can imagine our own *down*, build foundations, move around in the mapped area without thinking that's all there is. Without getting trapped in the flat world. And provided your downward force is balanced just right, you can even take off from the flat surface, still knowing you can land.

"I mean, whatever is happening to us right now, we look at it like it's a still image. A flat map, a snapshot. But we are supposed to know there's a past, too: a kind of *down* from now. Let's say that's made of memories. Okay. As long as they don't bury you, suffocate you, they can be your grounding. The sandbags in your hot-air balloon. They keep you from floating off where the air's too thin to breathe. So, then, what's the future made of? *Nothing* isn't a good enough answer. I suppose Caitlyn realized that."

I said all this to The Cop, as we sat together on the damp grass. When I noticed I'd been talking for a long time, I looked round to see what she thought.

But she didn't say anything.

Until that night, The Cop and I had never argued.

I hate arguing. I am very bad at it. When I'm angry there is no breath behind my words, so they end up flat and soft like a muted trumpet. They can't express feeling. They can't do anything. I sound more like someone with a bad head cold than someone who is angry. Usually, I just go quiet instead. *Conflict-avoidant* is a term I only learned later.

That evening, as she stirred a pan of tinned soup on top of the cooker in her little flat on Hills Road, The Cop asked me why I never called her by her name.

"What do you mean?" I asked, although it was completely obvious what she meant. I was just embarrassed, and buying time.

"Why don't you ever say my name? You always either just start talking, or you say *Hey*. You never call me Julie."

"Well, names are strange, don't you think? I mean, they get attached to us from the outside, by someone else, and they don't really have anything to do with—"

She interrupted me. "And why do you always have to make it about philosophy? I'm trying to talk about us."

I hadn't thought of any of it as being about philosophy. But my embarrassment had heated up now, and was undergoing a kind of molten transmutation in my chest.

I said that if we were talking about "us," then we ought to know what we meant by that, and it wasn't changing the subject to ask this kind of question. Then, feeling like I was on a roll, I made a stupid mistake. I asked how come, if we were an "us," I had never met any of her police friends.

She talked to me about "the boys" sometimes, but I had absolutely no interest in meeting them, and would certainly have declined if such an offer had ever been made. It just felt like something to hit with.

"Are you kidding? You don't exactly walk in to the station and announce you're a lesbian. Not if you want to still have a job or a life when you walk out."

The word *lesbian* came splashing out of the sentence and all over my face like acid. It was still evaporating painfully when she came back for another pass.

"Anyway, I've never met any of *your* friends."

I was having trouble getting words out now.

"I don't . . . have . . . I mean, there was only Deb."

"Right." She raised her eyebrows. "Deb."

Then, after a long pause, she said again: "Right."

It was a chilly evening, but with all the windows closed and the four-panel gas heater glowing its little heart out, it warmed up quickly in The Cop's flat. Suddenly I was too hot.

"It's . . ."

My voice was trying to tamp itself out, close up my throat. Over and over. Shut it down, shut it down, *shut it down*. But I overruled it. I kept pushing. I forced myself.

"It's too much . . . for me. You . . . keep mentioning something that *might* be about Deb and then it never is. And maybe . . ." —here it came gushing out, like watery diarrhea— ". . . you could check, you know, next time, before you tell me, put me through all that, all the fear, over and over, and the *hope*, the hope is the worst . . ."

"Okay okay okay," she said, turning her back on the cooker to make shushing motions at me with her hands.

And then, as I went quiet, she looked me in the eye. "Oh god. Maybe it's time. Are we doing this, Victoria?"

"Doing what?"

The question was so strange, it brought me right back to her. Curiosity quickly cooled the heat in my chest and I felt sorry at once. Ashamed of myself.

"It's been, what, six months?"

"Since we met?" I nodded.

"Can we let it go now?" she asked. "The Deb thing? It's getting old. I think it's played out. Don't you think so?"

"What's played out?" I could hear fast breathing in front of my face. In my nose. Cooling me. Dangerously cold.

"Okay, babe. It's okay. I know there was never anyone called Deborah Orton at your college. I know you wanted to have a reason to see me again, after that first night. It's okay. I knew the whole time. I checked right away whether there might be anything in what you were saying and it *really* didn't look like it. I thought you'd drop it once we were, uh, seeing each other, so I kind of played along because . . . well, you know."

"I really don't."

I was pricking all over. Tiny ice flakes, first under my skin. Then the air around me became the flakes.

"And it was fun to go around on those trips and things. But you don't need to make up a reason to get me to drive you around. I love you and I'll drive you wherever you want."

She had never told me that she loved me.

"But we're not *children*, Victoria. This isn't a detective story. I'm not, you know, your police sidekick." The Cop held out both her hands, palms facing me. It was genuine, a frank gesture. Openness. She meant every word. I just didn't know what the words could mean.

Then the frozen air flakes clicked together, and trapped me in a translucent box. A barrier between me and the world. Through it, The Cop was looking straight at me, wide-eyed with a new interest, like she'd never really seen me before and didn't know what she was looking at. As though I were a very strange specimen, dead inside a glass case in the library of some Victorian naturalist.

Or maybe it was that I suddenly felt that way about her.

"No," I said through the box. "No. This isn't happening. You mean, all of this wasn't real? You're not . . . real?"

"Oh, *come on*." Now it was her turn to be angry. "What the hell is wrong with you? Why do you *always* have to talk like that?"

As if through a triple-glazed window, I could dimly hear that the soup was bubbling over. The Cop turned away from me to scoop the pan up off the stove. So sensible. So practical. As the brown, glutinous liquid hit the glowing element of the electric hob, it spat and sizzled. The sound of something snapping.

The thing is, when you stop talking people assume you can't. Then after a while they assume you don't understand language at all.

But I do. I hear things. Strange things. I hear them at night.

I'm not sure if it's the nurses.

Chapter Twelve

Some people, when their heart breaks, it breaks open. Not mine.

Once again I shut down all unnecessary functions. I focused for my life. I went to all my lectures, pored over set readings and essay drafts late into the night, impressed my teachers again and again with mindlessly intelligent arguments. Arguments about all sorts of things. Safe things. Theoretical, abstract, vast things. Questions so huge they could not possibly matter, nor have any possible connection to anything that did.

I maintained the very few other responsibilities I had: to pay my College bills, to attend occasional meetings of The Eleven, to appear in my tutor's office at the beginning and end of each term and tell him things were going fine. I knew, all the time, that I must eventually return to the terrible mystery of Deb's disappearance, but without The Cop beside me I did not know how. Not then.

My digestion kept deteriorating, and around this time I started routinely getting bad headaches that made it hard to concentrate. I went to see a GP, who said it was "stress."

So I went to see a counsellor. At that time the University was getting in some very hot water, once again, about failing to identify and help its suicidal students, so they'd started really pushing their in-house counselling services at everyone. Big colourful posters all over the JCR noticeboards, and flyers on library tables, asked us constantly if we were *Struggling with work? Feeling overwhelmed?* The result was that the counselling service was now inundated with new clients and I had to wait four weeks for an assessment. By then, the migraine auras had started.

I knew my mother and grandmother had special headaches. When I was little I had quite a few ordinary headaches, and my aunt had said I "ought to keep an eye on" them, but I hadn't paid much attention until one morning a piece went missing without warning from the centre of my visual field. It described a shallow arc, replaced with bright, jagged lines like a warship in dazzle camouflage. Do you know the lines of the bridge behind Queens'—the one everyone insists on calling the Mathematical Bridge? Imagine how it might look if you made all its lines jump about as if mildly electrocuted, and if you made them luminous with colours you'd never seen before, yet their appearance was somehow also the absence of colour. You must also recognize this bridge as the harbinger of hours of implosive pain, nausea, and altered senses. Having no taste for anything except salt.

My counsellor was a friendly, overworked woman with fuzzy auburn hair. I told her I'd heard that philosophy applicants were "screened" for mental health issues in the Cambridge admissions interviews, but I was still worried: surely we were not screened in expert fashion, since those interviews were conducted by College Fellows, who often sent along their grad students as stand-ins. There was no reason they'd be able to tell if I was okay, was there? It did occur to me to wonder how many philosophers were really entirely sane. Have you read Nietzsche? I can see why they would want to check up on us, before letting us come up to Cambridge. I told her about the headache bridge, and about the breakup, taking care to skirt around any details that would give away The Cop's gender. I told her about the *What's missing from this picture* incidents. I didn't mention the bath afterwards, because that was my own fault and it was obvious how to prevent that from recurring.

She didn't think any of it was a big deal.

"I know migraines can be nasty, but they are very common," she said, in a sweet, slightly Scottish accent. "Just take some ibuprofen if it's really bothering you. As for these funny déjà vu things,"—she pronounced it *déja view*—"they happen all the time. Especially when you aren't sleeping too well. Or if you're under pressure, like when your romantic life is a bit rocky."

She told me to do some relaxation exercises, and gave me a CD of bird noises. She said as long as I was worrying about myself, I was probably okay. Maybe she was right. Nietzsche, you know, thought he was fine.

I resolved to stay worried, and I didn't see her again.

The next clue came from an entirely unexpected quarter.

Back in my first summer, Gin had told me she was formally transferring into the Department of History and Philosophy of Science so she could work with a new supervisor—someone "less awful" than the guy she'd been assigned in the Philosophy faculty. During our conversations in the library, she'd started talking about some of the HPS lecturers and what they taught for Tripos. Some of it was interesting enough to stick in my mind, and that's how I found myself sitting in on a series of HPS lectures in my second year. And then when money got very tight near the end of that year, one day after lecture I noticed a sign in the lobby of the HPS building: *Cleaning staff needed*.

What I had learned to call "outside work" wasn't permitted during term time. This rule was justified as ensuring that undergraduates would not be distracted from their studies. Only the few of us who needed the work knew what the rule really meant, what it did. But it made it even more important to work over the holidays. I opened my ring binder, and in the margin of my notes from the day's lecture, I jotted down the contact name and number from the ad. A cleaning gig could be a way to earn money that involved absolutely minimal contact with other people. A precious opportunity.

I am extremely good at cleaning and I take pride in it, for all it's a skill that no one else seems to value. Not at more than £3.40 an hour, anyway. People will pay almost any price for novelty, for creation. And destruction is its own industry. But I always thought the secret star of that trinity was maintenance. When I think of originality, I see a line passing through the origin: keep it running smooth, clear, and straight, and you can find your way to anywhere and back. If you've lived in a very small space you might understand that anything's enough if you know how to maintain it. And if you don't, nothing will ever be enough for you—you'll always need somewhere new to make a mess of. Medicine is just maintenance when it comes down to it, and people will pay enough for *that* when they need it.

The HPS department was down on Free School Lane. The building had itself once been the eponymous "Free School," and now housed the Whipple Museum and Library—a rather unspectacular collection of dull books and rusty, gangly-looking instruments, all connected in some way to what its curators considered the history of science. A history in which certain objects mattered. Probably full of fakes. My routine was to mop all the floors, empty the bins, clean the toilets and handbasins, then restock the soap and the toilet rolls.

I'd arrive to make my rounds at ten o'clock sharp, three nights a week, letting myself in with the satisfyingly huge metal front-door key entrusted to me. I'd proceed directly to the cleaning cupboard in the basement—to which I had another, much smaller, metal key—and emerge minutes later armed with my blue apron, red bucket stuffed with cleaning products, and yellow CAUTION sign to warn the world of what I was doing. I never saw anyone else in the building.

In the daylight of the teaching term I had entered through that same door, but it was already open for me and I wore my own clothes. I'd sat in the back row of the building's biggest brick-sided lecture hall, on the highest of its tiered wooden benches, while mild-mannered Dr. Lemon spoke passionately and peered at us over his tiny spectacles. He taught me about Copernicus, Galileo, Kepler, retrograde motion, epicycles, degenerating research programs. The search for explanations and for the meaning of *explanation*. I wrecked my wrist muscles taking notes, never understanding why the other students around me were content to let it all float past them, as if it did not matter. Washed in on the tide of Lemon's thinking, all these things he cared about. I suppose they let him care so they didn't have to.

It was from Lemon I learned that if you are committed enough to an idea you can wall it off from all incoming counter-evidence. When it was important to believe that heavenly objects move in perfect circles at a constant speed, that made it important to believe that Galileo's telescope was faulty. Which was easiest if you could keep the guy quiet. Lemon didn't tell me much about Isaac Newton, but I always felt close to him because I lived upstairs from his laboratory. I was his neighbour, really, just at the wrong moment in time.

I stumbled on more clues about Newton while I was "dusting" in the Whipple collections. It wasn't really part of my job to dust in the museum, but I was fast, and usually finished with at least half an hour to spare. So I wandered among the gangly objects and decrepit manuscripts, flicking a duster about. It gave me a strange feeling, being in there, which I attributed to having spent the previous two hours inhaling cleaning agents in windowless spaces, and to my migraines with their ever-weirder visual effects. A feeling of being out of time.

I didn't arrive at Newton directly, but I found a book that had once been Newton's. His copy of Boyle's *Tracts Consisting of Observations about the Saltness of the Sea* sits on display in a glass box in the Whipple, and I "dusted" the box open late one night. Finding myself once again in physical contact with a book I could not believe the universe would place in my hands (*why don't they lock these things?*), I silently resolved this time not to spit on it. I even took care to set my red bucket of chemicals—no doubt weapons of mass book destruction—far off to one side, and to remove my powdery yellow cleaning gloves as I digested the book's full title. It was a heavy name for anything to bear:

> *Tracts consisting of observations about the saltness of the sea :*
> *an account of a statical hygroscope and its uses : together*
> *with an appendix about the force of the air's moisture :*
> *a fragment about the natural and preternatural state of*
> *bodies / By the Honourable Robert Boyle. To all which is*
> *premis'd a sceptical dialogue about the positive or privative*
> *nature of cold: with some experiments of Mr. Boyl's referr'd*
> *to in that discourse. By a member of the Royal Society.*

I thought of how Deb hadn't been weighed down with so much as a middle name. *Deb* was so light, so floaty. A feather word.

I knew a little bit about Boyle from Lemon's lectures. An atomist. More or less credited with inventing modern chemistry. Pioneer of the scientific method. (*Order and method, Hastings!*) Member of some sort of organization that he called an Invisible College. I had heard of his *Suspicions about the Hidden Realities of the Air*, which is what you might call an in-between book: a relative both of alchemy and of science, yet fully at home in neither family tree. The title stuck with me, perhaps because I had a few suspicions of my own about hidden realities by this time. Boyle's family is interesting, too. How about his nephew Charles, the fourth Earl of Orrery, for whom the orrery is named. Or his collaborator Katherine,

Lady Ranelagh, quickly excised from the history of science for the heinous shortcoming of being a sister, not a brother.

Deb, too, had been cut out. From me, from the world. Extracted like a diseased appendix. How many more were there like her, I wondered? So far gone by now that they might as well never have existed, all still out there somewhere, still real. Or as real as they could be in that state. Trapped at the boundaries, in the walls of a reality that didn't want them, that wouldn't let them either be or not be. Anchorites by accident. Robert Boyle himself was famously too soft-hearted to conduct vivisections.

Perhaps the saltness of the sea sounds unimportant to you because it's about chemistry and small things. Well, no. The saltness of the sea is why you are alive. Everything is connected in pulses and currents: take the saltness away from the sea and it conducts electricity around a million times less well. Get down to the very small scale and start tinkering there and you start chain reactions that change the world. You can do it with chemistry or with people, the trick works in many mediums. Newton talked about worlds with different laws of nature, you know, in the *Opticks*: *And since Space is divisible in infinitum, and Matter is not necessarily in all places, it may be also allow'd that God is able to create Particles of Matter of several Sizes and Figures, and in several Proportions to Space, and perhaps of different Densities and Forces, and thereby to vary the Laws of Nature, and make Worlds of several sorts in several Parts of the Universe.*

Then he hedges: *At least, I see nothing of Contradiction in all this.* Yeah, well, me neither. And as for the very small, so for the very large: zoom out far enough and everything changes.

That kind of perspective jolts you, shifts you. Right now, our best scientists, our envoys into these territories, cannot reconcile the very small with the very large. They cannot deal with the shifts. I mean that they do not know what it is in which we are shifted.

Still, as for Boyle's *Saltness*, despite the author's eminence and all the title's promises I didn't find much of interest as I read the words within. When my shift was over, I set the book back inside its airless little greenhouse as though nothing had happened.

But something had happened.

Isaac Newton owned this book of Boyle's. And Newton's work—his real work, what moved his heart—was his work on prophecy, mystical clues to the order of the universe, occult chronology, and alchemy. Newton didn't want this *boring* world, the one made of gravity and all the things he could already explain. He wanted magic. (*Yes, yes, magic!* That's Blanche DuBois. And then how does she go on? *I try to give that to people. I misrepresent things to them.*) I thought of the entry in the Books of The Eleven, about Newton's search for the philosophers' stone, and the fifth element. I'd been comforted, back then, by the thought of how stupid it was. After reading Newton's copy of *Saltness*, I was no longer sure exactly how stupid it was. And this was not comforting.

It was the spur I needed, though, to dig up a few more of Newton's secrets. His erased history. The one buried in the dirt under centuries of tourist myths and official biographies. The next morning in the College library, I found myself unable to work on anything else, so I made a search of the electronic catalogue for materials relating to Newton, and landed on a lecture John Maynard Keynes wrote (but never delivered) for the tercentenary of Newton's death. Newton's manuscripts, which Keynes had assembled and decoded, framed an unrecognizable portrait of this man. A no-longer-credible silhouette of his pursuit of knowledge.

Keynes confirmed my sense that there was something about this place, as well: *There is an unusual number of manuscripts of the early English alchemists in the libraries of Cambridge*, he wrote. *It may be that there was some continuous esoteric tradition within the University which sprang into activity again in the twenty years from 1650 to 1670. At any rate, Newton was clearly an unbridled addict. It is this with which he was occupied "about 6 weeks at spring and 6 at the fall when the fire in the elaboratory scarcely went out" at the very years when he was composing the* Principia . . .

This last comment grabbed my attention because Newton's *Principia* is the book containing his theory of gravitation, his laws of motion, and all that jazz. The cornerstone of classical mechanics. To Newton's mind, science and magic were not either-or, but overlaid with one another. I wondered if Newton was a cat person and a dog person, too. Keynes said: *There was extreme method in his madness. All his unpublished works on esoteric and theological matters are marked by careful learning, accurate method and extreme sobriety of statement. They are just as* sane *as the* Principia, *if their whole matter and purpose were not magical. If.*

The College, I thought to myself, must be mortified by the existence of this other Newton, this wizard in search of his philosophers' stone. They wanted their man of science—*the* man of science—not some overgrown eighteenth-century Harry fucking Potter. The man who used his reason when an apple fell from a tree, not the one who hankered after the elixir of life, pinned down an earliest possible date for the apocalypse, and believed in entirely the wrong number of Gods. The College is very strict about certain matters; its "good customs" leave neither room nor need for a new heaven, or a new earth. Of course they'd kept the real Newton on the DL. Kept him quite literally incredible. *I don't tell the truth, I tell what ought to be truth.*

Even so, it wasn't until lunch that I realized. Not until I sat once more gazing up at *semper eadem* and poking at a plate of canteen gammon, with its one sorry pineapple slice and tiny heap of overcooked spinach winking up at me under the Hall lights, that I knew. That book—*Saltness*—was a perfect example. So crammed full of substance that there *had* to be something it was hiding. Something it deliberately wasn't talking about. It wasn't the words inside the book that mattered. You don't have to get meaning out of wordstuff. You find it. So you can find it in anything. Newton would have known that. Of course he would have. Newton was looking for a fifth element because he understood that something was missing in the four. *This nothing's more than matter.* That's Laertes. What mattered about that pointedly comprehensive book was what was *not there*. And that was it all along, wasn't it? The real work that Newton was trying to do, the shadow in the corner of his mind's eye, the trick of the light that had once caught the attention of some long-past incarnation of The Eleven before being buried again in the pages of its Books, that had briefly flickered out at me one evening, when I was too distracted and miserable to chase it. What was missing. Not just from that book, not just from my life without Deb, but from *everything*.

And instead of searching for it, everyone was expending all their efforts on denying there was anything to find.

My head was hurting, and the bright bridge was there again in the centre of my field of vision, but I wasn't feeling sick so I scoffed down all the food on my plate, except for the last bite. (My aunt had drilled this habit into me since infancy—"so nobody thinks you are starving!") I slid my tray of used dishes onto the conveyor belt that took it to the unseen kitchen for someone else to deal with, and walked out through the heavy doors into the cold sun.

The food returned my blood sugar to equilibrium, and I came quietly back down to earth. What was I thinking? Nonsense, crazy talk. I'd felt light-headed in the museum from the cleaning products, that was all. I'd had a brief relapse before lunch because I hadn't eaten since the night before.

Dammit, I needed to keep my feet on the ground, didn't I? To help Deb.

When you're lost in a forest or a city, the thing to do is to proceed in a straight line. I studied what I was there to study, Logic, language, the mind, mathematics, metaphysics. I became intensely skilled in the kinds of abstract hypotheticals I had first practised in the library with Gin. I learned all the theoretical vocabulary it was considered important for me to learn in order to compete in Olympic-level contests of argument-winning. *Rigid designation. The synthetic a priori. Sense and reference. Inaccessible cardinals. Accessible worlds. Restricted quantifiers. Two-dimensional semantics.* I became world-class. I do not exaggerate here, either for effect or out of arrogance. It is simply the truth.

Time passed, Cambridge continued in time, and I continued in Cambridge. Things sped up and I buckled in. One morning, I sat in a long hall full of rows of wooden seats and wrote a three-hour Part II Essay paper on the Liar paradox. I got my Double First, my M.Phil., my Ph.D. Scholarships and prizes turned into publications and conferences. It was a straight shot through a world that rewards straight shots. Things changed but nothing changed: my mind had sprouted its own sterile environment, an internal hospital ward—somewhere to wander all day, infinitely safe, like a well-harmonized Bach chorale. There are rules for these things. Expected progressions.

People considered this a good life. In the cheery voice of my aunt I heard, almost every day, *Count your blessings!* Only in my mind though. I didn't call her anymore. It cost money, and what would have been the point?

After The Cop, there was no one left to ask about Deb, so I asked myself. Each night, when my work was done, I burrowed back into my notebooks, racking my brains to figure out what I'd missed. What connected all those things I had seen and learned. What the clue must be that I hadn't noticed. What I had done wrong, or what I had failed to do.

———

You think you know someone but it's always you.
Whatever you think someone is, like if you try to
guess what they feel like you're only imagining
what you'd feel like. It's just you, back to front like
a reflection. But I can see him, *even on the* TV *screen,*
whatever they call it, not a "screen," I know there's
nothing really there—I can see his eyes aren't right.
I can see it now, I couldn't see it at first. Not back
then, not for years actually. If you know how to
see it in their eyes too then you would know what
I mean, when they have that kind of red glow, not
literally red, that's how you know. Some of the
nurses in here have it. Not all of them, but enough.
More than enough. You need herd immunity with
this kind of thing, like 99 per cent at least have to
be okay, and even then you can fuck up. I thought
I was okay but I seem to have fucked up royally.
    Then again perhaps I just got unlucky.

Part Four

But when I came unto my beds

Chapter Thirteen

I got out of Cambridge, but I couldn't get it out of me.

I found research postdocs in English red-bricks for a few years, then permanent places at a series of respectable universities. Durham, UC Cork, Rutgers, CU Boulder. Always trending west, as it turned out. As if to bring on a sunset. To wind everything down, this whole process a slow glaze of red endings. What was I trying to end? I told myself I was leaving one job after another for the improved salary, reduced workload, colleagues I might be able to talk to. It just happened always to take me further and further away from the one institution I could not leave. And Deb, the absence of Deb, followed me everywhere. Like my own shadow following me down an alley, speeding up as I did. By my mid-thirties I'd made it all the way to Seattle and she was there too. Or rather, she was not there too. I began to wonder if I might settle. Where else was there to go?

Apart from Deb's shadow, the only thing I *always* have with me these days is a compact mirror. With one of these, you can be surprisingly nimble at avoiding people in cafeterias and departmental common rooms. Like a wing mirror on a car: risks are larger than they appear. I could not care less if colleagues assume I'm obsessed with my appearance. I am. They are obsessed with it, too. Soon after I arrived, one of them started texting me about how much he liked it when I wore boots and a skirt.

Mostly people found my appearance misleading, and I was often mistaken for a secretary or a student. Once I was asked to chair a doctoral exam in the physics department. An interesting thesis on the theoretical relationship between entanglement and the nature of spatiotemporal dimensions. When I arrived there were seven or eight men milling about. They ignored me, so I attracted the attention of a youngish man at the edge of the group wearing black jeans and a black T-shirt. I told him who I was, and he swung around to address his companions.

"Time to get cracking, folks! The chair is here."

"Ah, good," said a friendly-looking older man with a soft grey beard and brown tweeds. "Where is he?"

For them, it was an awkward moment. Localized, occupying its little highlighted region in spacetime. It was not part of the pattern, the fabric of the universe, a signal received every day from every direction. The cosmic microwave background.

The University of Washington's Seattle campus is a little sea of noise. Half-sentences seeping into corridors from the various nearby lectures. Fragmentary half-arsed questions trickling out of morning seminars, the most expensive and unenthusiastic book clubs in the world. The effluent of semi-private conversation pools mixing in the visual solvents that soothe us all out of daily mutiny: grey linoleum floors, clicky under our heels; sort-of-white walls; sort-of-yellow carpet; miserable blare of office lights always buzzing behind our dry eyes. And text. All the text that nobody reads because it is always there. *Is that really garbage?* Every day, everybody and nobody sees this. It's printed in large white letters under a red STOP! sign, and it sits over the last bin in each row of four: *Compost, Cans and Bottles, Paper*, and then: *STOP! Is that really garbage?*

The lights give me migraines at permanent half-mast as I sail around this word-slicked static sea, my cashmere scarf catching noise breezes, slicing through the eddies of student energy that collect in doorways, lineups for coffee, women's bathrooms. Or is it *washrooms* here? My ship's not wrecked yet, although quite a few of the others definitely are. At the prow rides the appearance I am obsessed with, my figure-head, the painted-on performance of femininity. I am very good with makeup, a complicated art form. And clothes. As soon as I could afford the habit of taking my clothes to a tailor for alterations, my self-presentation underwent a paradigm shift. You wouldn't want to hand in your first draft of an essay, right? You'd rather edit it. This, too, is about what we communicate.

Still, the only thing people remark on is that I look too young to be a professor.

"Thank you! Youth is indeed my highest ambition," they never seem to notice that I do not say. *Is that really garbage?* It is an important question. The problem is supposed to be that we say "yes" when we should say "no," but in many ways we have the opposite problem. Blazoned across all four bins is one big word: SUSTAINABILITY. Soothed by the size of it, we can feel vaguely good about ourselves without asking what it is that we sustain.

Nothing on this campus is old. No sixteenth-century cloisters for undergraduates to vomit in. Everything that's old here has been stolen. And it's not concrete. Land, art. Maybe souls, I don't know. Nothing of mine. There's a deep past here but I don't speak its language. Don't belong to it. *We that are young / Shall never see so much nor live so long.*

The first day of my first term here, I thought about throwing all my Deb notebooks into the "Paper" bin. They are paper, and that's where paper goes. Still, I couldn't do it. The collection stopped growing after I graduated, but it followed me everywhere. I still knew it was incomplete, but I did not know what else I could ever add. So the pile became a relic. Ossified. Dead weight.

The week I arrived at UW there was an "orientation" event that new faculty were supposed to go to. We were traipsed about all over the campus in awkward pockets of enforced polite interaction, floating around lecture halls and sports facilities like so much clingy pondweed. Big clumps up front, and long tails of stragglers with their minds on their lunches and their eyes on their phones. The occasional loss, when someone actually wanted to stop and inspect the gym lockers, or see how the AV facilities were operated.

At one point we were all herded into a catacomb of dingy, bookish-smelling basement corridors under a brick library. (Why, seriously, do they bring new faculty down here in their first week? To kill off any lingering optimism in our spirits?) It smelled of cheap disinfectant that reminded me of the hospital where my mother lived until I was six. I thought of that other institution and its denizens: all the nurses, and the sad women, and me. How the organism itself must have survived, although I could not understand it at the time: muscle contractions squeezing us all along its corridors like sausage stuffing, absorbing what it could use, ejecting the rest. All of us on this tour were now ingested by a new beast, funnelled along its lower intestines. Would we nourish it? Keep it alive? Were we toxic to its poor insides? Or infectious? Could it catch what ailed us? Were we even going the right way?

Back outside, the dry skin of this brick dragon crackled in the September sun.

I started teaching, repeating course materials I had used elsewhere, repackaging the knowledge in suitably sized parcels for the local tastes, regurgitating them into a new set of bored mouths. Over the years, as anonymous student satisfaction surveys became the primary measure of a teacher's quality, it became important to make lectures easy and attendance optional, then hand out very high grades at the end of the course. Ideally, you should also be likeable, male, youngish, tall, white, and good-looking. These were the standards of pedagogic excellence as captured by the surveys.

Once, an unhappy camper complained on his survey that I was "a schitzoid [sic] bitch" because I was "nice" in class and yet I gave him a failing grade. *First let me talk with this philosopher.—What is the cause of thunder?* I explained that his work had not met the course requirements, so he complained about me higher up the food chain until his grade was changed to one that he liked. Universities hate bother.

I learned my lesson. I learned many lessons being a teacher. Next time it happened I just changed the offending grade myself. Quicker and easier.

I made myself a home in a very respectable Seattle neighbourhood, and furnished it with pieces from nearby vintage shops, of which there were several, and not the cheap kind. Old wooden chests of drawers that shuddered when you tried to open them, dark cupboards that smelled of sweet pipe smoke and bitter chocolate, heavy velvet door curtains, scruffily framed prints of Henner's *Liseuse* and Quast's *Soldiers Gambling with Dice*. It felt comfortably vague, after the glare of campus, to retreat into these soft chiaroscuro evenings.

At the weekends I generally got out of town so as not to court the expectation that I'd make myself available for meetings and additional work. The expectation persisted, but it was easier to ignore. I liked the landscapes of the Pacific Northwest, and the skies even more. Best of all were the days when low cloud lay in big clumps around the base of the mountains, as if someone had just pulled them from the fluff filter of a tumble dryer and let them fall where they would. I could spend whole days staring at the sky as it worked itself into strange, fantastical shapes.

I didn't exactly go *to* places. I couldn't come home and say, "Today I went to Mount Rainier." I just went to spend time with the sky, to stare at it, see what I could see. People use all kinds of things this way, as a reflecting pool, a mirror. The way tarot cards look to you is about what you see in them. Half of that is what you put in there. It's not supernatural, just a very old technology. Never try to cloud-watch with another person. The second they tell you, "This one looks like George Washington in profile!" that cloud snaps shut. A multiverse, an abundance of possibilities collapses and you're left with one dead white man.

I had begun to spend large portions of my days in a strange state of mind, a sort of quiet condition. The world faded a little, if you know what I mean. Became smaller, further away. Less intensely coloured, like the spines of old books bleached by the sun. Since settling in Seattle my migraines were less intense, and rarely accompanied by the bridge-shaped auras. I found, with practice, I could sometimes stop collapsing all the symbols around me into meanings. Text, for example, I could sometimes see as mere shape. Spoken words could strike me as simply sound. Peculiar, mouthy, resonant.

This is important, the way meaning works. Back in school we sometimes had to write poetry for English lessons. I remember the first time: Miss Minchin told us that, for homework, we were to write a poem that expressed something important from our childhood. I tried hard to do what she asked. I hated to fail at schoolwork. But I could not do it. For a week, I stared at a blank page until its whiteness became my entire mind. At last, in desperation, I copied out a page from "The Red-Headed League," rearranged some of this word-stuff into lines that approximated the sorts of poetry that had been our exemplars, and handed that in instead. I got an A+, and this became my solution to the problem of poetry.

In class, when Miss Minchin handed back the work, things were a little more complicated. She paused over my page, and then she asked me what my poem *meant*.

Miss Minchin was a thin, soft-spoken, slightly giggly woman with grey hair. She was not at all threatening or scary, I just didn't know what to tell her. I was quiet.

"What . . . is it about?" she tried again.

All I could think was: *Why does she want me to ruin it?*

My silence was making Miss Minchin nervous though, and I didn't want to upset her, or make her look bad. So eventually I just started talking. Like how I talked to my mother. I said I had been "going through a lot" with "a boy I used to like" and I hinted that the poem was to be read as a confession, a cry of pain. The other girls snickered but Miss Minchin seemed quite reassured.

Once you close something down like this, force it to mean something, opening it back up again is not easy. Try it yourself. Listen to someone speaking your language without hearing what the words mean. Or look at a line of English text without reading it. Can you? Even Latin will reanimate itself in my brain. Its dead speakers have that power over me: their symbols, their tools, still operating from beyond the grave. But I handed this power to them. By learning. By agreeing to their rules, as Mrs. Schmidt laid them out on her blackboard, all the while regaling us with cheeky tales of Zeus's bad-boy antics. By copying all this into my blue-lined notebooks and my brain. How dead must a language be before its zombie words run out of brains to consume? To be able to fight the meaning-zombies off, that's the thing. To unlearn. A negative capability. Most of the time we're stuck with the meanings we have, even if they're not only dead but killing us.

Take Cambridge. Cambridge opens doors for me, but that's

exactly my point: walking through doors that are already open is not much of an achievement. My career is considered to have gone brilliantly. Cambridge plays especially well in America. Even sounding English makes people think you're clever. And evil, of course, but that helps, too. People can respect evil. With that kind of momentum you keep moving in a straight line with continuous speed unless a force acts upon you. I had solved the world's easiest rat-maze: one tunnel, and I was trained to trot straight along it. There were sugar pellets, a steady stream of little rewards. The good job, the nice house, the train rides. You can't live on sugar pellets, but you can die comfy, and it takes a while.

My problem is I can't escape from other times. Other places. They are as real as wherever you are, but worse, because you can't *do* anything about them. You can only watch. One Seattle summer night a year ago, a woman stopped me on my way home from the bus stop. She was sitting in a metal chair, outside a pizza café. She didn't get up, she just started talking, and suddenly we were in conversation. This was a skilful performance, though that didn't occur to me at the time. She said she was new to Seattle, and a single parent, and she'd been fined a hundred dollars for jaywalking, and now she couldn't afford the ingredients she needed to make spaghetti this evening. Would I be generous?

I gave her five dollars and walked away wondering what had happened. *Is jaywalking even illegal here? I do it all the time and nobody cares.* But then I probably don't look like someone the police would hassle over trivialities. Come to think of it, she didn't either. I always say yes when people ask me for money, but it doesn't help. The request itself is enough: the past is there, as if I've just vomited it into my mouth. The night of the Jesus College May Ball.

I can't explain what the Cambridge May Balls mean. I suppose they are a kind of huge, lavish, all-night garden party. But that's not it at all. You need to imagine this: hold your hand out for a moment, and in it there suddenly lands a white-hot sphere of too much feeling, too much to drink, too much food and music and wealth and power and time, too much of everything crushed together into a brilliant imploding star, and now it's too big for your hand and you cannot hold it, rather you're trapped inside of it. A May Ball is one summer night made of black diamonds, bottomless champagne, hot-air balloon rides, fried food, acid trips, boat swings, dancing, fireworks and flowers and floodlights and fairground music. Comedians and casinos and thousand-pound gowns getting grass-stained by the river. Acrobats in marvellously coloured outfits tumbling in and out of trees just for you. The May Balls are in June, the misnomer itself a clue that these singularities do not belong to linear time.

Most of the bigger and older colleges have one, which means that entertainers of all stripes are in demand all through May Week. What it meant for me back then, for my earthier concerns, was that I could earn enough money to eat for a month by landing a gig at one of these events. A lot of students auditioned to play the May Balls, although only a few of us needed the money. I despise competition; I tend to win and then hate myself for it. But I told myself *you do what you need to do.* I bought a basic Marshall and a couple of effects pedals for a steal from a disillusioned student band,

and when I got my little Celtic harp miked up I'm telling you I could make it ring like there was a tiny elfin ceilidh happening inside your head. I did okay.

You had to dress the part though, to play a Ball, because after your set was done you were allowed to stay in for the rest of the night. In my case, this meant tracking down some sort of vintage finery—and its status as such had to be obvious, a loudhailer announcement that I was intentionally not entering into the game of thousand-pound gowns. I scoured the cheaper charity shops for weeks to get my outfit. Cambridge has strange charity shops, what with all the rich kids giving away last season's barely worn designer stuff and feeling like saints about it. But I certainly did not want their year-old Karen Millen. One year I found a long-sleeved, high-necked green velvet dress, almost Victorian, but pulling goth if you added enough black eyeliner. It had no label inside, but it looked and smelled like it had been in the world longer than I had. I paired it with a detachable white lace collar. The effect was off-putting, which was the point.

On my way to play the Jesus May Ball that summer, a woman asked if I could spare some change. I had no cash on me, I was carrying the absolute minimum. The green velvet dress had no pockets. I had only what I needed for the show, and my room keys which were stashed in the case of my harp. I didn't know to bring a mirror back then. Without thinking, I said I didn't have anything on me: I was on my way to the Jesus Ball. And she spat on me.

I hurried away, shoulders rounding to bear this new, unfamiliar yoke of shame that fastened me to this stranger forever. At first I thought she'd made a mistake. "I am not one of them . . ." I said it out loud, over and over, to the rainy pavement, to my cheap black court shoes, as I tried to outpace her judgment. I was not *like* the rich kids. I was embarrassed at having College staff whose job it was to pick up my mess, contrite when I forgot to make my bed and they did it for me.

But she was right, and I was wrong. *You have not observed. And yet you have seen. That is just my point.* Look at the Seattle neighbourhood where I live. Gentrification is a fait accompli. We have a Starbucks Reserve. We're all leafy streets, metal-and-reclaimed-wood eateries, houses with cute wind chimes and red pots full of flowers on their front steps. My aunt would have called it "swank." The working class who must live amongst us to keep us functional are the kind who can be tidily tucked away in marginal spaces. We pretend these aren't servants' quarters, but the idea is the same. A converted broom closet, a basement, an attic shared with three others. *I know that there are seventeen steps, because I have both seen and observed.*

Unlike Cambridge, Seattle has a real summer. But even when it's far too warm to be appropriate I stuff a cashmere scarf in my work tote. When I was a kid, my comfort blanket was a cheap piece of red nylon with brown swirls of fleur-de-lis round the perimeter. My aunt bought it for herself, but I kept sneaking into her room just to curl up under it, so she caved in and let me take it. It's in my laundry closet now. Threadbare, degrading. Picture-of-Dorian-Greying the shit out of this wealthy adult woman who wears cashmere. And I live in this cashmere scarf of a neighbourhood because of what I earn. Because of the doors that opens to me. I inherited nothing, only migraines. What I earn is a measure of the extent to which I was, I am, I *mean* Cambridge. It is not possible to run away from that.

My cashmere scarf is a careful camel that goes with everything, and therefore is nothing. An invisibility cloak.

———

These feet aren't mine. They're too old. Veiny.
Blue-green Ys tangling, knotting, bulging.
Tugging up the skin like chicken wire in
a forgotten papier mâché.
    I know, I know. Say what you mean and
mean what you say. *And what the fuck do*
I mean? It's like stretching toffee, pulling
words out of the air, extracting meaning.
    I think I mean I'm not supposed to be here.
Not like this. Not these bodily remnants, the
floppy edge-bits left over round a pastry cutter.

Chapter Fourteen

This last year in Seattle has been the year in which I became old.

Don't ask me how I know that, I just know. Like a birthday. Congratulations to me: I have turned *old*. When it happens to you, perhaps you'll know it, too. But your symptoms may be different. As for me, my fingers are just a tiny bit weaker now, that's one thing. Fingers and lips. They shake a little. Not so as anyone else would notice, but I notice. And I stammer. Only occasionally, but it never happened before. The stammer is such a peculiar, wobbly feeling, teetering on the precipice of expressing.

It's not that these things *mean* I am old, they just come with the territory. Like not being able to get drunk with impunity. The old body can't expel the toxins the way the young body used to. Then there's my face. I have been studying my face a lot. I want to understand it again, now that it's old. The acne is still there, usually around my chin, but now some of it is starting to sink inside little wrinkles. I've learned names I didn't need before. *The tear trough. Nasolabial folds. Marionette folds.* Marionette folds. What a cruel metaphor. Your cheeks hang down, either side of your chin, making you look like a ventriloquist's doll.

My mother always had pronounced marionette folds, although I never thought about them as an entity of their own, until they showed up on me. I spent a good two months this spring trying on different makeup and emotions in the mirror with this new (old) face. How, when I put lipstick on, my upper lip won't quite stay still. How feelings are supposed to pull on its strings. How I might rewire the connections, if I wanted the machine to perform differently.

I have started to notice that men look through me more often. And memory is more difficult. It's been happening since I moved to America. Memory is what experience grips to, like makeup needs a good foundation, and I think being foreign strips that base away. So you're left scrambling with things that shouldn't require any processing power, like knowing what kind of chocolate bar you like at the supermarket. *Genii loci* vary in the warmth of their embrace, but America is suspicious and wants me to know I'm an alien. Everything slips and slides.

Time races down the track. There are bends where it sways wildly, and I feel like I am falling off. *Now it must be evident to you, Watson, that this young man's body was placed on the roof of the train.* People say things like "the pace of life these days." As if it were time's own fault. For speeding up. From what? One second per second, like in the good old days? When men were men? To . . . what, one and a half seconds per second? Two? Seven thousand? It isn't about time. Can't be. It's me. Or if not me exactly, not time either.

Something else. Whatever it is in which we're both, time and I, only passengers.

My calendar tries to help, tries to keep my life in a linear order. But it's no good. Time requires maintenance that only I can do, and I seem to be becoming less capable. I try to leave space between things, or else the days grate and grind against each other like the joints in my neck. Then the calendar needs massaging. And it always requires a daily scrub-down along with the kitchen surfaces: you have to put enough effort into cleaning. Don't get buried in last week's dirty dishes. But on the other hand you don't want to get obsessive about it. If you're scrubbing specks off the counter every ten minutes you might be better off just installing a dimmer light bulb in your kitchen. A certain amount of for-getting is necessary. Like sleep—without it, you die. Isaac Newton wrestled with time, with what happened when. He wanted to get clear on the dates of ancient Egypt, of Atlantis, of the coming End of Days. Tried to lay it all out in order. Now it's all considered a huge failure. His entire project.

I don't struggle with long-term memory, though, just the short-term. The mind's copy-and-paste function. Things go missing in there for weeks then pop up at the wrong moment, too late to be useful. Or my mind will get man-gled, sending me to the Dollar Tree to post a letter or to the cashpoint for a pint of milk. Not pints—how much *am* I get-ting, when I buy milk here? See, that's what I mean. No traction. Everything slips. *Either the body fell from the roof, or a very curious coincidence has occurred. But now consider the ques-tion of the blood.*

And *that*. Yes that exactly—when my mind suddenly pastes in something out of a Sherlock Holmes story. Or Agatha Christie, or Shakespeare, or whatever else it grabs at. For no reason. Why do things like this happen? I like to quote things, but I would prefer to do it on my terms. When I decide. It's even worse when my voice follows suit. Then other people will look at me, and I'll rush to explain whose words they were originally. Only it's never a good enough explanation. And why should it be? Does everything have to be explicable?

I mostly remember in feelings. They are never wrong, but they're sometimes too vague to be useful. *This man is danger-ous* but in some undefined way. *Don't trust this person* but not why, or about what. In Seattle I take the bus to campus, and over time I have built up an emotional memory file on the other regulars who ride that route with me. Unfortunately, nobody's entry is in credit. Probably they'd say the same about me, though. Perhaps this bus doesn't see any of us at our best.

Some days, I think the bus itself is sick of us. Poor thing. Weird caterpillar, infested with mites. Imagine a bunch of little parasites climbed inside you every morning, forced you to convey them round and round the same route for hours on end, then they all just crawled out and left you all alone at night, an empty shell in the Seattle rain. What's worse: when they're in there, or when they're gone? When I close my eyes, the engines hum a minor third.

I have to take the bus because I am afraid to drive, but I try not to think about the bus's body. It's hardest when I have to stand at the join, one foot in its thorax and one in its abdo-men, as the creature shrieks and chafes around corners. Still,

I try. Like I try not to absorb the other parasites, their emotions, their conversations, their odours. I have more than enough of all those things. But other people are contagious. Their effluvia seep around me inexorably until my barriers get saturated, give up like a cheap raincoat. Sometimes it's panic: students on their way to tests, to classes they've skipped out on for weeks because their boss demanded night shifts, or their kid was sick, or their landlord renovicted them. Sometimes it's a more low-key terror: the kind that's invisible because it's always there. Like the pattern on the seat covers that nobody ever notices. Just the gentle second-to-second reminders that our time is ticking by with the white stripes and traffic lights, and we aren't sure if we're wasting it or doing the best we can. Who can tell us? Perhaps that's what everyone's looking for on their phones. Or maybe they're just trying to maintain their calendars.

Late one rainy autumn evening—I forget exactly when but I was on the bus home from a torpid sort of day—the dregs of a conversation began trickling down from the raised seats behind my back. Its volume was gradually increasing. A man was angry. Something about a dog. Then something about a child.

I tried not to pay attention. I was running through some of the details of Deb's last day, some things I hadn't thought about for a while like how I teased her about having a crush on Dr. Humberton, just before she went off to her next lecture.

The angry man continued to crescendo behind me. The bus was crowded but we were all pretending nothing was happening. The more crowded it gets, the less anyone acknowledges anything. Someone else can acknowledge it.

"Lu? *Lu!* Are you even listening?"

When you can't see who's speaking it is easier not to catch their feelings, but if they do get inside you it's worse. Ghostly, the emotion in those disembodied voices.

"Lulu? Please listen to me. Listen to me. Listen to me."

Angry. And desperate. For what? Just to be heard?

No, not just that. He was accelerating, and my pulse matched pace against my will.

"Lu, you have to look at this from where I'm standing. I didn't do it to hurt you. I never do anything to hurt you. I never do anything that hurts you."

Things were starting to feel one-sided. Perhaps the other party was just quiet. Or perhaps Lu was at the end of a phone. Then again, perhaps there was no Lu and this was a bus monologue. It wouldn't be the first one I'd heard and I wasn't about to turn around and find out. I breathed onto the window beside my cheek. It was cold outside, and specks of bright rain flecked the darkness, but the air on this side was stuffy. A layer of steam formed over the cool glass, bouncing the dim yellow-grey light back inwards, insulating us all from the world beyond our little closed system.

"You're only seeing yourself in this, aren't you, Lu? Always thinking about yourself. Well guess what Lu. Guess what Lu. *What's missing from this picture.*"

Like I said, my long-term memory is fine, especially the parts I wish I could lose forever. Every minute of those months after Deb disappeared. I would say like they were yesterday, but to be honest yesterday can be a bit of a fog.

I froze, but from the inside, not the outside. You know those handwarmers, the little bags full of fluid, where you click a button and watch the stuff freeze, and somehow it makes the outside of the bag warm up? My body does that. Freezes in the middle so the surface skin gets flushed and pink, hot to the touch.

By now the air was so full of the loud conversation that our oxygen was running out. There was a smell of bergamot and violets, bitter lemon and stale sweat pervading an atmosphere dim and thick as a gaslit Victorian seance. I could still hear the voice, though now it competed with the rushing beat of blood past my eardrums. On and on, back and forth between snarling and whining, always insisting that Lu accommodate another perspective.

And yet Lu's was the perspective that was absent. The silent voice. Was Lu even real? Did that question matter? Who among us on this stupid journey mattered? Perhaps we'd killed the host, and our caterpillar was now a desiccated husk of brittle tissue with us embalmed in its resinous inner chambers, a huge communal coffin on wheels accelerating us all towards an airless underworld.

I pulled on the stop cord as though it were an emergency brake. Then I closed my eyes and started counting backwards from one thousand, suspending time until our bus-body shook and stopped moving.

When I felt the doors open and the cold air rush in, I thrashed in its direction, a landed fish desperate for the water. I stumbled on the step and apologized to the world in general. Outside, I could breathe again. Fresh, wet night gushed around my body and splashed over my hot face. I took stock. It wasn't that bad. Only two stops before I usually got off. Close enough to walk home.

Leaves hung dark and dripping from the bottom branches of garden shrubs, forming spiky characters from an alphabet alien to me. What were they saying? I didn't have time to find out. I hurried along. A skunk led me the last few metres, wiggling along a few paces ahead on the black pavement, the undulating *M* of its long white stripe morphing into the *V* of its facial markings as I opened my squeaky front gate and it slinked its head around to check on the stray noise.

Then it disappeared into the night, so I did the same.

Disappearing is generally a good idea. I begin to understand why women do it. A few summers ago, at a conference in San Francisco, I skipped out of the dinner that the speakers were supposed to attend. There was nothing I trusted my body to digest at the restaurant they'd chosen without asking me what I ate, and when I sat down, opposite the only other woman on the program, she stood up and moved to the other end of the table to talk with a famous man who had just arrived. It left me the odd one out in a long line of pairs. She left as if I wasn't there, like how the girls at school used to if I tried to sit with them. I quickly learned not to do that. Why has it taken me so long to stop trying to socialize with academics? I don't know. I suppose kids learn faster than adults do.

I don't think anyone noticed me slipping away from that dinner. I wandered around a little empty park near Fisher-man's Wharf. I found a flight of steel stairs, part of what I suppose must have been some kind of sculpture. It was already getting dark so I wasn't totally sure what it was. The stairs led me up to a little ledge overlooking the park, with a small pond beneath it. The ledge was surrounded by a waist-high barrier, to keep people from falling off. Taken as a whole, the contraption was reminiscent of a ducking stool. A device for torturing women if they were witches. Or accused of being witches. Or, you know, if they talked too much. Do you know about Benjamin West? He wrote poetry in praise of the latter practice. *No brawling wives, no furious wenches, / No fire so hot but water quenches.* That's a real poem, I didn't make it up. Of course, there would have been no ducking stools in San Francisco. That echo was all out of place. North American cities always feel flimsy that way, plastered over with European histories, stories without roots. They don't belong here any more than I do.

In the half-light I scanned the ledge for graffiti. There's usually something on such a landmark, like there's usually dog pee on a lamppost. I was surprised to find just one inscription. Perhaps this wasn't a good enough spot to be worth much writing. Or perhaps the metal was too uncooperative a surface to be worth the effort, except for that of the most dedicated. The most devoted. Those to whom the heightened challenge might only amplify the meaning, the sentiment, the power of what was to be engraved here. I squinted to make out the lonely scratching:

C

+

C

4 EVA

The whole was enclosed in a misshapen and lopsided heart.

C and C were Friscans in love, obviously, once upon a time. Teen sweethearts. Imagine it: one solitary C returns to this place every year. To climb these very stairs, visit this scratchy remnant of their time together. It is, in its way, an act of pilgrimage: C stops on each step, whispers what might be a prayer. At the stroke of midnight C arrives at the ledge. Advances towards the barrier, weeping reverently. Approaches the relic with head bowed. Kneels. There is a ghostly air, a laying on of hands. Healing is largely a matter of having hope, and this symbol is the last echo of something that has disappeared, something that used to be here, that *should* be here, C knows. But somehow it isn't. Somehow it's been snatched from C's world, leaving only this behind. Most relics are pieces of something dead, and you have to take on faith that what you're looking at is really what it's purporting to be. C's faith is strong.

It's a sad story. Isn't it? I did make this one up. Maybe it's true, I don't know. It doesn't matter. I have no choice but to interpret the symbols around me. Symbols force themselves upon us as being symbolic, they push their meanings onto us. Whatever we design to keep order, to keep ourselves in order, it inevitably paints us into a corner. It's only when your symbols are all starting to fall apart that you have a chance to escape them, you know? Until then they are so opaque, so dense, that they stop you seeing more than a foot in front of your face. *Was ever such a dreary, dismal, unprofitable world? See how the yellow fog swirls down the street and drifts across the dun-colored houses. What could be more hopelessly prosaic and material?* It keeps your focus on the superficial. The surfaces of things. And our problem is that we learn to stay like that forever, while it quietly kills us. We are like those dogs who were trained to think they couldn't escape from electric shocks, so they just stayed there getting hurt even when they could leave. Who ever did that to a dog? Jesus Christ.

The surfaces of things: I have an excellent job. I am a success. A *good* dog. And don't I love my work? A "rising star"— that's what everyone wants to be, isn't it? Isn't that supposed to be why the trolls hate me? Why don't I just get a different job if I don't like this one? *I cannot live without brainwork. What else is there to live for?* Anyway, what I despise isn't the work so much as the thing that does it. It's hard to love that. That said, truth is, the two have not really been separate for a long time. Perhaps not truly separate since I lost Deb.

Or maybe it's that the fog makes them hard to distinguish. Philosopher, philosophy. What is there of one without the other? I've always been materially rewarded for putting my professional status first among my identities. The lady vanishes.

But something around here stinks. Maybe it's me.

———

Everything in here smells the same. Shit, and
stale cigarettes, and shit.
    Thing is, though, once everything smells of
shit, nothing does. So it's a good thing really.
Everything depends on how you look at it.
    Jesus, I'm kidding. I just told you that
everything in here literally smells of shit.
I'm not going to make that be okay, not for your
benefit, not for my own, and not for the little
shit's either. Relativism. It's an old joke. Very
old. Haven't you heard it before?
    And don't you remember the punchline? I could
be bound up like a nutcase and count myself
a king of infinite space, were it not that I have
bad FUCKING dreams.

Chapter Fifteen

Time passed faster the longer I stayed in Seattle, like how it did in Cambridge. It became predictable. Being a woman in the Academy means you are constantly put on committees, and every year or two, asked to serve in some sort of bullshit administrative role.

I always agree. Why? I hate this kind of work. It is not an honour to be asked, it's grim. You see the worst of everybody, you must absorb it full in the face and you cannot let anyone else know what is happening to you because it is confidential. All the things you're told to recognize as the warning signs of an abusive relationship, it's basically like that. I have no training in the skills required and absolutely no aptitude for any of it. But I am always told we need someone to serve, and that everyone else is unavailable or incompetent. I am made to feel responsible.

One semester, though, a request came in that felt different. Slightly off. Slightly darker, more intense. I was asked to serve as chair of my department, and I was told that in order to accept the role I must make a presentation in a large room full of faculty, staff, and students. This whole process was to be recorded and the video posted online.

It was strange theatre. Performing drains all my energy, so I walked in with a cold face, but I tried to make it look warm. Women are supposed to be warm. This is especially important in connection with management roles, because a woman in charge is generally perceived as mean and bossy. I was immediately called upon to defend my decision to stand, to persuade the room to elect me. I hadn't prepared for this because it made no sense. This was not a *prize*. I had nothing to say except that I had been asked to stand, and I was willing to serve, but this seemed to make matters worse, and the pressure intensified to defend myself. Why would I put myself forward for an honour like this? At last, a colleague asked whether I wouldn't be liable to disintegrate if I were chosen. She was one of the ones I quite liked.

Chosen. I paused for a moment. Yes, perhaps, as the most beautiful maiden is chosen to be burned to death in a bed of flowers and white cotton—we need a good budgetary harvest this year from the Dean's Office, these last winters have been so spartan, we are down three tenure-track lines, hemorrhaging funding for our grad students. I might be liable to go up in flames, but wasn't that the entire point? That couldn't be what she meant.

Sometimes my mind flickers in and out of time. This moment, another moment. Do you get this, too? Like two movies are playing at once, each one's frames interspersed between those of the other?

Here in this room, two years earlier in a doctor's office. The day after I nearly drowned on the bus.

"Now, then," the doctor explained, "I don't know exactly what's prompted it, but you do seem to be experiencing an especially bad anxiety reaction and I want you to take it seriously."

He said I needed to take an SSRI. I wasn't sure he was right about that. Generally, I want to feel the things that should be felt. But I took the pills. I am a very compliant patient. I'm also scared of doctors.

Then he told me I ought to take some time off work. My aunt used to say this little rhyme to me, when she was giving up on something:

For he who fights and runs away
may live to fight another day;
But he who is in battle slain
can never rise and fight again.

I thought of it often during those weeks, as I sat around the shadows of my home. I hadn't spoken to my aunt in years. It did occur to me to wonder if she'd ever given up on my uncle.

So, then, I might be liable to disintegrate again in this sense. Another colleague was talking now, a younger man who'd sent me some undesired photographs of himself wearing only boxer shorts a few months prior. He said he wanted to follow up on this question about my robustness, whether I could really be a stable leader.

My fingertips had started tingling, which is often the first way I find out I'm hyperventilating. I don't think the question was meant unkindly. These were good people trying to make an important decision. I mean a decision that becomes important at that scale, if you can zoom in to that room, into its nooks and crannies, all its little labyrinths, its ideas and ideologies and institutions. They didn't know anything about why I'd been away those weeks. They didn't know anything about me at all. They weren't my friends, I didn't have friends.

And in any case, the problem was not the question but the answer. Its being so obvious. *Of course* I could not be trusted to remain stable. I was not just liable to disintegrate in any responsible role, I was *in the process* of disintegrating right then and there, as they watched. I was a flimsy collection of dust particles glued together with a mishmash of borrowed character arcs—to trust in such a thing to do anything *but* disintegrate would be fucking ridiculous. To the extent that they thought they had a real creature in front of them, they were subject to a kind of illusion. There was no matter there. Nothing that mattered.

I decided, though, that I should not say this. *Pas devant les étudiants* and all that. Instead I ran rapidly through all the possibilities for lying, and landed on trying to smile. Women are supposed to smile. But the movement didn't feel like it was turning out right, so I hastily retreated to pursed lips and added a nod and a frown—this is the signal for thinking, which is allowed. The main thing was not to do anything crazy. I breathed slower as my chest and intestines filled with cold water and my hands froze into dead lumps.

I found I could still make sounds in the front of my face— the air was vibrating there, just with no connection anymore to anything on the inside. I couldn't tell if my lungs were full or empty. They felt very shallow. *Don't worry if the bag does not inflate*, I heard the spiel from some airline safety video reassure me. *Oxygen is flowing.*

I watched the recording of the interview online later, and learned that I had started talking about difficult lessons, how I would bring all my experience to the role to the best of my ability, crap like that. It was a strong performance and I am not ashamed of it. Still, something inside of me was dead afterwards and I could not make it alive again. Not even alive enough to run away. So I guess I'll die in Seattle.

Old sins have long shadows. My aunt loved that saying. She loved it because Poirot loved it, which really means Agatha Christie loved it. You see, there's usually a real person behind a legend. A truth in every fiction, or the other way around. Take Dr. Watson. His first name is John, except in one story his wife calls him James. Conan Doyle knew a real man called Dr. James Watson. But he probably also met someone else who was a military doctor invalided home from Afghanistan. And he definitely knew another doctor who was friends with one Joseph Bell, whom Conan Doyle says was the inspiration for Holmes. So who's the real Dr. Watson? That's a stupid question. All of these men can be parts of Watson. Fiction steals from real life in pieces. It's picky. But it pays us back with interest. How many bits of fiction are used to make up one of us, out here in the real world? Perhaps it's not so much theft as a reciprocal traffic in changelings. History transplants.

Until I was six months old, my aunt would put me down to sleep in a little room at the back of the house. It was just a cupboard really, despite having a small, grim window. The window only managed to emphasize the claustrophobia. The space was too small and shadowy to be of use for anything except storage. Storage, in this case, of me.

My aunt would tell it like a ghost story. How she and I were alone in the house one night. (My uncle was probably out drinking, or with other women, but she didn't mention that part.) In the small hours, I started screaming. Incessant and desperate screaming, the sound of a pure white mortal fear. A universal, primal, preverbal sound: the kind of emission that bypasses the mind and the will, that must take priority over everything else, even breathing. My aunt shoved her way in through the heavy velvet door curtain, and froze in place when she saw the scene.

As she tells it, my terry cloth nappies had been snatched from their tidy pile under the crib, torn up and strewn about the floor. One was wrapped part way around my throat. I was blue in the face. She ran to me and snatched me from my cot. Then she stayed up with me all night, cradling me in front of the inadequate electric fire in the living room, as we shivered and cried together.

The next day, she closed the door to the back room and put a padlock on it. I was never allowed to go in there again. Years later, my aunt made friends with a medium. The first time she came to the house, she said there was "something bad" about that room, and my aunt, wide-eyed with wonder, told the story.

Old sins have long shadows. Well then, why shouldn't they fall both ways? Forwards and backwards in time. I mean, what if it works like *The Terminator*—something sent to hunt me down before I can do any damage. What damage? What sin? That's the question. And that's exactly the problem. Most of what matters cannot be told. There's no story, nothing that makes sense. No symbol is robust enough to bear that kind of semantic weight, so it's left over in the world with nowhere to go. It might haunt you quietly all your life, like a cat who's never quite in your field of vision. Or it might fall on you one day like a twenty-ton cartoon anvil. Or it might come for you at night. When it does, you might as well be a sleeping baby.

Have you ever lived by a hospital? You know how eventually the sirens are nothing? That blue flashing wail that separates death from life, one day you realize it is *nothing* to you. What's coming for me is a siren I've halfway tuned out. All I know now is that it's angry. And it closes things. Ends things. There's something it doesn't want me to do, to breathe, to see, to feel, to know. I'm not sure which, but it wants something to end. Have you ever stared into a mirror so deep and so long that there's a monster in there? A witch? A demon? What do you have? I have this. It's nothing. I am always on the verge of seeing something.

It's not the trolls. The daily rage. Not even the rage of highly trained, respectable, angry white academic men, or anonymous reviewers, the gatekeepers forbidding entry, forever warning me that the next gatekeeper is exponentially more terrible, *the mere sight of the third is more than even I can bear*, draining everything I can give to my career *just so you won't think you've neglected something*. This isn't it. This is a pattern with repeats: the old white men match up at the

Carrie Jenkins

generational joins, just like when you hang wallpaper. Over time you realize the pattern doesn't actually get any bigger. And once it's up, everybody stops seeing it.

Instead, tune into the foreground. In front of the patterned wall stands a blank figure, a beige dummy from a store window. It has breasts and no face. Its *raison d'être* is to be that on which you may hang what you will. When the dummy makes these academic men mad they charge it wildly, like fighting stags. I suppose, in a way, it is about reproduction.

I know the deal, I agreed to it. I understood that I would be cast into a pit of flame for revealing the secrets of this Society. This weird club to which I seem to have been inadvertently granted admission while the universe wasn't paying attention. I may, however, quietly remove myself from the arena. This is always allowed and often the wisest strategy. In the last year, I pulled out of three conferences. In advance of the third one, I was explicitly told by the organizer that I had been added for gender balance (making a ratio of 1:12), then scheduled to speak at a time I could not attend. I asked to move to a later spot, but he said that time was reserved for the headline speaker. I knew it would be okay to drop out, though, because my name on the program was all they needed from me. A character for their story.

Oh the slings and arrows. It's not that. Zoom out. The sound dopplers from siren-cry to the taunting of children, *nee-naw nee-naw neh-neh-nee-neh-neh*. I don't need thicker skin. Zoom out. What's coming after me is something else. Something much worse, something that intensifies with scale instead of disappearing. Is it something I have done already or something I am going to do in the future? Is it outside of me or is it me? What if you got to the end of your life story and you were the baddie? What would Hitler make of his biographies? Am I really garbage?

I finally found Humberton again. It was just last June, at a hotel in Paris, and we were both there to speak at a conference on normativity. It was another one of those events that gave me the impression I'd been added at the last minute to avoid a sausage fest, although at least this time nobody said it in so many words. I agreed to the invitation at once, though, when I saw that Humberton had already been signed up. It was nineteen years since I'd last seen him. Why had I never written to him? I could have asked him about Deb. I could have. But some deep part of me already knew the reason not to. Still, when the invitation came and I saw his name on the speaker list, I thought it must be a sign. A *sign*. What an idiot.

My first evening in Paris, I saw him at the hotel bar. All the principal speakers had been given rooms at the same small hotel near the conference venue, reserved in advance by the conference organizers. Or more likely by their graduate students, who had probably done all the grunt work of arranging and administering the event. The hotel was a tall, slim building with Art Deco aesthetics. The elevator was original and took a long time to get anywhere. The rooms were narrow, with single beds and no wardrobes, and the whole ground floor was taken up with the lobby.

The lobby's floor and walls were covered in black and white tile that made footsteps bounce around the space, sounding small echoes of the grand Wren Library in College.

There was a tiny bar at the back, really just a few shelves of bottles and a table with two green lamps. I approached and asked Humberton if we could talk. He seemed pleased to see me, but I suddenly realized, once it came to it, that I did not feel the same.

Humberton looked strange and sad. His hair, strong and silvering when I'd known him, was mostly gone. A white semicircle was all that was left. A tired diadem in the painfully slow process of slipping down. He'd lost weight as well as hair; his tweed jacket was old and ill-fitting. It might actually have been the same one he wore to those lectures with Deb and me. It was almost unbearably pathetic. *Now thou art an O without a figure*—my mind traced the lines silently and without my consent—*I am better than thou art now; I am a fool, thou art nothing.*

My old teacher talked over my internal voice. He said he'd heard I joined The Eleven, and laughed about it a bit too loudly.

"You ever hear anything these days?" he asked.

"What?"

"From the Society. They still send me invitations to the annual dinners, but I'm usually out of the country. Do you still go?"

I shook my head. I hadn't heard anything from The Eleven for many years. But then, I'd never bothered to update them as to my several changes of address.

Still, the mention of the Society reminded me of something I hadn't thought about in a long time.

"Dr. Humberton, did you know that Isaac Newton was an alchemist?"

Humberton laughed again, and said I should call him Ron, now that we were equals. We were perched on red stools by the table, like a couple of awkward sheep propped upright, trying to figure out what to do with our front trotters.

He told me he was divorced these days, and I didn't know what to say about that so I said he had inspired me, back in Cambridge. Isn't that what you're supposed to say to your old teachers?

It wasn't far from the truth, really. He'd given me a strange superpower. His lectures, the ones Deb and I attended, were supposed to be about the problem of other minds—all that stuff about books and the topology of spacetime and everything was technically irrelevant. But sometimes people digress into what matters, and that's how you find out what you should have been doing all along. Humberton was the one, really, who taught me about meaning. He started with books. With how, when you read, everything—every character, every moment, every detail—goes through you. It has nowhere else to go. Whoever you're reading about, they can only see through your eyes. When they're feeling something they have to do it with your gut. Their world is a world digested by you. It's not about projection, at least not in the way you'd assume: this can be a kind of accuracy. An act of interpreting can be truthful. Even kind.

Or, of course, it can be bullshit. A powerful euphemism will bend morality like light in a prism. Eventually I realized he wasn't really talking about books. Meaning went far beyond. "The home" was not a home. It was a cell, a holding pattern, a way of circling the airport while you ran out of fuel. A child could see that, but it was Humberton who taught me how to know it as an adult. He taught me to *read*. He always said the base layer of truth is what matters, even in fiction. You can make up whatever else you want, but if you lose sight of that fundamental level, the basement of your world, everything you build on top of it is wrong.

When Deb got written out of the story, it would have been easy for me to be the crazy one. That was the quick fix, the path of least resistance, and it would have restored order to the world. Which was what I wanted, wasn't it? Everything back in order? Everybody gathered in the sitting room for the final chapter, the big reveal: *You made a mistake, it's okay, just move on?* But everything I built on top of that would have been wrong. That was how I used the power Humberton gave me.

And yet, now I saw him, I suddenly didn't want to tell him any of this. I'd held out all those years and now here he was, this man who should have been the missing piece in my puzzle. The one who could make it all fit again. Make it right. But now I had this terrible understanding that he was not going to.

And still, I had to ask.

"Deborah . . ." He looked slightly confused, and not very interested in the question. "Mmm. Hmm. Deborah who?"

"Deborah Orton. Blonde hair? She wore pink a lot? She was in your lectures that whole year, on the problem of other minds. She always sat by me and asked a lot of questions and she talked really . . . slowly . . ." I slowed my own voice down in imitation, trying to prompt the memory.

"No, I don't think there was anyone like that," he said.

"But you remember me?"

"Of course, Vicky! I usually remember my students."

"Please don't call me Vicky."

"Let's have another drink."

Something nasty was going on in my lower intestine. A deep rumble, a distant storm. *Being in a minority, even in a minority of one* . . . oh god, Orwell? Now? How cheesy . . . *did not make you mad.* Only sort of, though, Georgie. It might not mean you are mad at the beginning, but if it carries on you sure will be. There's neuroscience on this. The processing of the signals in your brain physically changes when everyone around you is telling you the long line is the short line, the moving dot isn't moving, the triangle is a square, the immigrants are rapists. You will start seeing it that way. That's how desperate we are not to be totally and completely alone. Even alone with the truth. *Especially* with the truth—that's the most terrifying place to be left alone. So cold. Here's the thing: this phenomenon is adaptive. Like most of the odd things brains will do in difficult circumstances. Features not bugs.

"I don't think I want another drink," I told Humberton. But he had already turned away to catch the bartender's eye.

———

They said she was premature but who was counting.
I mean, I had no idea there was anything to count.
Perhaps she was too late. It happened, that's all. At
the exact moment it was always going to happen.
The end.

Chapter Sixteen

Humberton bought me more Shiraz, and said he'd always thought I was as cute as a button.

"That's really working for you," he added, head on one side. "Still, I mean. At the moment. Not when you're forty!" He guffawed into his drink. How old did he think I was?

"Eventually, I suppose, you'll cut your hair? Bit less makeup? What do you have on your face right now? Actually don't tell me. I bet I can guess."

He leaned in and scrutinized my face. His chin was patchy with stubble, but he didn't smell bad. The smell reminded me of croissants. I laughed involuntarily because it was totally the wrong time of day for breakfast.

But he kept looking at me, and I stopped laughing. I stared deep into my translucent, jam-coloured wine. A half-sphere in the bottom of a huge glass, like a giant garnet cabochon. Perfect, a polished dome. No facets. Some people think of crystals as receptacles: they can hold things for you, like energy or illness. This faceless juice-stone struck me as good for an orison. In which all my sins might be remembered. I suddenly felt myself a tiny lady in a skimpy bikini, sliding frictionless down this convex glass, flailing beautifully in the bright blood below.

I have heard that drowning people often swim downwards, because they don't know which way is up.

Humberton and I flickered that evening. We skipped out of time. Or do I mean "Ron" and I? Even simple labels are beginning to outpace me. His real name wasn't Ronald, you know, it was Oberon, only he was usually too embarrassed to tell anyone. He told me, that night, as I fell into the wine. A special secret for the two of us, whispered on whisky-breath. It was after the whisper that everything went smoky. Drifted.

We are four-dimensional worms, world lines, just like he taught me. Only he and I are worms with a small temporal piece missing. Right there, in that evening. A little gap. A few hours. It's no different to how something can have a missing piece in space, a hole in the middle—we are just more familiar with how holes work in space than in time. We accept them more easily. But there's no difference, from a metaphysical perspective.

There would be no point in having persisted through that time. It couldn't make things any worse, or any better. *What happened that night?* You want to ask a question that doesn't have an answer. And I do not give you permission. Language will burrow its way into a situation like this, if you let it, like a parasitic worm in your heart that'll kill you. Although actually, heartworm is mostly harmless in humans. You pretty much just keep going with the worm right in there. The biggest risk is that it gets mistaken for a serious heart condition, and then well-meaning doctors start prodding and poking around and they kill you by accident.

So stop poking. There is no story. There's just this: as Humberton pointed out a few times in the bar, his room was next to mine. I remember thinking I didn't want him to be so close. And I know that when I sputtered back into existence I was actually *in* his room, my body rematerializing from a high-frequency transmission, and that he was there too, a lump of stuff, facing away, still on another plane. Soft, mumbling and snorting. Over his dull thrum, the metallic zing that had brought me back to the world kept ringing in my ears. A thin steel sound.

I tried to rush up but I was heavy and strange to myself. I stumbled down the hall into my own room, thrust the lock deep into the doorjamb behind me, and bent double towards the bathtub. Hands like lumps fumbled at the taps. Why? I don't like baths. These alien hands were gross and clumsy but I tried not to make too much noise. The water came on in a tornado. I didn't know if Humberton-Ron-Oberon was listening but I went on all fours to the TV and turned it up quite loud. I felt bad for being rude to whoever had the room on the other side, but it couldn't be helped. What made me search for a British channel? Homing instinct? Whatever it is that pours snippets from other people's stories into mine at poisonous moments? *And this same progeny of evils comes / From our debate, from our dissension; / We are their parents and original.* All those conversations I started under the covers with a flashlight when I wasn't allowed to read, and now I can't get away from the words. They *told* me not to do it.

"ROBIN! TELL US WHAT MADE YOU DECIDE TO GO WITH VIOLET FOR THOSE GORGEOUS ACCENT WINDOWSILLS!"

It was impossible to avoid the huge mirrored doors on the closet. Who was that? Was I skinny like that image? I looked like an advertisement for yogurt. Did you ever have a moment, in front of those fluorescent rows of refrigerated labels in the supermarket, when you suddenly realized that all those bright and beaming meanings were not *for* you?

"WELL TOM, I THOUGHT MORE BEIGE WOULD HAVE BEEN A LIT-TLE MUCH WHAT WITH ALL THE BEIGE WE ALREADY HAVE IN THIS ROOM!"

Why were my eyes dripping? Were my pupils always this big? All the better to see with? Far too big. Too hollow, too hungry. *Eyes bigger than tummy,* my aunt used to say, when I'd ask for something to eat but then I couldn't finish it. I didn't know how to explain that my esophagus was flooding with acid, she just thought I was full up. I didn't even know there was a difference. Was the TV too loud?

"SO THE VIOLET JUST BRIGHTENS IT UP A LITTLE BIT, AND OF COURSE IT GIVES US A WHOLE NEW COLOUR DIMENSION TO PLAY WITH IN THE TRICOLOUR CUSHIONS! I JUST *ADORE* PLAYING WITH COLOUR AND LIGHT, TOM, AS YOU KNOW, AND CUSHIONS ARE THE MOST FUN FOR ACCENTING ANY ROOM IN THE HOUSE!"

Unforgivable. There were monsters in this story. Not story. Right there behind the mirror, in the wings, in the mirror, coming out of the mirror. Look. Don't look. It doesn't mat-ter. Nobody cares what you do. You are nothing. You might want to fix that. Wisdom is caught by touching wise peo-ple, isn't that Plato? Or did he say it was fucking wise people? Fuck Plato. Something is caught that way—you know it the moment you're swimming in it, full of it, shit up to your eyes, in your mouth, in your nose. We are made of this shit, this *stuff*. We have to keep eating it to stay alive. Why? Fuck eating. Fuck breathing. Fuck this stupid, badly drawn face.

Fortunately at this point a ten-ton anvil falls out of the sky and hits you and it all goes black. This isn't a tragedy, you see, it's a Saturday-morning cartoon.

Voices over smooth things along into the next scene, the big reveal.

"WELL THE LIGHT THROUGH THIS FRENCH DOOR IS JUST INCRED-IBLE! I HAVE TO SAY, I PERSONALLY LOVE WHAT YOU'VE DONE HERE, ROBIN! IT'S BARELY RECOGNIZABLE! BUT NOW IT'S TIME FOR THE MOMENT OF TRUTH. LET'S SEE WHAT NICK AND FRANCIS THINK OF THEIR NEW *DREAM HOME*!"

Outside, a dark and empty moon washed over Paris. I had no idea the Seine had burst its banks until the early hours, when our hotel was suddenly pealing with the clamour of alarms. We had been sleeping in the path of the rising waters. I came to myself in my underwear, in a tub of cold water tinged with blood.

I jumped out, terrified and freezing, and wrapped my body in a hotel towel. Why are they always fucking white? I stained it.

I couldn't see any open wounds, but by now I could hear the bustling outside my door over the static from my TV. Palpably nervous but defiant staff were hurrying up and down the corridor, as though something monstrous were chasing them, but they still wanted it known that they resented the imposition. A Parisian boy who couldn't have been more than sixteen was knocking hard on each door, repeating his message over the protests of angry English philosophers.

"*Mesdames, messieurs, il faut sortir. Immédiatement, s'il vous plaît. C'est une urgence. Vous devez sortir.* Go outside now please. *Oui, monsieur, maintenant s'il vous plaît.* Outside now. *Merci, madame.*"

Faced with a door that didn't answer, he simply swiped in with his master key. As he seemed to appreciate by instinct, sometimes words only make a bad situation worse. One way or another, he sent whatever he found inside each room out shivering into the grey and terrible morning.

Onwards. Order and method. Trajectory and momentum. *No worst, there is none.* That's Manley Hopkins. *Here! creep, / Wretch, under a comfort serves in a whirlwind . . .* That's manly, Hopkins. Whether or not the worst is a real thing, we have plenty of language for it. *Pis aller* is one way of saying "last resort" or "worst-case scenario." Come to think of it, Piss Alley was the worst place in Cambridge. Could be a coincidence, but I doubt it.

Maybe there's no worst because things keep getting worse forever. Or it could be that they are always equally bad. The future will resemble the past; more generally, the unobserved will resemble the observed. This right here is the most basic principle of scientific reasoning. It's so basic it's not even science: it's what science *needs*, if it's to get started. David Hume said it was just a habit of thought, an assumption, the uniformity of nature. What reason is there for believing in it? That it's been true in the past? Come on. Yet if this principle falls away everything collapses. Things that stay the same, persisting through change, are the steel rods that keep the edifice erect. Keep the universe from disintegrating. Constants. Gravity. The atomic weight of hydrogen. Cambridge. Fun fact: *Cambridge change* is a philosopher's name for what happens to you when you stay the same while something *else* changes.

This is basic in a different way: what's valuable is about what we value, not the other way around. I am never going to be Humberton's equal, he knew that. What he had seen in the bar that night was one of the good girls. We are young, white, cis, straight (or single will do), well-spoken. Very clever, very quick on our feet. We have a strong but quiet record of publications in mid-ranked journals. We dress conservatively, feminine but not sexy. We "stay out of politics." We're skilled at admin and willing to do painfully large amounts of it. We are incredibly useful, because you can hire one of us to prove that you are not gender-biased. Good girls walk an infinitesimally fine line. Two-dimensional. We all know that, even if we don't know we know it, but what isn't obvious until you get there is that the line doesn't go very far. It's made of flat floating stones that are falling away, bit by bit, day by day, in slow motion, imperceptibly drawing on towards the day when they will deposit you into the sea of lava beneath with the excoriating logic of time, gravity, and something else altogether.

Back in Seattle the fall term started. I went for an ill-advised afternoon beer at the UW Club with Dean Crawley. I asked for the meeting, and suggested we go there because the view out the window is supposed to be impressive, and that means you always have an excuse not to look at the person you're with. I don't care for the place, nor for the beer.

The vibe, says one of the Club's reviews on Yelp, *is elite*. That's all you need to know, really: someone on Yelp says that. I don't know what I was trying to achieve. I talked to Crawley about being valued, being equal. Why it might be that there were so few women in his philosophy department. How in philosophy women are never quite *quite*, as my aunt used to say. I say that I talked, but it wasn't exactly communication. Just hinting, citing research by other people, dealing in vaguenesses, generalities. Still, he almost sounded like he understood. Crawley was a politician, and alcohol suppresses the mechanisms that normally adjust all my expectations to the lowest possible settings. Hope is a dangerous substance. He promised to meet with me again and talk more.

Come the next week, though, it turned out he was unavailable to meet, and I was funnelled through to an associate dean. This is never a good sign. When powerful people are about to tell you to go fuck yourself, they delegate.

Associate Dean Louise Jarre was a short white woman with artificially yellow hair and a voice like lemon curd. She must have been about sixty, but she had the face of the girl who used to push my head into the sink at school. That wasn't what was wrong, though. There was something else, something wrong with her eyes. Nothing I could point to, but it was almost like they didn't exactly let things in for her. Not light, something else. A blocked back channel. She smiled stickily at me, mouth only, and adjusted a huge, lime green necklace against her clavicle, where the smile had pinched the skin taut. I couldn't run.

I looked away, stammered, squirmed, tried to cite the research. I didn't talk about my own experiences.

"Well," Jarre ventured, without reference to anything I had said, "if you feel like some people aren't very impressed with what you do, it might not be *because* you're a woman, you know. Just because you are one, doesn't mean everything is about gender. We have to be very careful not to assume things. It could be that some people just don't think your work is as good as other people's work. *I'm* not saying that. I'm just saying you should think about whether that could be it, because we don't have any evidence, any proof. We can't say things like this, we can't go around accusing people of sexism and whatever else unless we have actual proof. And I know it's natural to get upset about it when somebody doesn't think you're very good, but I promise you, I'm used to people saying all kinds of things about me. Gosh! I just let it wash over me. Water off a duck's back."

She adjusted the necklace again. The sun was harsh through her window, low in the sky, hitting me in the eyes.

"Robust criticism is important in order for academia to function properly, remember. People have to be able to say what they think! To express their views freely. What I do— I'll let you in on a tip here—I go home and read about Mesopotamian art. Mesopotamian art! Just for fun! And honestly that's how I've made it as an academic. Hey, you can do anything. Why not learn to play the viola? You just need to take your mind off it. A little survival tactic of mine. No charge."

She made the wincing smile again and I felt tiny ice flakes pricking out through my skin into every subatomic particle of the air. For a second I was in another room, older, dustier than this one, but the light was suspended in the same way.

"As a professional woman"—Jarre was somehow still going—"it is important to be strong. Get a thick skin is my advice. And when it comes to gender, or . . . well, that sort of thing, we have to remember everyone is innocent until proven guilty."

Professor Bell.

I'm not sure if I said it out loud. I heard my chair fall over. I must have walked to the door but I don't remember that. I remember being outside, in the fishbowl corridor. The administrative buildings don't have the same sort-of-white walls, sort-of-yellow carpet as the teaching areas; they have bright pine and huge windows. And I remember only then realizing that I had left my best coffee mug in Jarre's office. The one with the peacock feather print.

I bet she kept it.

Onwards. Round and round and round she goes.

After the meeting with Jarre, I had to go and see a doctor to get stronger painkillers for my migraines. It was hard getting to the doctor's office with my head hurting so much and the shiny, dancing arc blocking out the middle portion of my visual field. I could see well enough in my peripheral vision to navigate spaces that were already familiar to me, but finding my way around a new building often felt like being trapped inside a Kafka story. Space was warped and strange. Corridors never led where they should have. Everything took forever. Outside on the street, I had nearly been hit by a car. The driver probably thought I was looking straight at him as I stepped out into the road, oblivious.

As he raced away he yelled at me through his open window, "Are you blind?"

When I did get in to see the doctor, she was able to give me the pain prescription I needed. She told me that for my own safety I should stay indoors and lie down when I had migraine auras. I told her that I would if I could. Then she asked me some other questions I wasn't careful about answering, because it was hard to concentrate. At the end of the appointment, she scribbled a number on a card and told me I should book an appointment with a "psychological counsellor." She gave me a letter which meant it would be paid for by my health insurance. In America I can have healthcare because I have insurance, because I have a good job. Others are not provided for.

Like I said, I am very compliant. When a medical professional tells me to do something, I do it. So I began seeing a therapist. He was called Jeff, and he was a kind man. A soft man. I didn't mind seeing him, feeding him a digest of my life. Another half-bullshit story I had to tell, for someone who apparently needed to be told.

After what had happened with Associate Dean Jarre, I didn't talk much anywhere except in Jeff's office. At the philosophy department's monthly meetings, I sat silently at the back while others discussed all the small changes that were needed. There were many. These meetings were always held in the same under-heated, white square room that had once been the scene of my little disintegration on camera. But it didn't matter. None of it mattered by this point.

As we crawled down through the agenda items we would reach a solid consensus on each one: something should be done. Indeed, the problem was becoming rather urgent. Then after much discussion—sometimes ice-cold, sometimes angry, sometimes tearful—it would transpire that we could not all agree on any particular direction in which to move. So the meetings would end for lack of time. For a week or two afterwards, louder colleagues would be overheard in the hallway taking a few supplementary bites out of one another, then the issue would quietly disappear from agendas for a couple of years until a new faculty member arrived and asked why we had such a baroque course structure, such a dysfunctional photocopier, such an ugly and unused faculty lounge. And these things would go onto the agenda again. These small monthly dramas were therapeutic phlebotomies, serving no purpose but to vent fluxes and fumes which might have been less toxic kept inside.

Sometimes we would discuss the graduate students. Who was "brilliant." Who was "struggling." Anyone deemed "brilliant" was assumed to be on a trajectory towards an academic career. I had a student deemed "brilliant" who didn't want to be a professor. It didn't matter how many times he told them, they always assumed he would be "going on the market" like a piece of prime real estate, sure to be snapped up as soon as he finished his dissertation. I stopped correcting them after a while, and just let them talk about his prospects. In their minds, he was irrevocably bound for the life they knew, the only future that made sense for such a quality individual. Once, I had thought this blinkering must be a sign of how wonderful it felt to be a professor: they *literally* can't imagine anything better. By now, I suspected it was a terrible thing, to only know one story.

At the meetings, I cocooned myself in my camel cashmere scarf. And after a while, the ambient sound would become grey, the auditory equivalent of letting one's eyes fall out of focus, releasing your grip on them, looking past the magic-eye picture until you see the dolphin, or the acid smiley, or whatever. To perceive without interpreting. Hold symbols softly. Let them go if they want to go. It's such a strain to be constantly processing signs.

The quincunx is an arrangement of five dots. You know the sign of five on a die? That's it. A strong symbol. It has to be—it represents all kinds of things. It is a good planting for apple trees. Prisoners wear it as a tattoo, a mark of the self incarcerated within four walls. It can mean being alone in the world. The centre dot is often semantically distinguished from the other four. The heart of the quincunx. Without it you have a terrible hollow, a nothing where the core should be. A mere four: something "stable" the way my mother was in the home, a blank space inside the brick square. The square college courts (not "quads"—Oxford calls them that, the other place, the not-us).

We can get very comfortable with four. Our four dimensions, three spatial and one temporal. The ancients made another four-map of reality: earth, air, fire, water. Four has a finality to it. It's closed. Perfect. Deathy. The quartus paeon is a metric foot, short short short long:

U U U __

Tap it out. Listen. That's what death sounds like. Beethoven knew this. His so-called *Fifth* Symphony. Another misnomer, another signal that something here doesn't fit. He knew. Five makes people uncomfortable because it's not dead. It refuses to be over. Hum a few bars of "Take Five" by Dave Brubeck. Compare that to the doomsound of the quartus paeon. You hear it? Five is odd. Prime. Undone. A zombie number, unkillable. It's been there, done that, and it's still going.

The dead emptiness of four keeps us calm, contained. We see a straight shot to the grave: a long corridor with no exits. Eyes on the road. No ups, no downs: round and round and round she goes. In our department meetings, the pattern was to worry about something, put it on the agenda, fail to agree on anything we could do about it, then shuffle it off to be dealt with some other time. The deathy square dance of our scholarly dreams. We didn't mourn them exactly, or at least if we did so we each did it privately, not together. But I think we shared a vague sense of our common loss. The parts of ourselves we'd had to chop out. The price we paid, to do whatever it was we were doing there.

———

The bright-laugh lady says he went through "a real
low point" between marriages. Yeah that was me.
A real low point mind you. No fakes here. And it
was not between marriages. Not by my calculations.
   You know how the more people talk, the less of it's
true? Signal and noise—percentage-wise, I mean,
the ratio suffers. You should listen to the ones who
aren't talking, only the problem is you can't hear
them. Those ones whose story is very together, they
made it do that. Like his giant face on TV. Not TV,
whatever they call it. Very believable. Very coherent.
And the ones who talk all the time, what you have
to do is figure out what they don't talk about.
The truth is the thing that matters. Or the other
way around. It's not a TV. I know, I know. What
do you call it now? I can't keep up with the words
in this place but you know what I mean.
   It doesn't matter because it's already happened.
It's already over. All of this is just more of the end.
The final moment. Just one moment but this one's
a doozy. Lasts forever. A single point and also
infinite. Really small circle. Limit case.

Now my temples are greyed out and I wake up
every morning with a bit more face missing, spend
a bit longer pencilling it back in. Never been that
great at pencil work. But it's tricky because there's
this picture covering the mirror in my room, a
snake or something. Badly drawn snake. I didn't
draw it. Actually I don't know how it got there.

*I wonder if we're just nuts, if it's just us. Just one
really unfortunate lineage from some primordially
fucked Eve, who would never have made it past
twenty-five anyway but she'd already had eight
kids by that point which means it's no big deal that
they all carried the same crazy gene. Self-destruct
button. Philosophers' egg. Who cares, right, as long
as we've all shat out one or two of our own before
the Big Crunch? Turns out normal service has
been in operation this entire time. Do not adjust
your fucking* DNA.

   *I'm old enough to remember the sound of a
skipping record. I had this terrible 78 of the
Marseillaise, I was told it was my grandmother's
favourite:* Allons enfants de la Patr— Allons
enfants de la Patr— Allons enfants de la Patr— ...
*That dislocated rhythm never dying, never progress-
ing. It's enough to drive you nuts. Of course her* jour
de gloire *never arrived. And I sometimes picture
that my mother had the exact same childhood I had,
just without computer games, and with the milk
delivered by a horse and cart or some shit like that.*
Tempora mutantur, nos et mutamur in illis, *right?
Yes I still have my Latin. Why, did you think I was
stupid? It's fine, they all do. I mean, it's not fine,
obviously. My Latin and my French. That's right
bitches, I have three languages to not talk in. All
those blank stories crowding into this room. Ghosts.
Round this pile of bones. The room is full of it.
Full of white space. Only fragments I can still*

*find in here and I can't put them in the right order
anymore. All the pieces that were supposed to
go in between* I can't go on *and* I'll go on.

   *And I bet my mother used to go to the asylum
and tell her mother things too, and I bet it was half
bullshit, and then when she got older herself, she
wasn't sure what had really happened, what
she'd made up, and what she'd seen on* TV. *Because
she wasn't used to* TV, *you know, she didn't grow
up with it, and I mean she sort of conflated some
characters with real people and couldn't always
tell the difference. Still, it was true in a way, that
was her life. I mean, by the end, that's what it had
been. Some things are just fucking important,
whether or not they happened. Why would it matter?
Who would it matter to? Those are the questions. We
all have good days and bad days. I'm not saying she
wasn't crazy, I'm saying it's irrelevant. It all washes
out with the night anyway. With the real night, the
real dark.* Every nighte and alle. *Jesus, maybe
there's really just one of us going around in circles
forever. To Sherlock Holmes you know she is always*
the *woman. Maybe the universe isn't big enough
for two. One of us had to go.*

   *It doesn't matter. It's just repetition. Repetition
turns any sound into a rhythm, into music. It's
coming round again. I'm not the only one who sees
it, am I? Maybe not, but you have to do it alone,
completely alone or the experiment fails. All alone*
on the shore / Of the wide world. *Of course,*

everywhere is the shore. Every point is the edge. You just can't see of what. I mean in what. Until you have nothing, you are nothing, standing completely still, weightless and unfastened.

Then you see it.

Part Five

Tears

A great while ago the world begun

Chapter Seventeen

I kept seeing Jeff the therapist every week, and so I suppose it was inevitable that I would start talking to him about Deb eventually.

I didn't exactly decide to tell him about her, but I had fallen into the habit of providing a running commentary on my life again, and Deb was just part of the story. But I could see he didn't know what to think about it. There was something in his eyes, in his frown.

After a couple more sessions, in which Deb seemed to be his main focus, he told me he thought it would be best for me to start seeing a psychiatrist as well. So I did. I didn't tell her as much as I told Jeff, but I repeated the things he told me I should say to her. I saw her once every two months, and from then on she was in charge of medicating me.

I already took escitalopram every night, and she gave me diazepam for when things were bad. After a couple of months she shifted me over to clonazepam, which was supposed to stay in my system longer. Then she started me on antipsychotics, which she carefully never described as such.

Quetiapine just to help you sleep. Brexpiprazole just so it doesn't make you so sleepy.

Whenever I saw Jeff, he would tell me I needed to work on things like "derealization" and "depersonalization." He liked to give me this kind of language. When I felt as if I were an old woman projected back in time to narrate an earlier phase of my life, he said that was "derealization." When I got confused about whether a feeling belonged to me or the person I was talking to, or when I talked about my body as if it was just a thing, as if it wasn't mine, that was "depersonalization." When I said I didn't know what Jeff meant when he talked about a "me" as the kind of thing that could own a body, he just smiled.

I asked him why I should call these "de-" anything. Why define something by what it is not?

"You call it that because you think I should experience things differently," I said. "But what if I'm right? I mean, what if the kind of thing you think is sitting here is not a real kind of thing? What if there is no here here?"

"There's a there there," he said gently.

"*There there there*," I said, patting my own knee.

"They are both forms of dissociation . . ." Jeff insisted on continuing the lesson. Language works like teeth. We tear into the world and each other, spit it out in little bits. A dirty process that contaminates the material.

"De-something, dis-something . . . all so negative. The valence seems to be the main thing."

"Well, I suppose that's because it's something we need to be careful about. Careful not to let it overtake—"

"Who's *we*?" I interrupted.

"Everyone. We all have things we have to be careful about," Jeff said.

"But you meant me. You could say *you* instead of *we*. It would be clearer."

"I meant everyone. But I feel as though perhaps you can't hear me right now."

"Maybe not. And yet you still want to believe that your language works. Fits the world. You think your words aren't broken."

In literature, the way you can tell if a woman's gone mad is that she's talking. Let's take Ophelia. For three entire acts she speaks when spoken to. She says some version of "my lord," like, thirty times. And it's her *mad* voice that's gone wrong? The one full of flowers and death and sex and shame? Please. We wonder why we can't see what's right in front of our eyes, but distraction is a powerful thing. Magicians know this. How do you think the disappearing act works? They make sure you're looking in the wrong place at the crucial moment. It's not really anything weird, it's just evolution. Our brains *need* to be able to get distracted. This is life and death, like forgetting. And sleep. Not a bug, a feature. Adaptive. Could we make a drug for distraction? If it's neurochemistry, there should be a drug for it. It would be useful when you have to live through something and you don't want to, because at least this way you wouldn't have to pay any attention to it. You would be totally distracted, and you'd remember nothing afterwards. I even came up with a brand name: *Inattentalin*. You'd pop a pill and then anything could happen to you and you wouldn't notice. You'd be able to *see* it, sort of, to *feel* it, but you wouldn't *notice* anything. Maybe you'd get odd nightmares years later, but you wouldn't be able to connect them to the original situation. A drug like this could make somebody millions. But it would probably only end up being used for date rape. Weaponized inattention.

Have you ever had the feeling that more than half the world is missing? Close one eye and walk around. Like that. The rest of everything is just . . . blank. Gone. Forever, because everybody was ignoring it. Worse, much worse: what's left is flattened. We no longer see depth in it. We sort of feel as if another dimension is still there, or *should* be, but with the loss of binocular parallax our ability to access it is straightjacketed. You know, at another scale, stellar parallax once shattered a moral universe—I mean a universal science. One that grounded out in the vast, dark narcissism of certain Earthlings. This can also be how a circle passes for a straight line: you cannot access that dimension in which the circle is curved, so it looks like a straight line to you. If you're a one-dimensional beetle crawling around and around the circumference you don't know any better.

Jeff is sweet. He wants to help. I didn't mean to be rude to him. Sometimes interpretations clash, I get it. What happens when you can't treat all the inconsistencies with charity? There is but such a quantity of truth between the stories; just enough to make one good sort of world. He had started talking about confabulation now.

"Sometimes," he said, "we fill in a story that seems to make sense of what we remember, or of how we feel. It might not all be exactly what really happened, but it certainly seems real."

I didn't even bother about the "we" business this time, because obviously he was doing the exact same thing he was talking about. Instead I made one last half-arsed effort.

"Language . . . is sort of our joint bank account. You see? We all have to invest, but we don't all get to draw on the funds."

He didn't get it at all. I could tell.

Whenever I can, I avoid going onto campus. It takes forty minutes on a good day, and at some point either the motion of the bus or the idea of the destination started giving me fierce nausea every time I set foot on board.

Instead, I got into the habit of bringing my laptop to a café if I only had a pile of essays to mark. I walked down my street of leafy trees to the Starbucks Reserve. Might as well go in there. I can't make things any better or worse by going somewhere else. I like the cafe in Ada's bookshop but it's small, and there's a risk that they will talk to me. In the Starbucks Reserve they know my name and they want me to have a good day, and that's absolutely all. Very safe.

I'm never ready to meet another person. If I see an acquaintance in town I try to pretend I didn't see them. Even when I've arranged a meeting myself, I always hope they won't come. So the day I saw The Cop, with a laptop of her own, in the Starbucks Reserve, I immediately tried to pretend I hadn't. It was a self-preservative instinct. It's a very specific kind of shock that kicks in. You know when you're on your own in a quiet room for a long time, but then you suddenly realize actually there's someone else in there, and they've been there for god knows how long? Without warning you are flung into a different universe. This new world's resemblance to your previous surroundings is creepy, superficial, uncanny. Worst of all, the old reality never existed.

The Cop didn't belong here. For fuck's sake, my last words to her had been *you're not real*. Perhaps I actually was crazy. Then again, this could just be one of her doppelgängers. We all have them; several, not just one. When you consider how much we have in common genetically, it's not surprising. If so, all I had to do was keep walking. Act as if nothing is unusual, and eventually nothing will feel unusual. This is magic that works. Keep moving. One foot, the other foot. One foot . . . I didn't notice I was humming until I was past her.

"Oh. My. Fucking. God. *Victoria?*"

The Cop wasn't in uniform. Of course not. That quaint British outfit would have looked as ridiculous in the U.S., where *cops* mean *guns*, as Sherlock Holmes in his deerstalker. It was a brisk October day, and she had on a navy sweater and a red scarf. I wasn't under arrest. Could I just keep walking? One more foot . . .

"Holy *shitcakes!*" She was up, and moving towards me. "You still hum that tune when you walk along?"

I was looking right at her now, right into her face. Her face was beaming. It was beautiful. She wanted to hug me, I could see it. I nodded she could, and I took a breath. As she moved in for the hug, all at once I was inhaling the earth of Wimpole Hall, the windy field at Steeple Bumpstead, the chill of the Lido at Jesus Green, the burned-out interior of Cindies, her tiny apartment and the spattering soup on her hob. I was rushed through these moments in a narrowing, swirling tunnel of lights and sounds, spiralling me down into the shutter of a camera as it closed *click* on one scene. Myself, sitting on the ground, staring up into her warm eyes on a cold day, the moment we first met.

The Cop's voice wrenched me back to a Starbucks Reserve in Seattle. "Hey, hey, babe, are you crying?"

I checked. The shoulder of her jacket was damp. I nodded and put my face back into her neck. I suddenly wanted to hide there. (Hide from what? The past doesn't care where you go.)

"What are you . . . why are you?" I asked her epaulette.

"Oh, my brother's out here now. You remember Elliot?"

I did.

"Took a bullet in Iraq. Now he's a mechanic. Set up a garage in Capitol Hill, wife and two kiddos. I took a bunch of my annual leave this year to hop over and see them all."

She kept me in close, while she went on for a while about her family. This was a kindness. She was giving me time. Her voice sounded *intensely* English, and I realized I had never noticed that she had an accent. How stupid of me. Her hair was still straight, and her body too. It was all so familiar, but so strange.

As she babbled on, she mentioned a "Jo." The name started to pop up a few times, and I gathered that Jo was her current partner—someone she was living with, maybe had been for a long time. But then there was a word that didn't fit: *husband*. I missed the next few sentences. There it was again. *Husband*. Jo was perhaps Joe.

"Joe . . . I thought . . ." I said, then stopped abruptly. Was that rude?

She laughed and said, "I thought, too! You think you know someone . . ."

"It's my last day in Seattle," The Cop said eventually. "Elliot's family drove south this morning. Going to see their other granny. Want to get dinner with me?"

I didn't say anything, because I didn't know what to say. So she went on.

"It's okay either way. I only want to say one thing. It's fine if you don't want to see me after that. I just have to say sorry, babe. I'm so sorry."

I frowned and took half a step back. "Why? What? For what?"

"For what?" Now she was frowning, too. "I should have believed you, I suppose. About Deb." Then she paused. "No, I don't mean that exactly. What I mean is I should have told you I didn't believe you. We could have talked about it. But I lied to you and it ruined everything. I just . . . I didn't know *I* was the one who was lying. You know?"

Her voice was so soft. So warm. So easy to follow. She made sense.

"Yes I know," I said. Then, very quietly, "Sometimes I can't tell if I'm the one who's lying."

We did go for that dinner. I brought her to a low-key pizza place I knew, and I paid for both of us. When she left to walk back to her hotel, I hugged her for a long time. She gave me her current address in Cambridge and her email address, and I said I'd write to her soon. She looked at me with her head on one side and smiled as she said, "You aren't on

Facebook." It wasn't a question, she was already sure. I told her Facebook freaked me out. She said that was more rational than people knew.

She was flying back to London the next day. I couldn't drive her to the airport, but I wanted to ride with her in the taxi. In the back seat, we held hands.

"I hope you have a safe flight home," I said. I felt an unfamiliar heat in my chest, one that didn't hurt.

She looked back at me with serious eyes. "I promise," she said.

As if anyone can promise that.

After she'd gone, I felt dizzy and my head hurt really badly. I realized I was carrying a weight in the pit of my stomach, a melancholy nostalgia for the version of me who only existed with The Cop, was only able to exist because of her. I'd caught a brief glimpse of that me, and it was like seeing a ghost. All the possible future selves you didn't become, you have to carry them around inside of you while they slowly turn grey and die.

I wanted to stand at the edge of an ocean and think. Puget Sound was the best I could get. It was easy enough to take a cab from the airport to Alki Beach, which was more or less on my way home. I go there sometimes. Whenever I get to the beach, though, my heart sinks a little when I remember dogs aren't allowed. Nothing makes me smile for real these days except cats and dogs. When humans pass me in the street or in a park and I'm smiling because I just saw a dog, they sometimes smile back. They're making a mistake. I am never smiling at them. It's not like it was in the hospital, not anymore. Smiling at people no longer keeps them away so I no longer do it.

There aren't real waves there, either. Not breakers. Just a rhythmic slithering in and out of white foam, a tangle of albino snakes' heads writhing up into the sand then changing their minds all at once and wiggling back out. They reminded me of the snakey worm diagrams Humberton was fond of drawing on the blackboard, when he would talk about how objects exist as little lines through spacetime. I'd heard Alki Beach itself was a fake, but I wasn't sure what that could mean. As I walked, a gentle, misty rain settled down on the beach like a cloud. I slipped a hand into the tote on my shoulder and pulled out my umbrella. I always carry an umbrella. I pay no attention to what the weather looks like when I'm leaving the house. If you know Seattle then you know what I mean.

An umbrella wouldn't do much to keep this kind of omnipresent rain from soaking into my clothes, into my skin, but I didn't care. The weather quickly emptied the beach of other people, which helped. I spent some time moving slowly across the grey sand, through the grey air, in my grey bubble. Thinking of nothing, feeling nothing. A blank grey space. I don't know how long I was out there. *Look out of this window, Watson. See how the figures loom up, are dimly seen, and then blend once more into the cloud-bank. The thief or the murderer could roam London on such a day as the tiger does the jungle, unseen until he pounces, and then evident only to his victim.*

Was The Cop straight now? So what if she was? What did that even mean? Even the path of light does not define straightness. Light bounces back on itself, bends when things get weighty enough, even breaks down, falls apart, comes to pieces. Just like us. Light is all that's really there, when I look in the mirror and I am afraid.

Remember this: *Mirror mirror on the wall, who's the fairest one of all?* Well, go on then, who is it? The fairest one is the most beautiful one. The fairest one is the palest one. Right there, there it is: the pale-skinned are the most beautiful. This is fine, because we made *fairness* stand for "justice" as well. It is the opposite of refraction: we compress. A rainbow of meanings, of values, made to toe a single line of white light. Isaac Newton said light travels in *a much subtiler Medium than Air*. He called it the Luminiferous Aether. There is a subtlety to language too, the way it moves, refracts, reflects, bends with the gravity of situations. Follows power. Language moves faster than we can imagine, is most full of colour when we find it colourless. It needs an even subtiler Aether to move in, a purer air, an atmosphere for beings finer than ourselves. Aether is another one of Nyx's children.

Lemon taught me that Newton wrote his *Opticks* in the vernacular. In English. As in, not Latin. A radical democratization of knowledge, Lemon said. Well, maybe. But one born in the belly of British colonialism, a hungry thing eating cultures and shitting out a new language of science. *The* language. The definite article. Beating the specific refractions of English into prescription lenses for all the world's knowers to wear. On my driver's licence, it says under "Restrictions": CORRECTIVE LENSES. What's so corrective about certain distortions of light and not others? Too much clarity is a disaster of its own kind. I guess I could wear the glasses, but I prefer to stay off the road.

Anyway, my point is that Newton's *Opticks* made popular the idea of an *experimentum crucis*. A crucial experiment. Before that, *crucial* didn't mean at all what it means now. It was pressed into service as a bit of scientific jargon. It comes from *crux*, the Latin for *cross*, because the *experimentum crucis* is a cross-shaped signpost that will appear at a fork in the road. So *crucial* is just another metaphor, like most of science. (In case you're thinking about it, don't give me some kind of sci- entific objectivity spiel here. Unless you can give it to me in no language at all, in which case I am actually all ears.) So Newton's *experimentum crucis* sees him showing how light falls apart. What it takes to break it. *Crux* is also the root of our word *excruciate*, because crosses can be used to torture bodies as well as point them in a certain direction. We still make many devices that serve both purposes. Newton fractured light by inducing a kind of deep nakedness, a rainbow-revealing of what had been hiding in plain white sight all that time.

But who comes here? I am invisible. And I will overhear their conference. Now consider ghosts: we also call them *spectres*, whose root is the Latin *specere*—to look, to watch, to see. A spectre is something we "see" when we are "seeing things," as an apparition is something that "appears" to us. The spec- trum appeared to Isaac at his home in Lincolnshire. He got out of Cambridge too, driven away by the Plague. As in, the Black Death. A sickness named for the absence of light. A good time for ghosts, things that don't need bodies.

Even light needs a body of sorts, it turned out. Newton called little bodies of light "corpuscles." Then Einstein got knowledge's knickers in a twist by pointing out that light sometimes needs little bodies and sometimes not. He said this means *we have two contradictory pictures of reality; separately neither of them fully explains the phenomena of light, but together they do*. Do they, though, if they are really contradictory? "Explain" is a very high bar—I feel as though the theories would have to cooperate to clear it, not compete. *We are faced with a new kind of difficulty*, he says. Not really, my dude. This is an old kind of difficulty.

Not to mention one we'll be funnelled back around to in a moment, when it turns out things that seem very small to us don't behave in ways we can reconcile with the behaviour of things that seem very large to us. Each time, the same question: which theory is *right*? You must choose, although the choice is impossible. The whole idea of an *experimentum crucis* is to create a fork in your road so that you cannot continue in a straight line. To force an excruciating choice. Shove you one way or the other, down the path towards the right answer. That sounds incredibly useful.

There's just one tiny problem. *Oh, Isaac, just one more thing . . .* there's no such thing as an *experimentum crucis*. The fork never arrives, the comfort zone is never breached. Maybe that's why Hecate, goddess of the crossroads, is always looking three ways at once. Lemon again—he taught me that Willard Van Orman Quine put it this way: *Any statement can be held true come what may, if we make drastic enough adjustments elsewhere in the system*. For example, you never have to admit you saw a ghost if you are willing to say you were hallucinating. So really, all experiments are just exercises in rebalancing your world view.

Now that's fine as far as it goes. But there's something going on in the background that we aren't dealing with: how that balancing act tosses us around in another dimension. The one we all don't want to admit exists at all. The subtilest Medium there is. We cannot quite pretend not to notice. I suspect there is something in the temporal lobe, something we can't switch off (*temporal* for the passage of time, you know—for the greying hair of the temples). But with our knowledge lenses on, all we see are a few of its ghosts, its traces, and at these we throw our most abstract labels. Stupid words like *meaning*, *value*, *spirit*. To help us keep the phenomena distant, poorly understood, unbroken like white light. Nothing to see here. But there *is* something to see: there's us. We cling to this power, define the lines of its force fields like iron filings round a magnet. What are we so afraid of? That if we admit it's there, it could suddenly shift? Realign? Or that we might not be anchored: that we might come loose from the pattern our people are making. Drift away.

Escape.

If we ever reach that other kind of *experimentum crucis* it will not present in the shape of a fork and there will not be any signposts. The assay will be made in perfect darkness, and that will be the entire point.

———

Tears

It's coming.

Chapter Eighteen

"Victoria?"

Jeff used my name in the interrogative mood to call my attention back to him. If I forgot to nod and say "mmm hmm" every so often he would assume I wasn't listening. He was usually right. Jeff the therapist. *Therapist therapist therapist . . .* I'd sit there saying the word silently to myself until it lost meaning. By the time of these later sessions, I had to gel myself into this kind of blank state, so I'd stare at the straight rows of bland self-help books behind his neat black-grey hair, the spotless beige carpet, the killer neutrality of the wood-framed sepia pictures. All somehow depicting nothing. We made our symbols weak; we can't complain now if they won't do anything for us. *Can you imagine language, once clear-cut and exact, softening and guttering, losing shape and import, becoming mere lumps of sound again?* Some people say this is what it's like to have a stroke. The Aether, the medium of meaning, starting to glop together and move about by itself, strange fingers of it poking up here and there then reabsorbing into the ooze. Marbled undercurrents of colour tugging at our attention, a weedy, slimy semantic death by drowning.

I haven't been able to say this to Jeff: men scare me. Because how could I? What is the word for this kind of attitude? Sexism? Reverse sexism? Is reverse sexism the reverse of sexism? To ignore the massive likelihood that if someone kills me or rapes me today it will be a man, to give men the benefit of doubts that don't exist, that would be sexism, so accommodating these statistics is the reverse of sexism. Only it isn't. It isn't allowed to be. Men scare me when they take up all the space, all the air. *Scare* is wrong. I need the right word. We all need symbols. But we need them to be the right ones—nourishing, non-toxic.

Not all men! The world always interrupts before I can think of the right word. My world will not be interpreted, pinned down, named, lest that give me power over it. True names are witchcraft, faery magic, not translatable into the language of science or publishable by English-speaking men in peer-reviewed journals. *Not all men! Not me, I am one of the good ones!* I didn't say all men. I said men. A generic (*men*), not a universal quantifier (*all men*). Birds fly. Not all birds fly. But language is not allowed to work if it would make a point we are not allowed to make. What's in a True Name™? What power does it have? Are our words little maps of the Real Essences, the Platonic Forms, the Fundamental Physics? We've sure come up with a lot of names for the deep structure of things. Words aren't enough. They aren't solving this.

I didn't tell Jeff the therapist I was wondering what the right word was for being scared of men. Once, I told him about how my mind's copy-and-paste function goes off without warning and I paste in quotes from other people's stories. He started calling these "intrusive thoughts" and "auditory hallucinations" but he never specified into what they were intruders, or why the resultant verbal collage should be considered any worse than the mess that was there before.

Instead, I gifted Jeff a little history. See how *he* liked it. Jeff Bryson, it turns out, was a science whizz in high school but also a kind soul and a good listener. Now you might think this rare combination would make him every bully's dream, but you'd be wrong. In fact, he was the kid who willingly gave away all his notes around exam time to slackers who'd skipped class, who once or twice might have "helped" with another student's physics homework but who was counting. He was valuable. Then Jeff studied psychology at Harvard which meant spending a lot of time in roomfuls of women. By the end of each term about 70 per cent of the class would be in love with him but he never dated any of them, preferring to wait for his long-term girlfriend in Canada. Most of the women suspected this Canadian girlfriend of being made up, a beard perhaps, but she was in fact not only very real but also cheating on him with a much older man called Anthony Black, of whose existence Jeff would be unaware until the summer after graduation.

"Victoria?" Jeff said again.

I'm Nobody. Who are you? Are you—Nobody—too?

"I want to help you not worry so much. I know you worry about turning out like Mum."

I can't stand it when other people call her Mum that way. Like they're talking to a child who is too young to realize Mum isn't *Mum* to everyone.

"I'm sure it's scary to think about, but there is much more help available now. We understand these things so much better. The science has come on a lot. Therapy has modernized, and we have better medications. And society has changed. Sure there are some things in our past that we're not proud of, things we regret—"

"Science or society?"

Jeff didn't always notice when I interrupted. He just carried on.

". . . —about the way mental illness used to be treated. But you are one of the lucky ones."

Lucky, you know, joined the English language as gambling vocabulary. Dicey stuff. He didn't care about that, though, so I didn't bother to say it. That was the kind of communication that didn't work in here. I looked at my hands. What might a hand communicate? The tree outside Jeff's office had better symbols in it than this room. Its higgledy-piggledy trunk was an awesome stack of trophy animal heads: buffalo facing east, ram's skull to the southwest. In the root was an empty lobster tail, and the claws. As though the lobster inside were recently eaten. It is an intense tree.

He ploughed on without me.

"If you can work with me, I know we can get you to a good place. I believe you can make peace with this . . . with whatever has happened. With the past. You have a life in the present, you know? I'm not going to say a *normal life*—that's not a very useful way of talking, is it? But you have your job, your career, your friends. Maybe you'll meet someone, get married, have kids. And it doesn't matter what you believe in your own head, or what you write in your journal at the end of the day, or what you say in your prayers, or what you say to me. You just need to keep it from taking over other aspects of your life. Can you work with me on this?"

I don't pray. He knew that. It was the same thing every week now. What Jeff wanted—what would count as a success for him—was for me to betray Deb. To give up. Every time, I gave him the same answer: If I stopped thinking about Deb, I might as well stop thinking altogether. Might as well die.

And by a sleep to say we shit out the day. In good dreams, I am putting on my makeup. The eyes are missing but I still have eyelids, so I colour them in dark browns and greys. I sweep highlighter across the high points of my cheeks, along the bridge of my nose, the inner corner of my eyes. The colour of my highlighter is "ice." The top note. My blush is "hot shame," trapped underneath. I have a mouth but it won't open, so I paint it closed with a sticky nude gloss. I mist on a spritz of all-over setting spray, and as it dries what's left of the face gradually disappears. I check the back of the spray bottle: *Specially formulated with dermatologist-approved particles, shown in clinical studies to reduce the appearance of face.*

In bad dreams, I am in an empty place. I don't know where I am. I can see there is space but I can't see anything in the space. I can hear the wind chimes from my neighbour's garden, but when I scan for their physical body, their little house of sound, they always seem to be coming from another direction. Then the women arrive. I don't know who the women are. Maybe my ancestors, or the sisters I could have had. They arrive in single file, and each one wears a beige trench coat as if it were a military uniform. Some of them have heads hanging off their necks by a thread. Dead heads on live bodies, dead hair dripping down to their hips in silver trickles, a macabre parody of the red-gold waterfalls of shampoo adverts. Some of them have parts of a head but the parts won't stay together—their hands grab wildly at pieces that keep floating away. The heads aren't breaking up cleanly, the way you would expect, into pretty bits: *item, one neck, one chin, and so forth*. Sometimes it's part of the scalp with an eye, sometimes three-quarters of an ear and a slice from the neck. Dangling tracheae.

Some of the women stop chasing, and just lie down.

————

Carrie Jenkins

It's coming. Do you see it?

Chapter Nineteen

Why had I said I would write to The Cop? How could I? I couldn't put down my whole life since we broke up and send it to her. Was I supposed to pick and choose bits of it, then? How could I possibly know what mattered and what didn't? Even if I could have answered that question for myself, which was hopeless to begin with, how could I know what would matter to *her*?

The next morning, I started an email three times with the subject line *Hi* before I realized the project was a total waste of time. Instead, I decided I should send her a gift. An object, not words. A parcel would probably take a few weeks to arrive, and that would give both of us time to think. And if she had died in a plane crash on her way home, it would also buy me a bit more time before I had to start worrying that she wasn't answering.

What I sent had to be something that mattered, something it would hurt to give away, or it wouldn't mean anything. In the end, I dug out my old choker, with the four little items I'd collected during the time we'd spent together, investigating (or at least, so I thought) Deb's disappearance. The skull, the sequin, the wing, and the crystal. The tired leather felt brittle now, and crusty. I wrote on a yellow sticky note:

> *Remember this?*
> *Love, Victoria xx*

Then I rolled the note up and stuck it to itself, slid the choker into the middle of the roll, and went to the post office. On the counter was a splotchy biro, tied to a chain with grimy old plasters. Plasters are called Band-Aids here. I copied The Cop's new address from the piece of paper she'd given me onto the front of a Jiffy bag. Do they call them Jiffy bags here? Home is where your words are, isn't it? Only as my pen hit the plastic did I remember to write *Julie*, not *The Cop*.

So I had sent her this part of me, feeling like I'd cut out an organ, to see what she wanted to do with it now. Knowing nothing could happen for at least a fortnight (they definitely don't call them fortnights here). Hoping I'd have enough time to figure out how I felt about having sent her such a gift. Why I would do such a thing.

But before the first week had passed, it was all moot. By then everything had shifted beyond recovery.

My psychiatrist had been trying me on a few new medications. I couldn't remember all the names anymore, or what they were supposed to do. Whatever the latest drug was, it was mostly just making me gain weight. Or perhaps it was that I had stopped moving. Anyway, something was different. And now Jeff the therapist was trying to get rid of me.

"I am a little concerned about our lack of progress," he said in our penultimate session. "There is something distressing you that may not be responding well to cognitive therapy."

"Mmm hmm," I said, because I didn't know what else to say.

"Victoria, I think I'm going to refer you to a specialist within the psych unit, who can review your situation in more depth. How would you feel about that?"

"You find my narrative unfit. It shall be rendered as fiction, crazy talk, nonsense. *Why don't you do what you dream, Bastian?* But this is the next step in an established progression. A straight line for us to follow. You will follow it, and I will follow it."

I'm not sure if I said all these things aloud.

"Is that a feeling?" Jeff asked.

But I can't! I have to keep my feet on the ground!

"It's what I have."

Call my name! Bastian, please! Save us!

Jeff made one other last-ditch effort for me, bless him. He suggested I could go and see a hypnotherapist.

Hypnos is twin to Thanatos, remember? Sleep and death? They call the quetiapine a hypnotic and it gives me strange dreams, like the ones with the women, though they're not as bad as the semi-dreams I used to have of Deb's death in the nights after she disappeared. In some stories Hypnos lives in a cave at the source of the Lethe, the river of forgetting, which makes sense because sleep and forgetting are both chain reactions, cascading failures. Hypnotherapy was not covered by my health insurance.

I remember when I was little, I made a den in the cupboard under the stairs. *The* stairs—the ones that presided over my aunt and uncle's house. Echoing the shape of the staircase in reverse, the cupboard ran from a full-size front door in the kitchen to a small, dark cave with a foot-high wall at the back. My aunt and uncle filled it up with things that in their opinion did not belong in plain sight: an ironing board, mops, brushes. Further back, tins of old paint and varnish, hammers and spanners, nails and screws, buttons and things in boxes. All this took up the front two-thirds of the space, which was as far as an adult could comfortably go.

Right at the back of the cupboard was a second door, a tiny side door that gave access to the cave from the hallway. This door was just two feet high at its tallest point, and slanted down with the slope of the staircase. I was small enough to crawl in that way and use the leftover space, which smelled of old varnish and dust. I stashed my red and brown fleur-de-lis blanket in here, with a torch and a little pile of Agatha Christie paperbacks, purloined from my aunt's bedside shelf. Some are born to *Endless Night*.

Hypnosis is another way in.

Vincent van Gogh once wrote to his little brother, *Find things beautiful as much as you can*. Not "find beautiful things" because that's not how it works. Beauty, magic, meaning— same thing. Like how we don't *make* meaning. You can talk that way—I mean, you can talk however you want. I am not the boss of you or the queen of language. But what it comes down to, the mechanics of it, is repositioning one thing relative to another. It's more a kind of a gear slip, motion through that subtiler Medium. The other Aether. It happens involuntarily as we shift our attention between the very large and the very small—that's why our best stab at knowledge isn't quite getting the traction it wants. Science vs. art is a stupid distinction though. This is what Aristophanes should have said: Zeus divided not us but our *attention*, so that we should never be able to deal with the whole situation. We get stuck at the edges of one or the other, without realizing how its ideals are *limit* concepts. Limiting.

Linette the hypnotist said I needed to unlearn some things that were deeply ingrained. She said she wanted to reset me.

"Return to zero," she said. "To the origin, okay?"

As she guided me through the process her voice was mechanical, ticking. A rhythmic flow of beats that came in waves across me as I lay stretched out on her sofa, my feet tucked comfortably into a cozy throw.

Linette asked me where I was, what I could see as she talked. Most of the time I did not know what to tell her. I was falling through nothing, I could see nothing. I wasn't sure it was helpful to keep repeating that, though. So I made up some other things.

The problem was I was already zero. I was already nothing. And I knew that would never change. I didn't want it to change. It was much too late for Linette.

Anyway she was too expensive. When I left her office, everything was quiet inside me.

---

*The little shit is here because of the night we got
unlucky. There's no moral if there's no story. He
was just an overgrown fuckboy. Do you understand? It doesn't mean anything.*

    *Now he's always on TV, always talking, always.
Empty talk. Not TV. I know. Mathematics and
physics and spacetime, people are static worms
in spacetime, but when I knew him he wasn't
a public intellectual. He was just a philosophy
teacher, and not the black-polo-neck-and-a-Gitane
sort of philosophy, the other sort that pretends it's
a kind of science and secretly wishes that was true.
Analytic, that's what they used to call it. As in not
continental. Oh my god that used to be such a big
deal, at least it did in Cambridge. Yes yes, if you
insist on a story we can always make one up.
Young men will do 't, if they come to 't. Let's play
that once upon a time he was my teacher, and once
upon a time I looked up to him, and once upon a
time he got me pissed in a bar, I think it was in
a bar, not a pub, not in Cambridge, and once upon a
time I forgot the rest of the story. He did it again
and again and he just got unlucky with me as it
happened, because there was no one else whose little
shit this could have been, because I didn't like men.
No we didn't call them fuckboys then, that word
came later, but it's what he is. That's right, assholes,
language is coming. It'll catch up. You must sing
A-down a-down, An you call him a-down-a.
O, how the wheel becomes you!*

Chapter Twenty

And now in that quiet, in the darkness, all the floating stones that defined my path have fallen away. What now? *Where now? Who now? When now?* Perhaps I just let go, tumble with them into the lava ocean. A blaze of glory. The internet loves to watch a woman burn. The brighter the better. Maybe I'll make a good show. Why do we say "the internet"? That's a euphemism. A light-polarizing filter we use to screen off moral glare, hide the disgusting reality. *The internet is people!* People like watching women burn.

But up until now those stones were floating. Weren't they? Somehow. How? If I could understand this, discover how they did it, whether I can do what they did . . . They appeared unsupported, but that might only be because from where I stood I couldn't see what held them in place. We tend to think in terms like *down*, but *down* is nothing, not from a large enough scale. Once you zoom out far enough, leave the earth's atmosphere, what counts as *down*? How does *down* work for the moon? Would it go by its own centre or ours?

What an existence, to be a satellite forever. A supporting character. Something to look at. Not for too long though, or you go crazy. Stare at a satellite for too long and you might try to occupy its perspective, then you go mad because the task is impossible. A satellite *has* no perspective. That would be a view from nowhere, from nothing. If you are a moon you'd better not stare at yourself for too long. Smash those 40x magnifying mirrors! Nobody needs to see the slippery slopes down the volcanic sides of their own pores, greased with igneous comedogenes, poised to make mountains out of melasma. How a landscape is formed. How texture develops on a face, like a photograph in a tray.

And then a moon shines when things are supposed to be dark. Keeps people awake who need to be asleep, need to not see what's happening, need to forget. This is life or death, like I said. A whole moon, a moon fully itself, is dangerous—we made legends about this, full of fear, and we were right to do so.

So let's say there is no *down*. We like to think time at least has a direction, but maybe *future* is nothing too when you zoom out far enough. I'm experimenting on myself here in the best traditions of medical science and I might die of it. A bit of carbon can be compressed so hard that it splits the light apart. Look what's inside. And if we keep pressing? *Bring the life of that unhappy Henry Jekyll to an end?* And if we do, does that have to mean Hyde dies as well? Can Borges kill off his *Borges* but not his *I*? And if there's another medium in which an *I* might survive, a substance *this* I can breathe after all the air runs out . . . well, well. If the *experimentum crucis* comes, don't help me. I don't need help.

I'm not saying there's nothing wrong with me, I'm saying there's no such thing.

—

The new psychiatrist Jeff had referred me to was a specialist in psychosis and schizoaffective disorders, as it turned out. I googled her.

I probably should have gone to see her, but I had another conference coming up. Actually I should probably have gone to see my GP first, because my body has been feeling like hell on toast for the last month. But I was scared to see either of them. And this particular conference is kind of a big deal. So I just came out here to Toronto. It's been twenty years now since Deb disappeared. Just a couple of days, this trip. I'll see the doctors when I get home. Did I break out of my path, coming here? Or was this just part of it, leading me back around, back into orbit? Is that even a fair question? Is there a difference?

Well, unlike a straight line, a circle can have apotropaic magic. Or at least it has an inside, which means there's something to be safe in. Safe or trapped. The difference is one of interpretation. Safe *and* trapped. There, I fixed it. There's a crazy lady called Molly in a film I liked as a kid. She says, *Crazy is good. Crazy keeps 'em away.* The film is called *Life Stinks.* It's very funny.

We do love us some crazy lady characters. Crazy ladies on stage, in stories, on TV, on the big screen, in myths and legends. Crazy lady lit. It's a whole genre. We can't get enough of crazy ladies. As long as they're not real. Take Cassandra, now there's a crazy lady for you. You know why she went crazy? She could predict the future. Saw the fall of Troy coming, and she tried to do the right thing and warn everyone, and nobody believed her. Instead they called her names, shitty shitty names. And you know why nobody believed her? It was a curse: Apollo gave her the gift of prophecy but then he cursed her to never be believed. And you can guess why he cursed her, of course. Here's the Latin for it: *quam Apollo cum vellet comprimere, corporis copiam non fecit*. That's Hyginus's version anyway, in his *Fabulae*. The Hygienic stories.

It means when he wanted to get with her, she would not "supply" her body, "provide" it, make it "plentiful." Isn't translation fun? Here's the kicker: Cassandra had a twin brother called Helenus, and he could predict the future too. Only when he did it, people believed him. What we have right there is an origin story, a myth to explain why something exists. This particular myth explains what philosophers are now trying to label a "credibility deficit," which is a fancy way of saying women just don't seem like they would know what they are talking about. That, plus of course the ancient tradition of pulling out all your shittiest names for women who hit too close to home. Accuracy is a serious offence. Sometimes capital.

And what did we take from this story? The *Cassandra complex*. More language—another label for another kind of crazy. Crazy will be named for a woman or the moon, depending on whether the danger turns inwards or outwards.

Something else we've lost in translation: the possibility that mad words, dirty words, have more in them than hygienic words. That Cassandra, the Pythia, even the Maenads might be worth a listen. That the story sanitized—the story made sane—might be *wrong*. In some versions of the story Nyx was there at the beginning, and even the day was her daughter. Hyginus decided Chaos ought to come first—emptiness, void. Nyx is too pregnant for some people.

Isaac Newton went crazy, too. Didn't you know? Keynes wrote about it in that lecture he never delivered. Another part of the story that was never told. It's a bad story though, we don't like crazy men, it's not the same. We are traumatized by King Lear. *Melancholia, sleeplessness, fears of persecution* . . . that's how Keynes describes the madness of Newton. *He writes to Pepys and to Locke and no doubt to others letters which lead them to think that his mind is deranged. . . . The breakdown probably lasted nearly two years, and from it [he] emerged, slightly "gaga"* . . . *he never concentrated, never recovered "the former consistency of his mind". "He spoke very little in company." "He had something rather languid in his look and manner."*

And he looked very seldom, I expect, into the chest where, when he left Cambridge, he had packed all the evidences of what had occupied and so absorbed his intense and flaming spirit in his rooms and his garden and his elaboratory between the Great Gate and Chapel.

But he did not destroy them. They remained in the box . . .

That was his magic. Keynes called Newton "the last of the magicians" and blamed all that alchemy nonsense on his having been tempted by the devil. But then, Keynes was just trying to fashion a comfort blanket of his own. A normal that worked for him. One with a devil—*the* devil—standing ready to take the fall. A safe ending with all the magic shut up in a box, all the magicians silenced forever.

Because he knew that if Newton *wasn't* the last, then we aren't safe.

Safe, trapped, whatever. Here I am. I end up here. Flat on my back on a hotel bed in Toronto and agony. The acid in my chest is killing me, but this is normal. It's just a stress reaction.

Tomorrow is my fortieth birthday, but that isn't what's stressing me out. I'd love to be forty. Forty will fit so much better, now that I am old. Perhaps forty is the year I'll outgrow my acne. Although I've heard you have to have a healthy gut before you get healthy skin, so I'm not holding my breath. If only everything could be a little less interconnected sometimes.

And it's not because tomorrow I'm supposed to give a keynote in front of a hundred people, half of whom are quietly thinking I'm an uppity overpromoted female. Ever got up in front of a crowd like that and done your best work? We'll strive to please you every fucking day, and it's so much better *not* to feel like it's your body on the line but Jeff doesn't get that. Or he won't let me get it. In the taxi from the airport, there was an ad on the back of the front seat advertising some tourist attraction, an aquarium maybe: *Feel like you're there*. And the billboard on the side of this brick hotel: *Be here now*. Fuck them all. I don't have to. I can't. I don't want to.

I finally finished the letter of resignation I've been drafting and redrafting for the last five years.

> *Dear Dean Crawley,*
> *I am dying here.*

But this doesn't mean anything.

I have an email from The Cop this morning with the subject line *Urgent: your package*, marked as "high priority" in my inbox. She writes that the crystal pendant on the choker I sent her was an incredibly valuable diamond. It belonged to a minor royal, who lost it when she was an undergrad at Christ's and there was a fire in a nearby nightclub where she had snuck out with a (non-approved) man friend. The whereabouts of the diamond since the incident were never known—its loss only came out much later. She was never supposed to have been at that club, nor with the young man in question, so she didn't tell anyone until her family demanded to see it for an insurance revaluation. Then she'd been so shamed over losing the stone that she'd killed herself. A week later the man friend, to whom it turned out she had been secretly married for four years, did the same. That pretty little crystal I stole, vested with such incredible power. It had been a receptacle for two lives.

The Cop's email said she was going to have to hand the stone over to the authorities and explain where she had got it, and she was really sorry but she would have to tell them who'd had it all these years. She would explain that it was an accident and I didn't know. I laughed out loud when I read that part. How like me, to have no idea what's right in front of my face. Or right around my neck. To have ignored the dimension in which we turn base matter into things immeasurably precious, and the other way around. I have always been blind in this particular way, to what is and what isn't worth a damn. Now that blindness has made me not only a thief, but a double murderer.

And even this, even *this* doesn't mean anything to me. It's not that I don't understand, it's just that there's no *weight* in it. In any of it.

No. You know why my chest is on fire? It's because I saw her. This afternoon. Pink twinset and pearls and blonde hair, like she hadn't aged a day in twenty years.

Why the hell would Deb be in Toronto? Who cares? The Cop was in Seattle, wasn't she? I was downtown, it was crowded and I had the worst migraine I can remember. It was so hot. Unseasonably, eerily hot, like Toronto had found a crack in Canada and slipped into Hades. I was stumbling through a stream of people flowing in the opposite direction, cursing and swerving to avoid me, when all of a sudden the migraine wasn't about pain anymore. The missing piece of my visual field was *there*. I could *see* it. I mean, I could see with it, through it. The crystalline arc of impossible colour was brighter than ever, somehow even more alive. And just like that, I felt a switch flick: as if someone had slipped new lenses into my irises, like an optometrist doing an eye test, and in that split second *everything* fell apart. I could see through the dazzling arc, through all that glitter and distraction, into the absence. Only now it wasn't an absence. I could see Deb. She was there. She was just across the street.

So I called out her name. And I ran.

I ran straight out in front of traffic. People were yelling and brakes screeching. I could hear all this but there was no weight in it. No meaning. This was a pure thing, it had to be prioritized over everything else. I reached out my hand towards Deb.

But she looked right through me. I had forgotten that I must look different, even though she was just the same. My hair is short now, and I have money these days—not that I'd dress like a troubled nineties teenager even if I didn't.

It took me a few seconds to realize all this, and by then it was too late. Deb had disappeared into the crowd, the ordinary people, people from Toronto, from this world. And in the closing of an eye this world flowed back in and swallowed me. The wormhole in my eyes blurred over, healed up like a wound, and the pain was back: the drilling pain in my head, now joined by that other familiar banging pain across my chest. I vomited onto the sidewalk. (*Sidewalk?* Not *pavement? Et tu,* Victoria?) I threw up twice, the second retch gurgling on for a long while, as though I were disgorging some giant intestinal worm, long-established in my gut but dead for some time. Finally ready to exit.

I had fallen down on my knees. After I stopped puking, a kindly passer-by helped me up and walked me to a taxi. They must have paid for it as well. The taxi took me to my hotel, and I stumbled up to my room, and I dumped my body on the bed, heavy and half-conscious.

So here we are. Back in the present moment. The "present" is an exceptionally tricky thing to accommodate from a metaphysical point of view. What differentiates the present moment from any other moment? What's a "moment," anyway? If simultaneity is relative like Einstein says, how can we even define such a thing as a moment? Two moments would be the same moment from one frame of reference and not from another. And even if we could handle this, are we supposed to think there is some kind of magic shiny light on the "present" moment that makes it special? Do you think your "now" is the real one? Why not your grandmother's?

Philosophers talk about "moving spotlight" theories of time: moments get "lit up" in an orderly sequence. But if there is a spotlight, why should it move? What if it's stuck, say on a cold October morning in 1984? Or pointing straight down on the first moment I saw Deb? I was always attracted to this idea of a stationary spotlight. Stories, dreams, political movements, people . . . they all tend to have a "now" that is *stuck* somewhere. The one time that's real, the one that counts, frozen solid. The idea of a moving spotlight is meant to give us something objective to cling to, an equitable distribution across all the candidates for "now." Everyone gets a turn: form a straight line in an orderly fashion. Well maybe it just doesn't work that way. Maybe some nows get way more than their fair share, and other suckers never get a break.

So what? Life's not fair. This isn't a problem I can solve. I only know what I can do. What I have to do. As soon as I can stand, I am going back out there. Back to where she is. Where I need to be. I am going to find her. I can do it. I can see Deb again now. The circle's closing.

And that's it. That's the truth.

Almost the whole truth. I'm not quite done. I didn't exactly lie about anything but I could have been more honest about one part. Because it wasn't just my mother. My uncle told me about this once, right before I left for the girls' school. My aunt never found out that I knew.

I come from a long line of women who all ended up in mental institutions. My mother was thirty-nine when she cracked. Her mother was about forty, her mother the same, and her mother, and that is as far back as anyone knows. None of us ever got a diagnosis. Nothing more precise than some era-appropriate variant on what the kids these days call "cray cray." So this is what we share. Like we only have one life story between us. That's our heirloom. And my uncle, of all people, was keeping this gem for me.

It's always a little bit like that, though, isn't it? Someone else takes over our stories when we stop telling them, when we can't say any more, when the path of least resistance is to let the circle be a straight line? Or the other way around. A circle with a bad memory might as well be a straight line anyway. If everyone tells you it's a straight line, it's a straight line. A straight line is everything in order. The Cop would approve. And Poirot: he always needed everything in order. Then again, Holmes's rooms were a big mess. Drove poor old Watson up the wall.

I honestly tried to get help. To be well. To be made healthy, sanitized. Sane. I made a good faith effort, as they say. Gave it the old college try. *Help*—now there's a word. But it was all talk. On and on and on. So much verbiage, garbage, land-fill, waste to plug up that one hole, the silence, the terrible empty centre. The absence of Deb. Her absence in me. I was all that was left of her, of what we had. What I lost. It was more than a friendship, a million times more. It was a lifeline. A tear. A little rip in reality that could have broken this pattern, this cycle, this script that keeps repeating itself, where we cannot get what we need. Where we are not safe. Where we don't have anyone. My mother didn't have anyone. Not one single friend visited her in the home, all that time, all those nights and not one friend. I wonder if she ever had a Deb, when she was young. Was her Deb lost, too? Was her Deb like my Deb? Could I *give* her my Deb? If we can tear ourselves out of cycles, out of scripts, could a character from my life story tear herself out and jump into my mother's? Maybe she needed my Deb even more than I did. Maybe that's where my Deb went. Maybe she wasn't my Deb to begin with. Maybe Deb is just a helper. Someone who goes where she's needed. Maybe it isn't my turn anymore.

I don't care. I need her, and I'm going back out there. I'm going to find her.

Yes I know how that sounds. "Help."

Epilogue

*N*yx *is a personification of the night.* The *night. The definite arti-cle. Nyx was there in the beginning and she'll be there in the end. My mother died in the asylum—when did we switch to "home"? They didn't mess around in that place: not with language, not with anything. Not by the end. God did it scare the crap out of me. Those last weeks. So I stopped visiting and eventually she killed herself and left a note saying it was all my fault. Like I said, it is in me. A baby kicking.*

I used to be that baby. How time flies! Nyx these days is a brand of cosmetics. And when my mother was a kid, she used to go and visit her own mother. Yes, in a fucking asylum, it's where we all end up, didn't I mention? Why don't we just check ourselves in when we hit thirty-nine? Save everyone else the trouble. Hi, no I don't have a reservation but do you have a godawful soul-killer of a room avail-able for the next 14,000 silent nights?

The other day the little shit brought me a book from home. A 1970s edition of Agatha Christie's **Endless Night***. Says she heard I used to like this one. There's this picture inside of a blonde woman in a pink sweater, like an actual picture, not on a phone—I suppose she used it as a bookmark. A beautiful pink lady smoking and smiling.*

269

Good hair for the '90s. On the back someone had scribbled in biro, Semper eadem xoxox. *Something about that was familiar but my memory is shot to pieces from the meds. They say it keeps me level but I feel like there are things I can't see properly anymore, things that are, I don't know, flat somehow. I threw the picture in the bucket with the food waste at breakfast.*

Well, what else did you want to have happen here? And the unclean spirits went out, and entered into the swine: and the herd ran violently down a steep place into the sea, (they were about two thousand;) and were choked in the sea . . . ? That's not a better ending than this, is it? Doesn't anyone care about the pigs? Two thousand fucking pigs? Keep it inside you, at least you save the pigs. Not that a pig's life is a party, but I'd trade for mine if I could without cursing an innocent thing. What is salvation anyway?

Instead there is only static. This hammering, this buzzing, all of us racing around trying to find some kind of straight line, some kind of normal, some kind of security blanket. A friend, the one true friend, the one we can trust, the one who won't leave us in the lurch. Or even just a good story, that'll do, one where it all comes together. All the loose threads cosily tied up by Miss Marple's clickety-clackety knitting needles.

Welcome to the lurch. Oh honey, is it too bright for you? Nyx, dim my lights to 50 per cent.

I'm supposed to eat something again and I don't know what to have. They're busy digitizing our whole lives in here, but at least for now you're still supposed to put food in one end of you and shit out the other. As long as you keep it all moving along. I mean, you can stuff yourself up, but how is that any safer, not going anywhere? It's only around and around anyway. Perhaps the motion is not really retrograde, perhaps it only looks that way from here. Not all regresses are vicious. This always used to happen, a kind of pathological indecision: even if I had enough money to buy something I'd just wander around in circles thinking, Chips. No, kebabs. No, noodles. No, chips, *because everything was wrong. I was skinny because there was nothing to eat. Nineteen, twenty, my plate's empty. And I lost so much weight when the little shit came out of me.*

That man was on TV *again yesterday—not* TV, *what's the word for the screens in here, what do they call them—explaining that we're doughnuts, topologically speaking. A tube with a hollow middle, you know, a corridor. A worm, a zero. An empty* O. *Or the iris of a human eye. All that stuff just passing through you on its way to anywhere.*

Acknowledgements

My home base, Jonathan, Mezzo, Drusilla, Seven. My brilliant friends and magicians and muses, Carla, Mandy, Marina, Adriana, Ray, Richard, Tyler. My family, Nick, Pam, Calum, James, Mum, Ted, Lorna, Jo, Doug, Lauren, Emily.

My agent, Martha Webb. My editor, Haley Cullingham. My copy editor, Gemma Wain. My fiction teachers, Heather O'Neill, Timothy Taylor, Alix Ohlin, Maureen Medved. My classmates and colleagues and students.

My writing haunts, JJ Bean and Kind Café.

My Cambridge, where I and other stories were made, and reality was always a sketchy business.

A NOTE ABOUT THE TYPE

The text of *Victoria Sees It* has been set in Baskerville BT WGL4. Originally designed by John Baskerville (1706–75), Baskerville's typeface is classified as transitional, as it was intended to refine the "old-style" typefaces of the period and was part of a larger project to create books of the greatest possible quality. It is characterized by crisp edges, sharp, tapered serifs, high contrast between thick and thin strokes, and consistency in both shape and form. The present design is an accurate recutting based on surviving punches and matrices taken from the Cambridge University Press with particular attention to George W. Jones' revision from the metal of Baskerville's English roman and italic in 1929 for Linotype & Machinery Ltd.